# Muscle for Hire

HEART OF FAME SERIES

# Muscle for Hire

## HEART OF FAME SERIES

## LEXXIE COUPER

Entangled Publishing, LLC
2614 South Timberline Road
Suite 109
Fort Collins, CO 80525
Visit our website at www.entangledpublishing.com.

Select Contemporary is an imprint of Entangled Publishing, LLC.

Edited by Heidi Shoham
Cover design by Liz Pelletier
Stock image by iStock

eBook ISBN 9781633759763
paperback ISBN 9781545362051

Manufactured in the United States of America

First Edition January 2013

**3 6109 00535 3591**

*Kirsten "Bellie" Bridge. For being my pimp and my friend.*

# Chapter One

A wall of screaming, squealing, crying young women — and some not-so-young women — threw themselves at Aslin Rhodes. He wasn't the object of their frenzied affection. That was for Chris Huntley, star of hit sitcom *Twice Too Many* and soon-to-be released action blockbuster, *Dead Even*. No, Aslin just happened to find himself between Chris and the wall of screaming, squealing, crying young and not-so-young women. Fifteen years working as the bodyguard of the world's biggest rock star, however, had prepared Aslin for all kinds of insanity, and this was no exception.

He planted his size-fourteen booted feet firmly on the footpath and with his arms wide, jaw bunched and muscles coiled, held back the frenzied horde. Just.

Movie-star groupies were more maniacal than rock-star groupies it seemed. At least those currently here trying to get their mits on Chris Huntley were. And, Aslin discovered, they were more prone to biting.

"Oi!" He flinched as a set of teeth sank into his forearm and he snapped his glare to a girl who looked no more than twelve snarling up at him from near his elbow. "Watch it."

"We're trying to," a middle-aged woman wearing a skin-tight *Twice Too Many* T-shirt snapped back, giving the teenager girl squashed between her and Aslin a shove. "But you're in the road."

Her fellow frenzied fans echoed her unhappiness with Aslin's presence, most resorting to names and insults regarding his British nationality. He'd never heard the words "fucking Pom" uttered so often by so many women. If the situation wasn't so surreal, he'd laugh.

"Seriously," he called out, still holding back the wall of hormone-induced lust with sheer strength and a wide arm span. "What are the odds Chris Huntley is going to—"

A loud groan drowned out the rest of Aslin's question. Almost as one, the women stopped pushing against him and fell back, their eyes swelling with tears, their expressions suicidal.

"He's gone," the woman in the *Twice Too Many* T-shirt moaned. Another collective sob sounded from the horde as surly glares turned to Aslin.

Aslin did his own turning, shooting a look at the space behind him where Chris Huntley and Nigel McQueen, *Dead Even's* famed director, had been sharing coffee. The harbour-side café was now empty of Hollywood-type persons, the normal run-of-the-mill patrons left behind smirking with bemused curiosity.

Aslin returned his focus to the women, only to find them dispersing on the esplanade. Most stared intently at their cameras and smartphones on which—Aslin assumed—

hundred of hastily snapped images of Chris sipping his latte were now stored.

He let out a chuckle and shook his head. He'd never get his head around the unhinged mentality of a frenzied fan. Fifteen years protecting Nick Blackthorne hadn't enlightened him, and he didn't see this small job illuminating it either.

*Maybe it's time you went back into the service, boyo? HRH's Defense Force would take you back in an instant.*

A dull pressure settled on Aslin's chest at the notion of returning to his post as a SAS Commando. He may not understand infatuated, borderline-loopy fans much, but he understood his country's need to be involved in the war in Afghanistan less.

There was a reason he'd left the United Kingdom Special Forces to become professional muscle for a rock star. *That* surreal career made more sense than the orders constantly given to him during—

"Mr. Rhodes?"

A male voice called from behind Aslin and he turned, an instinctual tension coiling through his body. He didn't like being caught unawares. It wasn't something that happened often.

A non-descript blue SUV sat parked beside the café's *al fresco* area, the rear passenger door open.

Aslin narrowed his eyes. That the SUV was there in the first place told him it wasn't as unimportant as it appeared. The whole area facing the harbour where he now stood was strictly an esplanade—no cars allowed. Added to the situation was the fact Aslin was at the café in the first place to meet the director of the film, and he suspected he knew who the owner of the voice was. There weren't *that* many men with American accents capable of flouting the laws in Sydney at the moment.

A soft snort sounded at the back of Aslin's throat and he began walking toward the waiting vehicle.

*Looks like your career in the movies is just about to begin, boyo.*

Stopping at the open door, he looked into the cabin and lifted his eyebrows at the sight of Chris Huntley smiling back at him.

"Nick told me you were good at keeping back the masses." The actor's smile turned into a grin. "But I have to say, I've never seen just one man intimidate so many women all by himself." Chris held out a hand as he shifted back deeper along the rear seat. "Nigel and I had planned to chat with you at the café, but…well, as you no doubt saw, it got a little crowded."

Aslin gave the actor a slight nod. "I saw."

Chris laughed. "Nick also told me you weren't one for a lot of wasted words. I see he's right." He waved his hand at the empty seat beside him. "Would you like to get in? Nigel got called back to the set and I'm due back in an hour, but I really wanted to chat first."

Aslin studied the man looking up at him from the SUV's interior. He was young, handsome and openly friendly. A target for all sorts of deluded and hysterical fans, especially given the sexual potency Aslin had noticed oozed from him when on screen.

*Are you thinking of a potential new boss?*

Since Nick's retirement from singing and his emersion in family life, Aslin had found himself at a loss for things to do. There was only so much a bodyguard could do in a small rural town in the Australian highlands, particularly when the rock star he guarded preferred to just hang out at home with his wife and son nowadays.

After a few months of watching Aslin attempt to find potential threats in the amiable citizens of Murriundah, Nick had finally rolled his eyes and told Aslin he had a job for him. Just a quick favour for a friend.

In Sydney.

On a film set.

Staring three big Hollywood actors.

"McQueen needs an advisor on all things menacing and commando, especially for Chris Huntley," Nick had said to Aslin with a grin. "I can tell you're bored out of your brain here, As. Get your arse to Sydney and be useful for a change, will you?"

And so here Aslin was now, ready to tell Hollywood— and an actor who so far hadn't played a single action role— how to do it right.

"Nigel said he'd meet us back on set, " Chris went on, his attention fixed on Aslin's face, as if storing away all sorts of little details. "He's getting his P.A. to arrange a trailer for you. It was meant to be ready now but apparently it's got a faulty pilot light on the stove." The actor shot a look at the empty seat at Aslin's knees, an almost nervous tension pulling at his forehead. "If you'd rather meet us both back there…"

From the corner of his eye, Aslin caught movement and he straightened a little, enough to notice the red-headed woman in the *Twice Too Many* T-shirt taking photos of the SUV. She gave him a wide smile, her expression suddenly predatory and smug.

A pulse ticked in his neck. The woman had worked out her prey was in the car. It was time to get Chris out of there.

As a rule, Aslin didn't get into a vehicle he wasn't driving himself, but with Ms. Too-Tight T-shirt hurrying towards him and the SUV's open door, he knew now wasn't the time to discuss the chauffeur situation.

Bending at the waist, he ducked through the opening, climbed into the SUV and slammed the door behind him. He'd arrange for his motorbike to be delivered to the film set. Better to stay with Huntley now that a fan knew the vehicle the actor travelled in.

"Hello, Mr. Rhodes." The same male voice that had called him earlier came from behind the driver's wheel. Aslin lifted his focus to the rearview mirror, finding a set of black Ray-Bans looking back at him. "Welcome aboard. I'm Jeff Coulten."

Aslin took in the broad width of the man's shoulders and the smooth strength in his neck. "Bodyguard?"

Jeff laughed. "Driver."

Chris let out his own chuckle. "I don't have a bodyguard, Aslin. May I call you Aslin? Jeff is what's left of my entourage."

Aslin cocked an eyebrow. "What's left of it?"

Chris reached up and snared his seat belt to buckle himself in. "I grew out of it." He gave Aslin a wide smile. "Ready?"

Before Aslin got a chance to ask for what, the thumping sounds of Linkin Park flooded the SUV's cabin, the engine roared into life and the car took off, throwing Aslin back into his seat as Jeff drove them away from the café and past the furiously photographing middle-aged fan.

*Welcome to the movie world, boyo,* Aslin thought, buckling himself in as quickly as he could. *Remind yourself to kick Nick in the arse when you see him again.*

Twenty minutes later—with quite a few of those minutes spent reminding Jeff Coulten Australians drove on the *left* side of the road—Aslin swore he'd never get in a car with what was left of Chris Huntley's entourage again. Not if the affable Jeff was driving. Thankfully, and somewhat remarkably, they'd made it to the film set in one piece, Jeff leaving Chris and Aslin at the fenced perimeter before tearing away, wheels spitting gravel out in his wake.

Chris threw Aslin a sideward glance, no doubt seeing the disapproval on Aslin's face. "He's a great guy, honest," he said as they began walking deeper into the area currently overrun with film crew. "And he's been my friend for years."

Aslin didn't reply. Instead, as always, he took in every detail of his surroundings, noting places where attacks could be made, objects that could be used as weapons, easy exit routes if needed. *Dead Even* was being filmed in part at the old Hyde Park Barracks near Sydney's CBD. According to Chris, the convict prison—normally a favourite destination for tourists—was now "the secret base for a clandestine, international defense-force network", code name Last Line. The actor had filled Aslin in on the drive, outlining the basic plot, providing details of his character—a "brooding, foreboding commando who comes into conflict with his superior's unjust, dubious orders"—and generally chatting away as if he and Aslin were long-lost mates. There was a boyish charm to Chris that Aslin found hard to resist. The young American reminded him a lot of Nick's teenage son. Young, eager and easy to laugh.

He could see why women threw themselves at him.

What he couldn't see was Chris in the role of a commando. Which was what Aslin had to make him.

It was going to be a challenge.

A small smile tugged on the corners of his mouth. He suppressed a chuckle. It was also going to be fun.

It seemed Nick Blackthorne's arse was going to be saved from a boot after all.

Two hours later, Aslin once again considered the rock star's butt overdue for a kick. Movie folk had an infuriating view of what a soldier of war was. They also had no clue — in Aslin's opinion — what looked believable and what didn't. He'd spent the last one-hundred-and-twenty minutes not just correcting one cliché after another from being captured on film, but trying to convince the director, Nigel McQueen, that a SAS British Commando, even a retired one, really *did* know how to hold a Desert Eagle handgun. And how to throw a punch.

The bloke was a nice enough fellow, but he had a warped and *wrong* sense of what actually happened during close combat.

"Don't worry, Aslin." Chris slapped his back as they walked off set, obviously unaware Aslin had broken arms and smashed jaws for lesser contact. "You'll get used to Nigel. He's stubborn, I know, but he's got a vision and he's true to it. It's why he's won so many awards." The actor laughed. "Having said that, I think what you did to the Second Unit stunt director illustrated his vision may be a bit off this time."

Aslin raised a contemplative eyebrow. In his opinion, the Second Unit stunt director was an idiot. What kind of so-called *expert* insisted it was impossible to down an opponent with a *harai tsurikomi ashi* without signposting it? After a good ten minutes arguing with the man that it could be done, Aslin had decided it was easier to just show him, putting the arrogant man on his back with the judo move mid-argument.

The stunt director had stormed off the set after that. Well, limped off the set. After Aslin had let him up off the ground.

Beside him, Chris chuckled again. "What are the chances your boss knew you were going to stir up trouble when he suggested you come on board the film?"

Aslin's lips twitched. "I suspect the odds are high."

A shout from behind turned both men around, Aslin stepping slightly forward and in front of Chris without thought.

"Chris." Nigel hurried toward them, his shaggy black hair flapping in the warm summer breeze. "You can't take off now. We need to check the dailies."

Chris slapped his forehead. "Ah fuck, that's right." He looked up at Aslin, an apologetic grimace pulling at his lips. "This'll take a while. Sorry. Can you come to my trailer in an hour or so? I want to get your take on my character's motivation."

Aslin gave him a brief nod. "Of course."

"I like what you gave us today, Mr. Rhodes." Nigel stuck out his hand, whiter-than-white teeth flashing from behind a wide smile as he shook Aslin's hand with a firm grip. "I'm not sure Ricco's ever coming back on set, but I like what you gave us. I look forward to seeing what you deliver tomorrow."

And with that, the film director and the actor walked away, leaving Aslin alone.

He watched them go, unable to suppress a snort as the personal assistants for both men came scurrying from the wings, water bottles in hand, mobile phones offered, fruit baskets hanging from bent elbows.

*And you thought the demands of a rock star indulgent.*

At the thought of his boss, Aslin pulled his phone from his hip pocket and dialed Nick's number.

"You missing me already, Uncle As?"

Aslin didn't bother answering the chuckled jest. "Am I being interviewed for a job by Chris Huntley, Nick? Are you trying to get rid of me?"

On the other end of the phone, the man who was once the world's biggest rock star and was now happy to be just a husband and dad laughed. "No, As. It's not. But let's be serious, mate, you can't hang around Murriundah looking out for insane groupies that *might* come after me or Lauren or Josh. The day I announced my retirement, they started to move on to the next new big thing. When was the last time you had to prevent a fan launching themselves at me? Seriously? Chris on the other hand..." Nick left the sentence unfinished.

Aslin's gut clenched. Nick was correct. The Blackthorne groupies and fans had tapered off over the last few months, only the odd truly die-hard willing to make the long trip to the small town Nick now called home. When that happened, a state-of-the-art security system kept Nick and his family safe from unwanted guests when they were at home, and the protective residents of Murriundah looked out for their famous neighbours when they were in public. Which left Aslin almost redundant. But if he wasn't Nick Blackthorne's bodyguard, what was he?

"Listen, As," Nick went on, his voice relaxed and calm, and for one brief, stupid moment Aslin longed for the days when Nick was the wild rocker who had no fucking clue what he was doing from one second to the next. "Do what you're there for — be the bad-arse Pommie commando and tell those Hollywood guys how to do it right. When you're finished, we'll talk about what's next, okay?"

Ending the call after promising to get Chris's autograph for Josh's latest girlfriend, Aslin wandered around the film set, charting everything he saw for later consideration. He had to admit to himself, it was a bizarre experience. He'd grown up in the London slums, the middle child of five boys who all knew how to fight by the time they were eight. Aslin joined the British Army at the age of seventeen in a last-ditch effort to avoid ending up like his older brothers—who were already serving time. His years as a SAS soldier, of existing as a vital member of a unit, followed by his life as Nick's bodyguard had given him little time to exist as an individual. Now here he was, alone, with a possibility before him he was eighty-five percent certain he didn't want.

But if not a bodyguard to a celebrity, than what? What kind of career options did an ex-bodyguard, ex-commando have?

And did Aslin want any of them?

*Do you even know who you are now, boyo? Or are you just muscle for hire?*

The question was unsettling. And without answer. At least none presented itself in the time that lapsed as Aslin toured the film set.

Forty-five minutes later, part-frustrated, part-irritated, he made his way to the massive, ostentatious manor on wheels that was Chris Huntley's trailer.

He stopped a few yards away when he noticed a tall, slim woman dressed in faded denim jeans and a snug black T-shirt trying to jimmy open the door.

Her back was to him, her long, toned legs braced apart as she wriggled something thin and silver between the door and the frame near the lock. A thick ponytail the colour of spun wheat spilled from the back of her baseball cap, fanning over her shoulders and ribcage as she shifted her position, no doubt to put more weight behind her attempt to access Chris's trailer.

For a quick second Aslin, was struck by the sublime perfection of her physique — the latent strength in her firm limbs, the confidence in her stance. And then the sheer gall of what she was doing hit him and he moved. Fast.

Silent.

He snared her right wrist with one hand, spun her around to face him, his expression set in an intimidating glower — and ended up on his back in a blur of colour as she kicked his legs right out from under him.

*Fuck.*

A booted heel rammed under his chin, mashing into his flesh as the woman glared down at him, her fists loosely clenched at her face. "Want to explain what you're —"

He didn't let her finish. Twisting to his left, he slammed his forearm into the side of her calf, rolling to his feet and driving her back — butt first — against the trailer.

A second later, she dropped into a crouch, escaped his pinning arm and smashed a fist into his balls.

He staggered back a step. But only one. The pain was excruciating, agonizing, but he'd learnt to shut pain out a long time ago. Fixing his stare on the woman's face, he whipped out his right hand, feigning an attempt to grab her arm even as he swooped his left foot against her right ankle.

And ended up on his arse, again, the wind knocked from him, when she spun off the ground in a tight circle and drove her heel into his chest.

*What the hell?*

The thought had barely formed in his head when two firm thighs slammed into his ribcage, right under his armpits, squeezing him with phenomenal crushing strength as one fist balled in the front of his shirt and the other bunched behind her head. "Nice try, buddy." A soft American accent turned the words to a mocking snarl. "But not good enough." Brilliant blue eyes glared down at him, thick dark lashes framing their obvious anger. "Now tell me who the fuck you are and what the hell you think you're —"

"Holy shit, Rowan!" A male voice called out, and a distant part of Aslin's mind recognised it as Chris Huntley's. "What have you done to Nick Blackthorne's bodyguard?"

The woman straddling Aslin didn't move a muscle. Aslin could tell. Every muscle in *his* body was tuned into hers.

"What's Nick Blackthorne's bodyguard doing here?" the woman — Rowan — asked without lifting her pinning stare from Aslin's face. "And why did he try to grab me?"

From the corner of Aslin's eye, he saw feet come to a stop on the concrete beside his head, but he didn't tear his focus from the woman atop him. His nerve-endings sparked and fired. He'd been put on his back by a woman? How the hell had he been put on his back by a woman? Who the hell was she?

"I don't know why he tried to grab you." Chris laughed. "Did you piss him off?"

Blue eyes flickered, holding Aslin motionless. And then the woman was standing, in a move so fluid and quick he couldn't stop the slither of appreciation threading through his disbelief.

"Funny, Huntley," she said, stepping over him like he no longer mattered. "Now shut up and say hello to me. It's been too long since we saw each other."

From his place on the ground, Aslin watched her reach out and wrap her smooth, firmly toned arms around the actor, giving him a hug that was relaxed and warm. She kissed Chris's cheek, a grin playing with the corners of her lips. Lips, Aslin couldn't help but notice, that were full and naturally pink.

"Ugh," Chris laughed, stepping out of the woman's hug. "Girl germs."

The woman swiped at his jaw in a friendly punch, a shallow dimple creasing the smooth flesh of her cheek. "Shut up, you idiot."

Chris laughed again, dropped a kiss on that very dimple, and then turned to Aslin. Aslin who was still lying shocked on the ground.

Aslin who'd just had his arse handed to him by a woman no taller than his chin.

"Aslin Rhodes," Chris said, his eyes twinkling with mirth. "Allow me to introduce my sister, Rowan Hemsworth."

# Chapter Two

The situation, in Rowan's opinion, wasn't acceptable. For starters, the last thing she wanted was her brother forming a relationship with the bodyguard of the famous wild boy of rock. She'd worked too hard to keep Chris grounded for him to suddenly be exposed to the lifestyle and stories Aslin Rhodes would no doubt regale him with. The life of a successful actor was already fraught with temptation for Chris. Rowan didn't want the potential decadence of celebrity leeching into his ear via the stories told by a walking, talking mountain of muscle.

She watched Chris hand the silent bodyguard an icepack. Her brother was already enamored with the Brit. It was obvious in the easy smile on his face. This was not how she'd hoped the shoot in Australia would go. Getting Chris away from all the yes-men and fawning hanger-oners in L.A. was meant to help him grasp a more real perspective on life, not skew it to hell.

And the other thing unsettling her? The one she was trying to ignore?

Rowan slid a quick sideward glance at Aslin Rhodes. Her stomach clenched. The Brit was unsettling. His towering height, his impressive strength, his speed, the way his body moved when fighting her, like oiled smoke and liquid steel. It had only been a short kerfuffle between them, but it was enough to tell Rowan she may not be the victor if it happened again. The element of surprise had been her greatest advantage this time, but that element was gone. If she had to face off against Aslin again, she didn't know if she'd win. And *that*, ladies and gentlemen, was very unsettling. Because the very real possibility of being bested by the Brit not only made her angry, it made her…

*Horny.*

Damn it, on a level she didn't want to acknowledge let alone analyse, the man currently holding an icepack to his groin turned her on.

Rowan bit back a curse. She hadn't flown halfway around the world to be turned on by an Englishman, no matter how killer his biceps and moves. She'd flown to Sydney to look after her kid brother. Aslin Rhodes could just fuck —

*Me?*

"And then Ricco stormed off…sis? Are you listening to me?"

Rowan jerked her stare back to Chris, dismayed by the fact both he and the Brit had caught her unfocussed.

She pulled an exasperated face at her brother. "Of course I'm listening. What I'm wondering is, now Mr. Rhodes has apparently pissed off the stunt director to the point where Ricco has gone AWOL, who is going to co-ordinate and choreograph all the fight and stunt scenes?" She folded her arms across her breasts—breasts that for some stupid reason felt much fuller and rounder when Aslin's gaze moved to her. "After all, *I'm* not allowed to do it, am I?"

Chris laughed, a boyish chuckle the world was in love with and she'd heard her whole life. "You know why you can't be the stunt coordinator." He tossed a grin at the still-silent Englishman. "But I'm certain I could pull some strings and Aslin could do it. The bodyguard union and the stunt-workers union would have to be connected somehow, right?"

Rhodes cocked an eyebrow. Just one. "I'm here to show you how to be a soldier, Chris. That's it."

The calm statement sank into the pit of Rowan's belly. Maybe it was the British accent, or the undeniable power lurking beneath his steady words. Whatever it was, it made her pussy contract with a greedy urgency she hadn't experienced since…well, since ever.

Great. She was attracted to a grunt. Awesome.

She leveled a glare at the man, ignoring how goddamn handsome and intimidating he was, even holding an icepack to his groin. "What do you know about being a soldier? Aren't you just a bodyguard?"

The question was petulant, but Rowan couldn't help it. She didn't like her base reaction to the man. It made her feel out of control. Weak.

One thing Rowan Hemsworth *wasn't* was weak. She had the black belts—plural—to prove it.

"Aslin was once an elite soldier. An SAS Commando in the United Kingdom Special Forces." Chris grinned at her and, for the first time since entering his trailer, Rowan recognised his wicked sense of humour brimming below his boyish front. Her kid brother was enjoying himself. A lot. Which meant *he* could detect how…affected she was by Rhodes.

Rowan ground her teeth and gave Chris a look, the one that said she was going to give him a damn good nipple-cripple when they were alone.

She didn't miss the fact that, once again, she was sidestepping the situation. The hired grunt *wasn't* just brainless muscle with a sexy accent. Which made him all the more dangerous to her.

Rowan turned to look at Rhodes, her sex constricting with impatient want again. She narrowed her eyes. "What kind of SAS Commando gets his ass handed to him by a woman?"

With that same fluid power she'd noted earlier in his moves, Rhodes placed the icepack on the table and gave her a slow smile.

She really wished he hadn't. It turned his handsome, intimidating face into something so close to mischievous sex-god she knew she'd be picturing him that night when she masturbated in the shower. And in bed. And—

"The kind who won't let it happen again."

Rhode's deep voice played over Rowan's senses in a caress of sound and unspoken promise. A ripple of something delicious shot through her and her nipples pinched into tight tips.

Oh God, he was…

She jutted her chin, desperate to haul back her poise. She'd kicked his butt only a few moments ago. So why did she feel like she was the loser now? "You think you can take me?"

Rhode ran his gaze over her, from eyes, to toes and back to her eyes again. "I think I can take you."

A heavy silence pressed down on Rowan and the trailer was suddenly hot. Tiny. And then, to her left, Chris burst out laughing. "Oh man, and to think I was pissed you were coming to Australia, sis."

Aslin gave her brother a curious look. "Why would you be angry?"

"'Cause Rowan here is the fun police, Aslin." Chris grinned at her, the patented Chris Huntley smirk that had earned him the Sexiest-Man-Alive mantle twice since his sitcom hit the air. "She's the one who made me get rid of my entourage. She's the one who keeps me on a strict macrobiotic diet. She's the one who makes sure I run a freaking marathon a day to keep in shape. And she's the one who kicks my butt—like she kicked yours, apparently—if I go out partying too hard."

Rowan straightened her spine and fixed her brother with a pointed glare. "*She* is also the one who made you audition for this role, who keeps your damn feet on the ground when the studio suits kiss your ass so much you float, and the one who tries to do what's best for you. In other words, your big sister."

Chris's answering laugh bounced around the trailer. "I know, I know. And you know I love you, Rowie."

As always, the proclamation knocked the fire out of Rowan's ire. Their parents had died when Chris was only sixteen, both killed when a break and enter of their family home went wrong. Horribly wrong.

That one night had changed everything for the siblings, Rowan doing everything in her power since to never *ever* be defenseless again, Chris using humour to suffocate his grief.

They only truly had each other. That was until Chris's acting dream became a reality and fame and fortune brought a slew of *invaluable* people into his life. So many of them that for a while Rowan had wondered if she was relevant any more. However, the one thing she *could* do was look out for him, protect him from those who would take advantage of his easygoing nature. She did that very well. Still, she always got stupidly choked up when Chris uttered the word Rowie, his childhood nickname for her, no matter how hard she tried to stay calm and stoic and stern.

She let out a ragged breath. God help her if anyone knew she was marshmallow inside. It wouldn't do her reputation as Chris's menacing, prickly sister any good.

Which was all the more reason to keep Aslin Rhodes at a distance. The fact she was turned on just by looking at him was the final nail in the coffin.

"Okay." Chris slapped his hands together, smiling at Rhodes before turning to Rowan. "Now we've got that outta the way, tell me how the World Cup went, sis. Did you win?"

Rowan felt Aslin's steady gaze on her. For some stupid reason it made her pulse quicken. She nodded at her brother, determined to ignore her ridiculous reaction to the Brit. "I did."

Chris nodded back. "Of course you did." He turned to Rhodes who, Rowan could tell, was still looking at her. "Rowie is five-times Taekwondo World Champion. As well as a ninth degree Master in Jiu-jitsu. Oh, and she really knows how to swing a...what do you call it, sis? That long stick?"

"A bò."

Rowan's heart beat faster at Rhodes' deep voice.

Chris snapped his fingers. "That's it. A bò."

Rowan wanted to fidget. She didn't know why, but the unwavering attention of Aslin Rhodes was disturbing her.

Disturbing her. Arousing her. Making her want to throw Chris from his own trailer and beg the British super soldier to have wild, monkey sex with her.

A thick throb pulsed in Rowan's core and she pressed her thighs together, willing it to go away.

But it wouldn't. Not when she couldn't escape Aslin's focus. Not when she saw his nostrils flare as he watched her.

Not when her stare locked with his.

Damn it, this was unexpected.

"So." Chris jolted to his feet, the action so abrupt Rowan flinched. "Does my sister want to join me and Aslin and Nigel for dinner? Apparently, we're going out on the harbour on Russell Crowe's yacht. Sounds like fun, right?"

Rowan watched Aslin's nostrils flare again, a minute tension coiling in his sizeable shoulders. She narrowed her eyes. Did he not want her there?

Tearing her stare from his, she smiled at her brother. "Sure. Just let me have a shower and change my clothes. I've been wearing these jeans since Quebec."

"I thought I could smell something." Chris grinned. "The shower is on the left. Where's your luggage?"

"Outside next to the step." Unable to help herself, Rowan slid Aslin a sideward glance. "Where I put them before being attacked."

Chris laughed, slapping Rhodes on the back. "I think she's dissing you, Aslin."

The British ex-commando's lips curled. "I think you're right."

He didn't move. Not for a strained second, and then— with that same oiled perfection she'd noted in him earlier— he turned and opened Chris's trailer door.

Her brother dropped a wink at Rowan and, as Aslin

turned his attention back into the trailer, ducked passed the Brit's intimidating frame out the door.

Only to tumble, face first, onto the ground.

Rowan leapt to her feet. "What the fuck?"

She moved, but Rhodes moved faster, out the door to crouch beside Chris before she could even make it to the threshold.

"Geez." Chris was pushing himself up onto all fours, Aslin's long-fingered hands helping him even as the Brit scanned the immediate area with an unblinking stare. "Where'd the freaking steps go?"

A frown pulled at Rowan's forehead as she studied the bottom of the doorway. Just as Chris had muttered, the steel steps leading up to the trailer's only entry were gone.

She jumped to the ground and joined Aslin by her brother's side. Chris was now sitting on his backside, his fingers taking hesitant swipes at his face. Blood trickled from a split beside his eyebrow and a ragged graze on his cheek. Around them, Rowan could hear people running. The film's star had been injured. That was enough for any film crew to go into panic mode.

Squatting beside her brother, she turned her focus to the spot below the open door.

The steps were still there, but skewed off to the side, the top level nowhere near where a foot would land. They looked like they'd been kicked aside, maybe bumped by a passing cart, but to her memory, there'd been no resonating bump through the trailer.

Of course, it may have happened while she was fixating on Rhodes's effect on her state of mind? Damn it.

She frowned. She didn't believe that. But if the steps weren't moved by accident, than who—

"Chris, are you okay?"

Rowan swung her attention up to Nigel McQueen, who now stood beside Chris and Aslin, worry etching his Hollywood-handsome face.

"Yeah, yeah." Chris waved a dismissive hand, a grin playing on his lips. "The ground broke my fall." He ran his fingers across the cut still oozing blood above his eye and winced. "Did a damn good job of it too."

Nigel threw a hard glare at the misplaced steps before turning to Aslin. "Do you know what happened?"

Rowan's pulse thumped hard in her throat, her belly knotting. Why ask Aslin? Didn't she—

"Someone moved the steps."

The Brit's deep voice sounded like calm thunder rumbling through Rowan's irrational insecurity.

"On purpose?" Shock cut through Nigel's question.

"If it was an accident I would have heard or felt it in the trailer."

Rowan's heart punched at her breastbone. Rhodes had just echoed her own thoughts, almost word for word.

So why did that fill her with cold trepidation? And squirmy arousal?

Nigel's forehead creased with a frown. "You think someone's trying to hurt Chris?"

Aslin studied the skewed steps for a few seconds, and Rowan noticed everyone—including herself, damn it— seemed to be holding their breath.

"Trying to cause harm to *someone* in his trailer," he said, returning his focus to Nigel. "It may not be Chris."

A sharp bark of a laugh burst passed Rowan's lips. "You think someone's trying to hurt you or me?"

Chris snorted. "I'd like to see them try."

Rowan whacked her brother's shoulder with the back of her hand. "Screw you, squirt."

"Hey! Don't hurt the talent." He pulled a wounded expression, and if it wasn't for the blood still trickling from the gash on his eyebrow, Rowan would have whacked him again.

Rowan rolled her eyes just as Aslin let out a low chuckle, and before she knew what she was doing, she was giving the Brit a wide grin.

"The talent already *is* hurt." Thank God, Nigel's gruff statement shattered the ridiculous moment.

Rowan lurched to her feet, her belly not just knotting, but twisting and churning as well. She didn't *want* to connect with Aslin Rhodes. He would bring nothing to her brother's already unnatural reality. He was an unwanted distraction.

"The paramedics have arrived, Mr. McQueen."

Rowan blinked at Nigel's personal assistant, the young man appearing from nowhere at his side.

"I don't need the paramedics," Chris protested.

"Of course you don't." Nigel shook his head. "But the studio will bust my ass if I don't get you looked at by a medical professional. The film's insurance policy and all. How much *is* that face of yours insured for exactly?"

Rowan snapped her stare to her brother, not even attempting to hide her shock. "You insured your face? Oh, Chris, I thought we talked about that kind of pretentious crap?"

Chris chuckled. "Shut up, sis." He placed his palms on the ground beside his butt and pushed himself to his feet.

And stumbled sideward.

Straight into Aslin's chest. "Whoa…"

Aslin closed his large hands around Chris's shoulders,

stabilizing him. "Steady there, lad." The Brit shot Rowan a look over Chris head. The concern in his eyes made her throat tight and her heart beat faster.

Oh God, she couldn't fall for him. She could *not* fall for—

"I feel…" Chris frowned at Rowan, "…odd."

"And that's my cue to get you to the hospital." Nigel stepped forward and slipped his arm around Chris's back.

Chris shook his head, and then moaned. "Might be a good idea. Aslin, can you take care of my sister for me?"

Rowan mouth fell open just as her pulse surged into a maniacal sprint in her throat. "Take care…? What, you don't think I'm coming to the hospital with—"

Her blustered argument was cut short by the screeching halt of an ambulance beside them.

Chris grinned at her. "Nope. I don't. I'm fine." He paused as a female paramedic climbed out of the driver's side and hurried toward him. A very cute paramedic, Rowan couldn't help but notice. Chris's grin turned flirty, bordering on kilowatt intensity as he focused it on the young woman inspecting his wound. "Exceptionally fine."

He flicked Rowan a look and she wanted to groan at the devilish mischief in his eyes. "Now go. I'm sure Aslin knows exactly how to show you a good time."

Rowan scowled at him. "Chris."

"Is that okay, Aslin?" He ignored her, giving the Brit a wide smile. "Can you look after Rowie while I go to the hospital? If I let her come, she'll just intimidate all the doctors and nurses into giving me a CAT scan or something equally horrible."

"Chris," she tried again.

"I can take care of your sister," Aslin said.

To Rowan's horror, her cheeks flooded with heat, but whether it was the far-too sexy sound of his accent or the utterly confident calm of his tone, she didn't know. Both made her think instantly of being *taken* by him—his head buried between her thighs, his tongue rasping over her clit as his hands roamed her body...

The throb in her pussy grew thicker, hotter, and she looked at him, noting the ambiguous expression on his face, the quiet strength in his body. She opened her mouth to protest, to tell him—and her brother—to piss off, but he spoke before she could.

"I know exactly what to do with her." The edges of his lips curled a little, his gaze holding hers. "Exactly."

Rowan's mouth went dry. Even as her sex constricted and the crotch of her panties grew damp.

Oh boy. This was *not* what she expected.

What the fuck did she do now?

# Chapter Three

The sweat trickled down Aslin's temples, but he ignored it. His muscles burned, flooded with energy. He studied Rowan, his heart pounding, his body on fire. Fuck, he'd never felt so charged. If he didn't know any better, he'd say his veins flowed with concentrated adrenaline. And lust.

Who would have thought it?

He sucked in a swift breath. He'd never been a man for self-delusion. When he recognised in himself a want, desire or opinion, he acknowledged it and, if possible, acted on it. His time as Nick's bodyguard had taught him about the dangers and vices of self-indulgence, and his years in Her Majesty's service taught him self-discipline and control.

That he was sexually attracted to Chris Huntley's sister was a given.

What he was going to do about it wasn't.

His blood on fire, he studied the American as she rocked back and forth. Her exquisitely fit body was beyond sublime, her long thighs firm and toned. Her hips rolled with confident purpose, the rhythm moving through her close to perfection as she rode the mechanical bull between her legs.

Another cheer reverberated around the Buckshot Saloon, one of Sydney's most popular American-themed nightclubs, as the mechanical bull lurched to the left with violent speed. The crowd cheered louder as Rowan clung on with all the skill of a professional rodeo rider.

She let out a squeal of laughter, her smile wide and open. When he'd first brought her here—after a good hour's worth of crawling through Sydney's peak-hour traffic on his bike, her inner thighs pressed against his hips, the tips of her breasts brushing his back whenever he braked—she'd looked at him like he'd grown an extra head.

"Seriously?" She'd cocked an eyebrow at him, her long blonde hair scraped back in a ponytail his fingers just itched to release. "This is what you think I want right now?"

A thick spasm had claimed Aslin's cock at her choice of words. He'd known what he wanted right there and then, but despite the desire he'd seen in Rowan's eyes every time she'd turned her gaze on him back in Chris's trailer, he didn't think it was right to suggest it. For one thing, he'd also noticed anger in her eyes. And confusion.

So instead he'd brought her here, to the Buckshot, a place guaranteed to give anyone who enjoyed testing their physical limits a good time. If nothing else, the mechanical bull allowed them both to work off their pent-up tension.

Out in the middle of the riding area, Rowan whiplashed backward, one arm arcing behind her head as the machine between her legs took a savage nosedive. Every man with a pulse watched her, enrapt. Aslin couldn't miss that. He'd scanned the crowd after his own go on the bull, biting back a growl at what he saw. The second Rowan had taken his place, had swung one long, black-leather-clad leg over the saddle, every male in the club had paused, drinks forgotten in their hands, stares locked on the woman astride the machine.

Every single one of them, Aslin suspected, would have traded places with the bull in a heartbeat.

Sitting at their table on the perimeter of the riding mat, Aslin didn't doubt many of those men were preparing to make their move when Rowan finished her turn.

The way she rode the mechanical bull, the way her body moved, the way her breasts strained against the snug black T-shirt she wore, the way her laughter escaped her in breathless gasps…hell, even the sexy American accent that filled the club every time she called out, "Yeah! Oh boy, that's it, that's it!" was turning the audience of red-blooded males into a frenzied pack with only one thing on its collective mind. Rutting.

*Or is that just you?*

Aslin drew a slow breath and let his gaze move from the vision of Rowan riding the bull to the crowd watching the show. No. It wasn't just him. More than one man stared at her, more than one disgruntled girlfriend or wife glared at their partner's mesmerized face.

This very moment in the Buckshot Saloon, Rowan Hemsworth was as lusted after as her brother was every day.

A sharp buzzer sounded over the cheers and hollers, signaling Rowan's time had ended.

The bull's erratic gyrations slowed, coming to a standstill a few seconds later.

"Now *that* was very impressive," the Buckshot's MC congratulated into a microphone as he approached Rowan, who was now sliding off the bull to the mat. "Am I allowed to say it's your American blood?"

Rowan laughed and Aslin couldn't help but notice his cock grew thicker at the relaxed sound. She had a horny laugh—throaty and sensual. "Not if you want to keep standing."

The MC chuckled, threaded his fingers through hers and lifted her arm above her head. "Give the little lady a hand, everyone. Six and a half minutes."

The crowd burst out with raucous cheers, clapping and more than one wolf-whistle. Rowan grinned, dropped into a little curtsey and began walking toward where Aslin sat at their table.

As predicted, she was stopped twice before she made it. Both times her would-be suitors indicated in the direction of the bar with their hands, their gaze devouring her with open interest. Both times she flashed her dimple at them and shook her head, her cheeks high with colour.

Both times, the desire to stand up and cross to her while the men chatted her up shot through Aslin. He kept his arse in his seat however. For two reasons. One, he had no claim on her and if she wanted to have a drink with a man she met here tonight she could, as much as he didn't like the idea at all. And two, she didn't like to be treated like she needed to be looked after. He could tell already. Not just because she was one of only three people in the world who'd managed to put him on his arse, but by the way she held herself, the way she'd challenged him when they first met. And by her martial art skill.

You didn't take the world Taekwondo championship multiple times over if you needed protection.

Which was interesting, because by nature he was drawn to people who needed to be protected, and yet Rowan turned him on more than any woman he'd ever met. What did that say?

"I beat you."

He smiled at Rowan's smug gloat as she sank into the

seat opposite him. Her breasts were still heaving, her voice still a little breathless. It was a deliciously arousing sight and his cock responded. At this rate, he'd need to unzip his jeans soon for fear of breaking his dick. And then he'd be unable to stand up without poking himself in the eye.

She grinned, dimple creasing her smooth cheek. "One whole minute longer. *And* I got two drink offers. How many did you get?"

He chuckled, unable to help himself. Christ, her accent was sexy. "One. While you were on the bull."

An unreadable expression fell over Rowan's face at his proclamation. "Really?"

He nodded again, holding up his half-consumed soda water. "From the waitress. She asked if I wanted a refill."

Rowan rolled her eyes. "So, your humour is just as lame as your fighting technique, I see."

"It would seem so."

She picked up her own drink—a scotch, straight up—and raised it to her lips. "Do you come here often?"

"Is that a pick-up line?"

"Answer the question, soldier."

"Is that an order?"

"It is. I've beaten you twice in a twenty-four-hour period. Victor's privilege."

"I see." He lifted his own glass to his mouth and took a drink, enjoying the icy liquid flowing over his tongue and down his throat. He was hot. Hot and aroused. "In that case, no. Never been here before."

She contemplated his answer, her gaze on his face just as confident as her body language. Her posture was beautiful, her spine straight, her shoulders the same, nothing in her position telling him she was unnerved by their banter. And yet, her breasts still rose and fell with alacrity. He knew she wasn't breathless from her rodeo ride—her level of fitness was obvious to him from the second she put him on his back at the film site. Which meant she was affected by him. It would be very enjoyable to see her lose control completely.

To be the one responsible for such release.

"So, out of the blue, you brought an American to an American bar you've never been to before. What if it sucked?"

"Then I would have taken you somewhere else."

The corners of her lips curled. "Where?"

"The local paintball arena."

She burst out laughing. "You really know how to show a girl a good time, Aslin Rhodes."

He took another drink of his soda water, doing his damndest to ignore the urgent pressure in his cock. "Thank you."

"So tell me, how does a super soldier end up being a bodyguard for a rock star?" She leant forward, the nightclub's muted light glinting in her eyes. "Did you get wounded?"

Aslin shook his head. "No. I just needed a change of scenery."

"And now you're working on a Hollywood movie." She sipped her scotch, studying him over the brim of the glass. "Planning on becoming an actor next?"

He shook his head, holding her inspection. "I don't suit the lifestyle. Besides, I have a very limited range. Stoic and menacing."

"Don't suit the lifestyle?" Her eyes narrowed. "After all those years as Nick Blackthorne's bodyguard? I would have thought you'd be *used* to the lifestyle? I've read the stories about his indulgences. The wild parties, the women, the excesses. Surely you miss it? You were in among it for so long, right? I bet more than one fan or record-label executive offered whatever you wanted for a chance at Nick."

He took another drink. "The stories aren't all true."

She cocked an eyebrow. "Really?"

Aslin knew exactly what Rowan was doing. Weighing up the man who had suddenly become a part of her brother's life, no matter how recently—or vaguely. He held her gaze with his, understanding her actions this afternoon a little more. She may not need protecting, but in her opinion her brother did. From the life fame delivered. He understood that. He'd done his best during his years as Nick's bodyguard to protect him from the wildness, especially when he was still in his twenties. It hadn't been easy. At times, he was still surprised Nick had survived it all.

*And that's what she fears, boyo. Her brother getting caught up in it…and maybe not walking away with his life.*

"I won't lead him astray," he said. "Nor tell him any tales of Nick's wild days."

A calm stillness fell over Rowan. She stared at him, a fine muscle in her jaw bunching. "I would hurt you if you did."

"I know."

She didn't take her focus from his face. "I'm serious. He's too important to me to lose to the lifestyle. He doesn't need another party buddy or drinking chum. Or someone to help him spend his money or to tag along to celebrity dinners and award shows. If you think you can gain something from him, if you think he's a free ride to your next *change of scenery*, you're sorely mistaken."

Warm approval rolled through Aslin. It threaded through the base physical attraction he felt for Rowan. There was so much more to this woman than just a gorgeous body and sexy strength. She was protective, stubborn and not afraid to face any challenge to those she loved.

The realization was unsettling. It made the heavy pressure in his groin all the more exquisite and painful. Mindless fucking wasn't mindless when the woman he was fucking stirred him on an emotional level as well. And Christ, did Rowan Hemsworth stir him on an emotional level.

His blood roared in his ears. The adrenaline still lingering in his veins from his earlier mechanical-bull ride surged through him again, this time fed by an excitement far more potent.

He could fall for Rowan Hemsworth if he let himself. Hard. Fast.

The thought made his mouth dry. He'd had numerous lovers in his time, but nothing serious. Protecting Nick—and then Lauren and Josh—had been his priority. He met his sexual desires when needed and went back to work. But that work, that life, was almost in his past. What did that mean for everything else in his life?

"So tell me, super soldier—" Rowan's stare held his, a shadow deep in her eyes Aslin longed to understand, "— what exactly *are* you hoping to achieve working on *Dead Even* with my brother?"

*To get to know you better.*

The words, the confession, almost slipped from him. They were there, right on his tongue. They made his heart thump harder and his stomach coil. Instead, he leant forward, drew his gaze level with Rowan's and said, "To make him the most believable super soldier Hollywood has ever seen."

"Oh well, in that case—" she chinked her glass against his, a smile playing with her lips, "—here's to super soldiers on and off screen."

She downed her scotch in a single mouthful and then ran the tip of her tongue along her top lip. Aslin stared at the small pink tip of flesh, hypnotized. He wondered what it would feel like sliding against his. Would she taste of scotch if he kissed her now? Or would her mouth be sweet and warm?

Would he lose himself in the kiss? Would she moan into his mouth and wrap her arms around his back?

Would she press her hips to his?

Would she—

"Here's your fries." A woman's voice sounded to Aslin's right. He started, snapping his stare up to the waitress leaning over their table. "And your ketchup."

She placed a large basket of thin, hot chips between them, followed by a red plastic bottle. A disconnected part of Aslin's unsettled mind told him it was tomato sauce, not ketchup the waitress was giving them, another part thanking bloody Christ she'd arrived when she had. His cock was threatening to burst free of his fly. He needed the distraction from his overwhelming response to Rowan.

Rowan smiled up at the woman, her cheeks flushed. "Thank you. These look delicious."

Aslin bit back a growl. He'd never experienced such a predicament. The need to fuck Rowan so badly twisted through his overwhelming desire to do nothing but get to know all about her—her dreams, her hopes. It was…it was….fuck, he didn't know what it was. Confusing?

Disorientating?

Scary.

A snort left him at the word. Since when had he been scared of anything?

"So." Rowan's low voice drew his attention back to her face. Her cheeks were still flushed, her lips moist, as if she'd licked them again. "Tell me more about Aslin Rhodes. Married? Girlfriend? Dog? Cat?"

He chuckled, forcing some semblance of calm through

his wired muscles. "No. No. No and no. You pretty much know it all, I'm afraid. Ex-SAS commando for the United Kingdom Special Forces, followed by fifteen years as Nick Blackthorne's bodyguard. And now advisor to the film *Dead Even*. That's my story."

"Wow. I don't know what's sadder? The fact that's your story, or that you summed it up in one sentence."

Aslin raised what was left of his soda water to his lips. "Two, actually."

Rowan narrowed her eyes again. "There's that lame humour again. I thought you British were meant to be funny."

"No, that's the Irish. And sometimes the Scots. Billy Connelly is bloody funny, don't you think?" He snared a hot chip from the bowl between them and tossed it into his mouth. "Now," he spoke around the deep-fried strip of potato, "your turn. Why can't you be stunt co-ordinator on the film? I suspect you'd do a very impressive job."

"I'm not a member of the union. Film folk are very particular about their unions." She smiled, a hint of her dimple making Aslin's gut clench. "And thank you. I think I would too. Next question?"

"Huntley? Hemsworth? Which is the real name?"

Rowan picked up the sauce bottle, squeezed a steady stream of the condiment onto half the chips and then plucked one from the bowl. "Hemsworth. But when Chris went to register his name with the Screen Actors Guild there already *was* a Chris Hemsworth."

"The current Thor."

She nodded, popped the chip into her mouth and selected another one. "The current Thor. So Chris went with Huntley, which was our mother's maiden name." A stillness fell over her and her gaze lost focus for a moment. A heartbeat. Long enough for Aslin to see a raw pain in her eyes.

And then she grinned, as if the shadow had never been there, and tossed another chip past her lips. "These fries are really good."

"I'm glad you like them."

"The perfect texture, the perfect length—" she plucked a long chip from the bowl, dipped its end into some tomato sauce and held it up for inspection, dimple denting her cheek. "—sweet but a little salty."

As Aslin watched, she placed it—end first—into her mouth, and then sucked the salt from the tips of her fingers. A groan threatened to escape him. Low and deep in his chest. His balls tightened. Christ, why did he imagine it was his dick sinking past her lips, not the potato?

He jerked his stare from her mouth to her eyes, his jaw bunching.

Rowan stared back at him, unmoving. Motionless.

Fuck. He wanted her. Right at this sodding moment, he wanted her more than breath. On a carnal level. On a filthy level. He wanted to bury his cock in her pussy and fuck her until she screamed his name with release. He wanted—

"I don't want to be attracted to you." Her voice was steady. Direct.

Aslin sucked in a sharp breath, her abrupt statement like a punch to the guts.

"Being attracted to anyone isn't part of my plans," she continued as if discussing the weather. "I don't have time for it. But…" She stopped, her teeth catching her bottom lip.

"You are," Aslin finished for her, his groin a thick knot, his heart pounding. "You are attracted to me."

Rowan nodded, her gaze holding his. "Yes. Very. I've tried to play it cool, but I've spent most of the night thinking about what it would be like to fuck you. To be fucked by you."

The thick tension in Aslin's groin throbbed. Hard. Urgent. Demanding attention. He swallowed, every muscle in his body coiled. "And?"

"And I think the best course of action is to find out. As soon as possible." She paused. For a heartbeat. "If you're interested."

*If you're interested.*

The question hung on the air. Aslin stared at her. Was she kidding? It was all he could do not to shove the table between them away, snare her ponytail in his fist and crush her mouth with his. His cock was a pole of rigid agony. His blood roared in his ears.

*If you're interested.*

"Well? Are you?" Her soft voice played over his scorched nerve-endings. Her American accent sent fresh lust into his balls.

Without a word, he rose to his feet and rounded the table to stand before her. Curling his fingers around her firmly toned upper arm, he hauled her off her feet with a single tug and captured her lips in a searing kiss.

He plundered her mouth straight away. He didn't care they were in a public bar. He didn't give a sodding rat's arse. He wanted her. She wanted him. It was simple.

Her tongue lashed over his, hungry and aggressive. He groaned, the sound a testament to his desire. Rowan raked her nails down his chest, her hands exploring his torso before returning to his pecs. She brushed her fingers over his nipples, sending shards of wet electricity into his groin. His cock pulsed in his jeans, and Rowan moaned into his mouth, pushing her hips harder to his.

Aslin's head swam. He tore his lips from hers, holding her arms with a firm grip as he stared down into her eyes.

"My hotel is—"

"I can't wait that long," she cut him off, her voice a rasping breath. "I need…"

He didn't let her finish. He spun on his heel and strode through the club, heading for the back door. He'd spent enough time escorting Nick from frenzied venues to know every club and bar had one. He also knew this area of Sydney well enough to know the back door of the Buckshot Saloon would lead directly to a narrow alley.

An alley was perfect for filthy, carnal fucking.

Raw, primitive sex.

Warm, slender fingers threaded through his as he pushed open the door to the staff area. He didn't need to turn to know it was Rowan. He'd felt those fingers on his body once already today and he recognised their fierce strength. Five steps later, he shoved open the kitchen door. No one stopped him. No one ever did. His height, his build, his expression… all of it spoke of certain pain if anyone tried. It was one of the reasons he'd been such an effective bodyguard. He radiated deadly promise.

Behind him, Rowan followed, her hand holding his, her strides long and purposeful. He could feel it in the way she kept pace with him.

It was a powerful aphrodisiac. Knowing she was as capable as he. His cock throbbed and jerked in his jeans, straining for release.

Five more steps later, without a word or even a glance at any of the surprised nightclub staff, Aslin flattened his hand on the Buckshot's kitchen door, pushed it open and stepped through it into the alley beyond.

Two steps after that, he heard it slam shut, plunging the alley back into shadowy darkness again. Just as he turned and snared Rowan's waist with one hooked arm.

Their lips came together, hard and savage and brutal. The kiss was wild. He crushed her to his body and fucked her mouth with his tongue, her moans of rapture heating his lust. She clung to him, her fingernails scraping at the back of his neck as he drove her backward to the brick wall behind her.

She cried out, throwing her head back, wrapping her right leg around his thigh. He dragged his lips down the column of her throat, biting, sucking as he went. Her flesh was soft and smooth, velvet beneath his tongue, lips and teeth. He couldn't get enough. He wanted to feel more of her. All of her.

Driving his hand under the hemline of her shirt, he captured her breast, cupping it with punishing force. She whimpered, grinding her sex to the bulge in his jeans. The pressure almost undid him. He pinched her erect nipple through the satin of her bra, reveling in the raw moan falling from her at the course touch.

"Fuck, yes," Rowan panted, wrapping her leg tighter around the backs of his thighs. "That feels good."

He pumped up against her spread pussy, his mind telling him they were still fully clothed, his lust telling him he was sinking into her heat. His cock ached. His balls were rock hard and swollen. Every thrust he made drove him closer to the edge. Every scoring rake of Rowan's nails on his shoulders, his neck, pushed him closer.

He crushed her lips with his again, plundering her mouth with his tongue before capturing her bottom lip with his teeth. She groaned, ramming her sex to his constrained erection, raking her hands down his chest.

A sharp tearing sound, followed by a second of displaced cool air, told Aslin she'd ripped his shirt open. He didn't care. Not when her fingers found his nipples and pinched them.

Hard.

Pain sheared through him, exquisite and primal. He sucked in a sharp breath, teeth clenched, eyes closed. And then let out a low moan as Rowan closed her lips and teeth around one tight nipple and sucked on it.

Hot steel flooded his already engorged dick. He fisted his hand around her ponytail and yanked her head upward, tearing her mouth from his flesh. She gazed up at him, her lips wet and pink, her eyes fogged with desire.

"If you want to stop," he ground out, his heart hammering, "now's the time to say so."

Rowan shook her head. "Shut the fuck up and fuck me, soldier."

He smothered her command with his mouth, snaring the back of her bent leg with a firm grip and yanking it higher. Holding it there as he took what he wanted from her mouth—his pleasure, her need. Every time he swiped his tongue over hers, she whimpered. Every time he thrust into the wet well of her mouth, she rolled her sex against his erection. It was exactly what he'd known it would be— carnal and filthy.

It was perfect. And yet, he wanted more.

Not just to be inside her, but more…

*Later. Later.*

The thought purred through his head, like the licking caress of a whip. He broke their kiss again, pulling away just enough to watch as his hand bunched up her shirt and revealed her breast to him.

She let out a raspy, "yes", her head rolling on the brick wall, her lips parted and moist with his saliva. "Suck it," she whispered. "Suck it."

He did. Cupping the swell of her flesh with his hand, he bowed his back and took her nipple in his mouth, suckling on its distended form through the black satin of her bra.

"Fuck, yes!" She bucked against him, her nails scraping over his shoulders beneath his gaping shirt. "That's it. Harder. Harder."

Her feverish demands drove him wild. His blood surged through his veins in rivers of molten lust and desire. Throbbing through his cock.

He lashed her nipple with his tongue. Sucked it. Bit it. She whimpered, her hands tugging on his hair, tight fistfuls that sent wicked ribbons of pain through Aslin's scalp.

*Christ, gonna...close...*

The unhinged thought tore his mouth from her breast. Or maybe it was the frantic tugging of her fingers on his belt buckle.

He straightened, flattening his hands on the wall either side of her head as he stared down into her eyes. He gazed into her face as she released his belt, popped the button of his fly and then lowered its zipper.

His pulse pounded in his ears. His heart smashed fast in his chest. He drew a slow breath, biting back his groan as Rowan's talented fingers parted his fly, allowing his cock — thick and stiff and swollen with desire — to spring free of his jeans.

"So the commando goes commando does he?" she murmured, the realization he wore no briefs or boxers making the dimple in her cheek flash.

"The commando does."

"Does the commando have a condom in his wallet?"

Aslin's heart thumped harder. "The commando — "

The recorded sound of Chris Huntley shouting, *"Answer your freaking phone, sis!"* cut Aslin's answer short.

He blinked, the actor's voice yelling the same words again a cold blade stabbing at the inferno of his need.

Rowan's eyes widened. Her body tensed. And then she was pushing at Aslin's chest. No, not just pushing at it, shoving it. Driving him backward, her cheeks suddenly pink, her hands—only a second earlier undoing his belt and fly—now scrambling at her pocket, Chris's recorded voice shouting *Answer your freaking phone, sis!* coming from her hip.

Aslin stood motionless, his blood roaring in his ears, and watched her pull a mobile phone from her pocket. Her gaze flicked to his, her cheeks red, and then she turned away, swiping her thumb across the screen of the phone before ramming it to her ear. "What's up, Chris?"

Whatever her brother said next, Aslin didn't hear. What he *did* hear was Rowan say, "Nothing, I'm not doing anything. Don't leave until I get there, okay?"

And when she turned back to him, the woman that faced him was the same woman he'd met back on the film site. The same woman who had put him on his back and dismissed him like a gnat.

*That* woman looked at him, tucked her shirt back into her snug leather pants and said, "Dinner was lovely, thank you. Mind zipping your fly now. I've somewhere else I have to be."

# Chapter Four

Rhodes insisted on taking her to the hospital, which really was damn annoying because her body still burned with the memory of his touch. Still craved for more.

Sitting behind him on his bike, she held onto the rear grab handles in a death grip, determined not to lean into his back. She couldn't risk any more body contact with him. Not if she wanted to keep her sanity. And dignity.

All it would take was the feel of his strong muscled back pressing to her breasts and she would be gone.

So she clung to the Ducati's rear handles, anchored her weight to the pillion-passenger seat with her inner thighs and prayed for a smooth, red-light-free journey.

What was only a twenty-five-minute trip felt more like a lifetime of exquisite torture, her body thrumming with sexual need, the powerful vibrations from the motorcycle between her spread legs sinking into her already stimulated clit. By the time they pulled into the hospital's parking area, she was damn near on the cusp of an orgasm.

She practically threw herself from Aslin's bike, her pussy throbbing, her pulse pounding, her nipples so hard they hurt.

Thank God Chris was waiting for her in the ER. If it weren't for that simple fact, she'd probably do something completely stupid like beg Aslin to fuck her there and then.

Again.

She didn't bother to slow down as she hurried toward the hospital's access elevator. Nor did she check if Aslin was following her. He was. She not only heard his footfalls behind her on the concrete—long strides that echoed around the underground parking area like a slow tattoo—she felt his gaze on her back. Steady. Direct.

Intense.

It made her pussy squeeze. Damn it.

A childish part of her wanted to break into a sprint, dash to the elevator door and get inside before Aslin could join her. It would be easier than standing in the small, confined space with him.

She didn't know what unsettled her more, the way her stupid body was behaving around him, or that he hadn't tried to broach the subject of what had occurred in the alley between them before Chris called.

Either was bad enough.

*For Christ's sake, woman. Control yourself.*

Easier thought than done, especially when his hard, tall body brushed against her back, his oh-so-perfectly muscled arm extended past her and his index finger depressed the elevator button just as she was about to jab at it.

She sucked in a sharp breath.

Control. She needed to find her control. And her focus. Her brother had called for help. That's what she needed to concentrate on, not Rhodes and his sexy-assed muscles, sexy-assed accent and sexy-assed…everything else.

It wasn't until the door closed, imprisoning them both in the small metal space, that she realized she was still holding her breath. Or maybe it was when Aslin moved with silent speed to stand directly in front of her, both hands pressing to the wall behind her head, his intense dark stare capturing her.

"This isn't finished, Rowan." His British accent sent shards of wet tension into her sex. "So don't think it is."

She swallowed, the pit of her belly a churning, twisting mess that had nothing to do with the elevator's rapid ascent to the ER level. "W-what isn't?"

His nostrils flared. "What started in the alley. It's not finished."

Before she could respond, the elevator bounced to a halt, a soft chime screamed through the heavy silence and the door slid open with a clunking jolt.

The smell hit Rowan first—the stinging odor of disinfectant. She stiffened, the memory of the night her parents were killed slamming into her like a fist. Five hours waiting in the ER after the break and enter that changed her and Chris's lives, covered in her mother's blood as the doctors tried to save the unsavable, Chris sitting beside her, shell-shocked, a cop doing his best to get answers from Rowan that weren't coming—who did it, what they looked like, how it happened.

Aslin's stare on her face narrowed. For a heartbeat. And then he turned and, with a gentle pressure she didn't realize she wanted until it was there, smoothed his hand to the small of her back and walked them from the elevator into the ER's waiting rooms.

"Hey, is that Nick Blackthorne's bodyguard?"

Aslin's hand grew firm on her back at the muttered question, a second before a blinding flash detonated to

Rowan's right. And another. Rowan flinched. Which was stupid given how many times she's been photographed while out with Chris.

"*Enough*," a female voice ripe with contempt rose over the sounds of the crowded floor. "I told you scavengers to bugger off already. Stay and I'll order colonoscopies for the lot of you."

Rowan jerked her attention toward the nurse storming toward her and Aslin, her mouth falling open. Now *there* was an intimidating woman. Five eight plus, one hundred and seventy pounds at least, and scowling like a grizzly with a sore tooth.

Rowan heard Nick Blackthorne's name uttered again a second before another flash fired, and then the nurse wasn't just storming towards the scurrying photographer, she was running. If Rowan hadn't been so damn flustered with the whole situation, she would have been impressed.

But she was flustered.

On every level imaginable.

Worried. Turned on. Out of control. Haunted.

Why the hell had she come to Australia in the first—

"He's here, Rowan."

Rowan snapped her stare to her left, finding Nigel McQueen standing at an open door under a sign that clearly said *Medical Staff Only*.

"He's fine—" *Dead Even's* director held up his hands—palms out—as if to placate an expected tirade before it began, "—but word must have leaked to the public he was here, because by the time the doc was ready to discharge him the paps had arrived." He flicked Aslin—towering over Rowan on her left—a quick look. "I've never seen so many supposedly injured paparazzi in one place. Thank God you came, Rhodes."

The obvious relief in Nigel's voice at the Brit's presence pissed Rowan off. She ground her teeth and stepped away from the man. His fingers slipped from the base of her spine, a loss of contact that should have made her glad.

*Should* have.

She drove her nails into her palms and glared at McQueen. "Where is he? Take me to him now."

"This way." The director turned and began to walk away.

Rowan nodded at Aslin. "Thanks for bringing me here. I'll catch a taxi back to Chris's trailer lat—"

"Chris wants to see Aslin too." Nigel's voice cut her dismissal short. "He said the two of you would be together."

Hot tension squirmed through Rowan's belly, but from Nigel's words or the look Aslin gave her that echoed exactly what he'd told her in the elevator—that it wasn't over—she didn't know.

*Of course you know. It's both.*

It *was* both. She was pissed Chris had made a connection with the bodyguard. And she was unnerved that she had as well.

Without a word, she walked through the door. A white flash popped behind her, telling her at least one paparazzo had risked being given a colonoscopy to get a photo of Nick Blackthorne's bodyguard. On a detached level, she wondered if images of Aslin without the rock star sold, and then she saw her brother sitting propped against a pile of pillows on a hospital bed, a white butterfly bandage stuck to his eyebrow and all thoughts of the paparazzi vanished.

"Hey, sis." A wide grin split Chris's world-famous face. He cocked his head to the side a little, no doubt in an attempt to show her his wound. "Looks like I'm going to need to make a claim on my insurance. What do you think, Aslin? Will it make me more believable as a seasoned commando?"

"Definitely," Aslin's deep rumble behind her made Rowan's belly knot. "All us commandos have scars."

Before she could stop herself, she turned and cast a steady inspection over Aslin's hawkishly handsome face. There was a ghost of a scar along his strong right jaw line, a thin straight line that—to her practiced eye—looked like the result of a blade or knife of some kind, and a smaller, thicker scar just above his left eyebrow near his temple. Neither detracted from the understated sensuality radiating from him. In fact, they only emphasized it. In a menacing, primitive way.

Oh boy. She was pathetic.

"Like what you see?"

A fiery blush flooded Rowan's cheeks at Aslin's murmured question. She started, jerking her attention back to her brother. Only to find Chris grinning at her.

*Great. Just great.*

"Rowan and Aslin sitting in a tree," her brother sang off-key, his eyes sparkling with mischief. "Kay. Eye. Ess. Ess. Eye. En—"

She thumped him in the shoulder with a fist. "Shut the fuck up."

He laughed.

Behind her, Aslin chuckled. Chuckled.

"Probably not a good idea to hit the patient." An older man dressed in a white coat appeared at the foot Chris's bed, a disapproving frown on his seamed face. He reached for the chart, the wrinkles in his forehead deepening. "Hmm. Your vitals are still a little erratic, Mr. Huntley. I'm thinking I'd like to keep you in overnight for observation."

Rowan stiffened. "What's going on, doctor?"

The elder gentleman lifted an eyebrow at her. "Apart from being punched in the shoulder, you mean?"

Chris snorted. "Gotcha there, sis."

"Sister?" The doctor made a *tsk tsk* sound.

Rowan bit back a retort. No matter how much she wanted to tell the old coot to shut up, now wasn't the time. "Is Chris okay?"

"He's fine, Rowan," Nigel answered. Apparently because the doctor decided he needed to check Chris's eyesight. "A mild concussion. But the studio bosses will feel happier if Chris stays overnight."

Rowan looked at the doctor currently studying her brother's right eye. "Just a concussion?"

The doctor didn't break off his inspection of Chris's eyeball. "I believe so. But I want to be sure."

"Awesome." Rowan pulled a face at her brother. "First night in Australia and I'm sleeping in a hospital room. Way to go, squirt."

The doctor straightened. "I don't know how you do things in America, but unless the patient is possibly going to die, overnight visitors are not allowed in the hospital rooms."

Rowan frowned. "But he's my brother."

Chris smirked at her. "And he's alive. Yay. Now take off. I thought I was getting out tonight but it looks like I'm staying put."

"So I came all this way for what?"

Her brother looked at her. "To go buy me a toothbrush?"

She crossed her arms. "Seriously?"

The clatter of the hospital chart dropping back into its holder prevented Chris from saying whatever he was going to say. It was probably for the best. By the gleam in his eye, it would have made Rowan want to punch his shoulder again.

"That's enough for the evening, I think," the doctor spoke up. He fixed her with a steady glower, obviously not impressed with any of them. "You can come collect Mr.

Huntley tomorrow, but now he needs rest."

Rowan studied her brother's grinning face, her belly tight. She couldn't help but notice the deep purple bruise smudging his cheek. He'd been very lucky, it seemed. The fall from the trailer could have really hurt him, and as much as the idea pained her, his good looks were part of his career. If his face had been damaged, his nose broken, it would have impacted the filming of *Dead Even* and may have had an adverse effect on his future roles.

Damn it. It was times like these she wished he were a normal brother, with a normal job. Like a dog walker or something. She wouldn't need to be constantly worrying about stuff like this, superficial stuff, surreal stuff, if he was a dog walker.

"Don't worry, miss," the doctor continued, his glower replaced with calm sympathy. "We are well aware of who your brother is. The media and any unauthorized personnel will not be allowed access to him or the ward he stays in. There will be no need for his bodyguard to stay."

The word bodyguard sent a hot lick of something delicious through Rowan's agitation. She threw the silent Aslin a quick look over her shoulder, her pulse pounding faster at the sight of his towering strength and undeniable presence.

For a worrying moment, she longed to feel his warm, strong hand on the small of her back again. To lean against his hard body and surrender to the attraction she felt for him.

That same hot lick teased her again at the thought. Why *couldn't* she lean on him? Would it truly be so bad?

"Thanks, doc." Nigel's voice jerked her from the ridiculous question, and she focused her attention on the film director. "Aslin, can I trouble you to take Rowan…"

He stopped, giving Rowan a frown. "Where are you staying, Rowan?"

She blinked. She hadn't booked into a hotel room yet. She hadn't planned on her brother ending up in the ER. Just like she hadn't planned to spend the evening being seduced by a British super-soldier.

Or making out with said soldier in an alley behind a bar.

"She can crash in my suite tonight," Chris piped up. "But after that you're on your own, sis. You cramp my style too much."

Nigel laughed. Even the doctor chuckled.

Rowan glared at them all. "Your style? Falling flat on your face, you mean?"

Chris smirked. "That's the one."

"Fun's over," the doctor said. "Time for everyone to go. Mr. McQueen, as the person who brought Mr. Huntley in, can I get you to sign some paper work at the nurses desk, please?"

"Sure thing, doc." Nigel extended his arm across Chris, and Rowan almost yelped when Aslin brushed against her to complete the handshake. "Thanks for taking care of Rowan for us, Aslin. Back to normal on set tomorrow, okay? Shall we say ten a.m.?"

"We shall," Aslin answered.

Or at least she thought he did. All she could hear was the roaring of her blood in her ears. With just one small touch of his body—his chest on her shoulder, of all things—she was almost panting with need. God, how was she going to survive the motorcycle ride to Chris's hotel?

"Give me a kiss, sis." Chris chuckled. "And stop freaking out."

Heart far too fast for its own good, Rowan leant forward and dropped a kiss on her brother's cheek, right beside the blooming purple bruise. "I'm not freaking out," she muttered.

Chris laughed. "Yes, you are," he shot back, his voice low. "And I know exactly why and it has nothing to do with me." He slid a quick look over her shoulder, a shoulder still tingling from Aslin's contact.

A thick lump formed in Rowan's throat. She forgot sometimes how astute and observant her brother was. The world knew him as a sexy, handsome funny-man, a guy with a quick wit and a killer smile, and sometimes she herself was guilty of pigeon-holing him the same way. But he was more than that. He was smart and perceptive and tuned into her moods as only a brother who'd survived a nightmare with his sister could be.

"Love you, Rowie," he murmured into her ear. "Now fuck off and have some fun for a change, will you?"

Rowan swallowed, unable to find any words. Instead, she gave her brother a quick nod, straightened and stepped back from his bed.

"Okay, Mr. Huntley," the doctor said, just as a tall male nurse arrived and released the locking mechanism on the bed's casters. "Time to exit left. Or is the appropriate term 'That's a wrap'?" The elder gentleman chuckled, slid his pen into his top pocket and gave Rowan a smile. "Do not stress, miss. Your brother will be fine." And with that, and a quick inclination of his head to Aslin, he left.

As did Chris, the male nurse pulling the bed from its place without warning and maneuvering him away.

"I was about to say welcome to the weird world of film making, Mr. Rhodes—" Nigel chuckled, "—but I suspect the music world is equally weird, right?"

"Somewhat." A shiver rippled up Rowan's spine at Aslin's voice. Damn it, when was she going to stop reacting to his accent?

Never?

Nigel laughed and then turned to her. "Rowan, Tilly has Chris's hotel key. She's waiting on set until she hears from me. Give her a call to let her know you're on your way to collect them."

Rowan nodded. "Thanks, Nigel."

The director cast them both a contemplative look, as if seeing something he hadn't expected, and then strode through the private room toward another door on the other side.

Which left Rowan alone with Aslin.

Again.

For some stupid reason her mouth went dry.

When Aslin placed his hand on the small of her back—the very place she'd been aching for it to be since he removed it—she jumped.

She lifted her stare up to his face, her lips prickling with a sudden rush of blood. "I…" she began.

A crooked smile pulled at one corner of his mouth. "Let's go. There's things that need to be done."

Rowan's heart smashed against her breastbone. She swallowed, her stomach muscles clenching. "Aslin, what we did—"

His dark gaze grew intense. "Isn't finished." And with that, he directed her from the room out into the ER waiting area beyond.

There were no camera flashes to been seen as they crossed the floor. She didn't hear any more mutters of Nick Blackthorne's name from the surrounding seats, nor the word *bodyguard* whispered, but the tension in Aslin's body as they walked to the elevator told Rowan he suspected the paparazzi were still lurking there.

Or maybe he was tense because of her? Maybe, despite

how calm and cool he seemed, he was just as disturbed by the sexual chemistry between them both?

She didn't let herself ponder the possibility. When they stepped into the elevator, she pulled her cell phone from her hip pocket and dialed Chris's personal assistant's number, refusing to look at Aslin as she waited for Tilly to answer.

She heard him chuckle, a low rumble that made her sex throb, and then Tilly, in her subtle Californian accent, was saying, "Oh my God, Ms. Hemsworth, is Mr. Huntley okay?" in her ear.

The duration of the trip down to the parking level was spent arranging with Tilly to meet at Chris's trailer within the hour. Rowan kept her stare on the closed elevator doors the whole time. It was gutless coward's way to deal with a situation, but all Rowan could manage. The whole thing was too overwhelming. Too confronting and confusing. Better to spend longer than normal talking to Chris's perky personal assistant than deal with the...the...*thing* hanging between her and the Brit. Not until she got her head around it. And decided on the next course of action.

She was still talking to Tilly—enquiring about Chris's food intake while she'd been in Canada, of all things—when she and Aslin crossed the parking level to his Ducati. Their footfalls bounced around the quiet space, a soft tempo that rivaled the rapid beating of her heart. By the time Tilly said goodbye, Rowan was so tense, so on-edge, she could barely draw breath.

Getting back onto the Ducati was insane.

Pressing her chest and belly to Aslin's broad back, nudging his butt cheeks with her spread pussy, hugging his hips with her inner thighs...all insane. God, at this rate she would come the second he started the bike.

Long, firm fingers circled her upper arms a heartbeat

before a tall, hard body appeared directly before her. She stiffened, her stare clashing with Aslin's. "You can't ignore me forever, Rowan," he spoke, that sexy British accent doing wicked things to her senses. "Especially when I do this."

He lowered his head and captured her lips with his, his tongue delving into her mouth with velvet ease.

She didn't fight him. There was no point. She wanted this kiss, this touch as much as he did. Maybe more. She'd denied her sexual needs for a long time, putting Chris's wellbeing above everything else except her driving need to never be weak and vulnerable again. The number of dates she'd been on since *Twice Too Many* hit the air could be counted on two hands. If she wasn't looking out for her brother, protecting him in the only way she knew how, she was working out in the dojo, training, sweating out the fears and the nightmares of her parents' murders until she was nothing but a well-honed machine capable of breaking a fully-grown man in two with a simple jiu-jitsu move. And yet here she was now, rendered vulnerable to an emotion far more all-consuming than fear and terror.

Here she was, surrendering to a fully grown man's mastery over her body with no more fight than a whimpered groan.

Surrendering willingly. Despite the fact they were in a parking lot. Despite the fact her brother was somewhere in the hospital above her, injured due to a suspicious situation.

Surrendering and aching for more. Aching for Aslin's total and utter possession of her body.

Weak.

Vulnerable.

Defeated.

Oh God, she'd never felt so damn on fire. So damn alive.

She pressed her hips to his, rolled them, wanting to feel

the solid steel of his erection trapped by his jeans grind against the curve of her sex.

He growled into her mouth. That was the only word for it, a growl, animalistic and dominating. Her pussy turned to liquid need at the purely male sound. She raked her nails over his shoulder, knotted her fingers in the hair at his nape. He lashed his tongue against hers, his rigid cock pressing into her belly.

Her head swam. Her sex throbbed. She gave herself over to his control, the kiss igniting a need within her she could no longer ignore.

He circled his hands around her waist and, without tearing his lips from hers, hauled her from the ground. She moaned into his mouth as he spun her around and deposited her onto the seat of his bike, wrapped her legs around his hips and slammed his trapped cock to the junction of her thighs.

# Chapter Five

The last place Aslin wanted to make love to Rowan was on the back of his motorbike. First against a wall in an alleyway, now an uneven bike seat in a cold, concrete parking lot. The trouble was the second, the very second, she looked up at him with those mesmerizing blue eyes of hers, any sodding notion of controlling his lust vanished.

Kissing her wasn't enough.

He needed to be inside her. Now.

He dug his fingers into the firm muscles of her arse cheeks and squeezed, pressing his cock to her heat as he did so. Pleasurable pain shot through his groin and he groaned into her mouth, hauling her harder to his erection. She raked at his shoulders with her nails, her thighs squeezing his hips, her own moans loud in the near-empty parking level.

*Stop, boyo. Not here. Not like this…*

But he couldn't. His hands roamed her legs, up her ribcage, over her breasts. She gasped into his mouth when he pinched one nipple through her shirt, her nails scraping at the back of his neck in response. He liked it. A lot. He'd never been one for BDSM, but the pain Rowan wrought on his body was delicious.

Pinching her nipple again, he steeled himself against the agony of her nails on his flesh. The pain came, sending fresh hot blood surging through his straining dick and he groaned again. More pain followed, pleasurable pain, when she snared a fistful of his hair and tugged. Fast and hard.

He tore his mouth from her lips, sucking in a steady breath as he stared down into her eyes. "I can fuck you here and now, Rowan. On my bike. Where anyone can stumble upon us. I don't care. I'm beyond caring. But it's your call. I don't want you to—"

A sudden white flash bleached Rowan's face, followed by another, and another.

Aslin spun around, his glare falling on a familiar man standing but a few feet away, a large SLR camera held up to his face.

Aslin's gut clenched, cold fury storming through him.

Holston.

"Now that's what I call an action shot, Rhodes," the notorious Australian paparazzo called out, removing the memory card from the camera with swift hands. "You been taking lessons from that boss of yours?" He shoved the card into his back pocket with a smirk. "How is Nick by the way? Fucking around on his wife yet? I was hoping you'd lead me to him, but instead I found—"

Rowan stiffened in Aslin's arms. For a second. Only one. And then she was off his bike and sprinting toward Holston, a feline grace claiming her body.

The paparazzo froze. His mouth gaped, sheer shock on his face as Rowan flung her body into the most elegant spinning kick Aslin had ever seen, her heel smashing into

Holston's jaw with a crunching thud.

The photographer stumbled sideways and fell to his knees. His camera clattered to the concrete, skittering across the ground just as Rowan's leg completed its blurring arc.

It was poetry in motion. Aslin had never seen anything so beautiful. So perfect.

"Fuckin' bitch!" Holston screeched, desperately trying to regain his feet. "You fucking—"

Rowan's foot struck out in a blurring streak. There was a distinct cracking sound, a surprised yelp from the photographer and then Holston's camera was flying through the air, rising, rising...

And then smashing down to the ground in pieces.

"Now try and take our photo, fucker," Rowan's coldly calm voice reached Aslin. "Or better still, get a real job."

She turned and walked back to Aslin, as if she hadn't just put the most infamous paparazzo in the country on the ground.

Aslin cocked an eyebrow. "That was interesting."

She looked up at him. "That was an interruption." Her glare slid behind him and she shook her head. "Don't even think about it."

Aslin twisted at the waist, a grin pulling at his lips at the sight of Holston frozen in an awkward half-crouch. How many years had he wanted to beat the shit out of the bastard? How many times had the sod invaded Nick's world and Aslin had been forced to pull punches longing to be swung?

Hell, how many cameras wielded by Holston had Aslin himself smashed before the paparazzo learned to swap memory cards before Aslin could get to him? Too many to count, but none were as beautifully destroyed as Rowan's effortless kick.

"You'll pay for this, Rhodes," Holston snarled, still motionless.

Aslin chuckled. "I've heard that before."

"Didn't think you'd need a chick to do your dirty work."

Aslin shook his head. "Mate, I'd shut up while you can still talk." He turned back to Rowan, his smile stretching wider. "I was wrong. That wasn't interesting, that was impressive."

"Thank you. Now can we get out of here? I want to take these boots off and disinfect them ASAP."

"Bitch!" Holston yelled behind Aslin. "The cops are going to hear about this!"

Aslin unclipped his helmet from its secure lock and handed it to Rowan. "Think you've made a new friend."

Rowan pulled a face. "Oh goody. Shall we ask him to join—watch out!"

Aslin spun at her shout. Just in time to duck under the camera Holtson wildly flung at his head. He punched a fist upward into the man's flabby solar-plexus. Just one punch. But it was enough.

Holston doubled over, face red, and then crumpled to his arse with a fat plop.

"Now that," Rowan said, "was impressive."

Aslin stood, casting the coughing, groaning photographer a steady inspection. "You'll never learn, Holston."

"Fucking Pom," Holston mumbled, head down, arm wrapped around his gut.

With a shake of his head, Aslin turned back to Rowan. "Still want to ask him to join us?"

Disgust pulled at Rowan's lips. Lips Aslin had tasted such a short while ago. "No."

He recognised the anger in her face. He'd seen it on Nick Blackthorne's face so many times in the years he'd protected the rock star it was etched in his psyche. He'd watched it simmer in Lauren's eyes since Nick re-entered her life. No doubt, for Rowan it had always been directed at the scum invading her famous brother's privacy. Tonight however, that scum had invaded her own.

And it sickened her.

Shooting Holston one last look and finding the paparazzo glaring at him with sullen eyes, broken camera in hand, Aslin climbed onto his bike.

"Fucking Pom," Holston muttered.

With a chuckle, Aslin removed the helmet lent to him by one of *Dead Even's* film crew from the handlebar. "As always, Holston—" he grinned at the surly photographer, a deeper part of his mind all too aware that Rowan had climbed onto the pillion seat and was now sliding her thighs against his hips, "—it's been a pleasure."

He didn't bother to wait to see if Holston responded. Pulling the borrowed helmet over his head, he leant forward, started the Ducati's ignition and revved the throttle.

He wanted to get Rowan away from the bastard ASAP. He wanted to take her somewhere private. Somewhere safe.

Tearing through the night streets of Sydney, he headed for the old Hyde Park Barracks. He didn't question his need to protect her. It was who he was. It was ridiculous, of course, given that she'd just handed Holston his arse with that exquisite spinning kick, but there it was. He not only wanted to fuck her, he wanted to guard her from anything that may upset or unsettle her. One day, no not even that, half a day, and he was completely focused on her emotional and physical safety.

A tight fist of disquiet twisted in his gut. Maybe he really *was* just a bodyguard? A man with nothing more significant to offer the world than his muscles? Was that truly it?

The answer didn't come to him before they arrived at the film location.

Nor when he climbed off his bike and crossed to Chris's trailer before Rowan could slide from the pillion seat.

The silence of the surrounding area put him on edge. As did the darkness lurking around them, barely penetrated by the weak glow thrown by the sparse lights scattered around the fenced-off film set. It was ludicrous to think any possible threat hid in their depths, but he moved as if there was.

Too many years knowing no other way had left its mark. With the suspicious tampering of the trailer's steps gnawing away at the back of his mind, Aslin couldn't stop his wary alertness.

Especially when Rowan was so close.

When the door to Chris's trailer slammed open, his hand reached for a gun he hadn't worn on his hip for over sixteen years.

"Hiya, Ms. Hemsworth." Chris's personal assistant skipped down the once-again aligned steps, a black bag hanging from her fingers. "I've packed Mr. Huntley's hotel key, his cell, a change of underwear and three bottles of coconut water."

"Thanks, Tilly."

As always, Aslin's body reacted to Rowan's soft American accent. He wished he could understand why. Hell, Nick had lived in New York until returning to Australia, which meant Aslin had too, in a smaller apartment one floor down. An American accent wasn't exotic and unusual to his ears at all. And yet every word Rowan said sounded sinfully sexy.

Every word. Even something as innocuous as, "thanks."

He stood and watched the two women, enjoying the way Rowan's dimple flashed as she smiled at Tilly.

*Who are you kidding, boyo? It's not just her dimple. It's*

*everything. And the way she handled Holston is just the icing on a very delicious cake.*

A cake he really wanted to eat.

The crude thought made his cock pulse in his jeans. A dull ache shot through its length down into his balls, telling him he'd come close to erupting more than once in the last twelve hours.

He drew a slow breath, forcing calm into his muscles.

And tensed instantly when a soft scratching sound rasped on the concrete to his left.

Turning his head, he scanned the blackness engulfing the area beyond Chris's trailer. The hair on the back of his neck prickled.

There were eyes upon him. He could feel them.

Somewhere in the shadows, someone was—

"Bye, Mr. Rhodes."

Aslin started at Tilly's call. He jerked his stare around, just in time to watch the young woman run past him. Straight into the arms of the tall, heavy-set man in a *Dead Even* T-shirt currently walking out of the darkness.

The man met Aslin's gaze for a microsecond, and then he was kissing Tilly, his hands gripping her backside before he straightened again.

"I'll see you tomorrow, Ms. Hemsworth," Tilly called over her shoulder as she and the man made their way back into the shadows.

"She can do better," Rowan muttered beside Aslin. He looked down at her, noticing the frown pulling at her eyebrows.

"Trouble?"

"Just a bit of a loser." She pulled a face. "He used to be part of Chris's entourage. Now he's the key grip on the film. I think Chris got him the job because he felt sorry about ending his gravy train."

Aslin returned his scrutiny to the place Tilly and the key grip had disappeared into the night. The hairs on the back of his neck still tingled.

He didn't like it. His gut told him something was wrong.

"Can you give me a lift to Chris's hotel, please?"

Rowan's question drew his attention back to her. She stood on his right, the black bag Tilly had passed to her now hanging over her shoulder, his helmet in her left hand. Those blue eyes of hers seemed to shimmer with an emotion he couldn't read, a tension stealing through her body once more.

He understood. Twice they'd been interrupted. Twice she'd been given the opportunity to question her actions. He knew she fought what she was feeling for him—the base, physical attraction—and he also knew a thirty-minute bike ride to the Sydney Park Hyatt would only evoke her sexual need again. Holding on to him, her sex pressed to his arse, her breasts crushed to his back…

His cock throbbed.

Christ, *his* sexual need was well and truly evoked just thinking about it.

*Then do something about it. Once and for all.*

"I can," he said, stepping to stand directly in front of her. He gazed down at her, the subtle scent of her perfume, the delicate kiss of her body heat teasing his senses. "But tell me, what's going to happen when we get there?"

For a moment, it looked like Rowan wasn't going to answer. She looked away, her jaw bunched, her stare fixed on the shadows behind her brother's trailer. "I don't know," she finally said, her voice a low husky whisper.

The urge to capture her lips with his almost undid Aslin's control. He stood motionless, his blood roaring in his ears, his heart hammering in his chest. "You can't fight this forever, Rowan."

She let out a strangled chuckle. "I'm not in Australia forever."

"All the more reason not to fight it."

His answer was arrogant. Dominating. He knew that. But Christ, his control was being pushed to its limit. He studied her profile, watching the conflict raging war on her mind and body pull her eyebrows in a deep frown. He almost kissed her, just to ease her stress.

But stopped, just as the muscles in his lower back began to flex.

No. He couldn't. Not while she was so torn. Not while he was so aroused. If he kissed her now, he wouldn't stop.

Straightening, he turned and crossed the dimly lit stretch of pavement to Chris's trailer. Another urge was twisting through him, one that had everything to do with Rowan and nothing to do with sexual hunger. He wanted to enter her brother's on-set residence first. He'd spent his life listening to his gut and his gut was telling him there was something off.

He hadn't let himself think about the disturbed trailer steps. Hadn't allowed himself to ponder the fact they'd been moved on purpose. His concentration had been too distracted by Rowan. But now he was here…

Pausing at the steps, he ran a narrow-eyed inspection over them.

"Someone had to unscrew them," Rowan said beside him, her voice low. Serious.

He inclined his head, casting her a quick look.

"I had the same thought you did when it first happened." A soft snort escaped her. "In fact, I was pissed about that fact. Still am. A little."

Aslin cocked an eyebrow at her.

She shrugged. "I'm competitive. What can I say?"

He suppressed the smile wanting to play with his lips. "Do you know anyone who would want to hurt your brother?"

She shook her head.

Aslin's gut clenched. Without another word, he climbed into the trailer.

It looked the same as it had the last time he was in there, with the exception the icepack he'd used earlier on his Rowan-punched balls was nowhere to be seen, and the bottle of water Chris had been drinking from was no longer sitting on the small table.

Tilly, no doubt.

Three lamps threw soft yellow light around the space, causing shadows to leap and dance over the walls as Aslin moved deeper into the trailer.

His gut clenched some more.

Off. It felt off.

*But there's nothing wrong here, boyo.*

There wasn't. But that didn't make him feel any less on edge.

A noise behind him told him Rowan had followed him inside. "I'll just grab my bag and we can go," she said as he turned to face her. "Tilly gave me everything else I need."

He watched her scoop her backpack up from the trailer's luxurious leather sofa and hook its straps over her over shoulders. Even in such a simple action, her body moved with fluid strength. He couldn't help but be impressed. If he had a checklist of every attribute his woman should have, Rowan Hemsworth met them all.

*Christ, what are you, Rhodes? A caveman?*

He wasn't. He was intelligent, educated and level-headed. But everything about Rowan—everything— brought out a primitive male response in him. The kind that wanted nothing more than to snare a fistful of her hair, drag her back to his cave and claim her as his mate. Solely his mate. And heaven help anyone who wanted to argue with him about that fact.

"Ready?"

Rowan studied him. If she was aware how close he was to slamming the door shut and throwing her on the bed, she didn't show it.

He inclined his head.

A security guard met them as they were exiting the trailer, a torch beam drilling into Aslin's eyes. Rowan flashed her *Dead Even* film set pass at him a second before the man apologized and directed the light at their feet.

"Do you have a pass, sir?"

Aslin pulled his own pass from his back pocket and held it out to the guard.

The man bathed the plastic I.D. card in white light for a moment. "Thanks, Mr. Rhodes," he said, lifting his scrutiny to Aslin's face. "Don't forget to check in with the gate guard when you leave."

"Is there a problem?"

The guard shook his head. "Just the normal over-zealous fans trying to get at Chris Huntley. We busted a fairly determined woman earlier this afternoon trying to con her way in. She said she was with the catering firm." He chuckled. "Staggers me the lengths these women will go to. The old duck would have had more chance if she wasn't wearing a *Twice Too Many* T-shirt."

Aslin's nerve-endings fired. He narrowed his eyes. "Did she have red hair? Obviously dyed?"

The guard nodded. "Yep, that's the one. Real charmer

she was. Never heard so many swear words come out of the mouth of a woman before, and I've worked security at a Nick Blackthorne concert." He made a snorting sound. "Now there's some seriously zealous fans. I had to save the guy's girlfriend years ago when a group of squealing women turned on her during the show." He shook his head again. "Insane. Just insane."

"Wow," Rowan spoke beside Aslin. "Didn't Blackthorne's bodyguard protect her?"

"Not during the show, he didn't." The guard pulled a face. "But I've never been convinced about these celebrity bodyguards. They all carry on like they're invincible. Reckon one hard punch and they'd be out like a light."

"I think you're right," Rowan agreed. Aslin didn't need to look at her to know she was trying not to laugh. "I suspect they are a bunch of pussies." She paused, a prickling heat on his profile telling him she wasn't looking at the guard anymore. He slid his gaze to her, the laughter in her eyes making his stomach clench. "Pussies in designer leather jackets, of course."

"Hell, yeah." The guard snorted. "Wonder what they'd be like in a real fight? Too worried about getting their clothes damaged, I reckon." He shook his head, as if disgusted by the notion.

For a dangerous moment, the urge to lean forward, gaze into the man's eyes and introduce himself came over Aslin. If for no other reason than to see him squirm. Instead, he ground his teeth and pocketed his I.D. pass. Beside him, Rowan chuckled.

"Anyways." The guard gave them both a wide smile. "I better keep doing my rounds. Don't forget about the gate guard. Sorry 'bout the light in your eyes and all."

"No worries," Aslin said. "You're just doing your job."

Beside him, Rowan burst out laughing.

Five minutes later, they were on his bike heading for Chris's harbour-side hotel.

Rowan's thighs hugged his hips, her body heat a constant promise of what might happen when they arrived at Chris's penthouse suite in the Park Hyatt.

Aslin's head swam at the thought. Would they finally surrender to the overwhelming sexual chemistry between them? His dick throbbed, stiff with anticipation. That the thrumming of his bike's powerful engine radiated through his balls only sweetened the pleasure in his groin.

When he pulled in front of the hotel, every muscle in his body was on fire.

He planted his foot on the road, killed the engine and held his bike steady as Rowan climbed off. The absence of her body pressed to his sent a chill through his heat. An emptiness he wasn't prepared for stole through his soul.

*Are you falling for her already, boyo?*

Throat thick, he slid the visor of his borrowed helmet up and turned to see her remove his helmet from her head.

She stood motionless beside his bike, her ponytail falling over her shoulder in a tumble of messy waves, her gaze unreadable as it found his face.

He drew a steadying breath. "Wait for me in the lobby."

She didn't answer. Instead, her teeth caught her bottom lip.

"Evening, sir, ma'am. Are you checking in?"

The cheerful voice to Rowan's left jerked Aslin's stare from her face. The hotel's parking valet stood beside her, bestowing them both with a wide smile.

Before Aslin could answer, Rowan shook her head. "No. He's just dropping me off."

Aslin's gut clenched. He controlled his frown. "Am I?"

Rowan nodded, her teeth no longer worrying her bottom lip. "This is too much, Aslin. Too much too quickly. I want you, but I realized on the ride here I need to take a breath. To think."

Beside her, the valet cleared his throat. "Shall I—"

Aslin didn't move his focus from her face. "It's just sex, Rowan."

She shook her head, her eyebrows pulling into a brief frown. "No. It isn't. And that's the issue."

The parking valet mumbled something and then, head down, cheeks red, hurried away.

Aslin ground his teeth. She was correct. It wasn't. He knew it, and so did she.

Rowan let out a sigh. "I wasn't ready for this. It's a problem I'm not prepared for, and I don't know what to do next."

"Fuck me," Aslin growled. "And let me fuck you. Simple."

She chuckled. "Not simple at all. And I can see through your bluster, soldier boy. You're as freaked out by this whole thing as I am."

His gut knotted. That she could read him so well already should have angered him. It didn't. It only highlighted exactly what she was saying—what was between them had the potential to be so much more than sex. And he could tell it scared her.

*And it doesn't you?*

"Rowan," he began, but she shook her head and took a step backward, hugging his helmet to her breasts. "Goodnight, Rhodes. I'll see you tomorrow on set."

And before he could utter another word, she turned and strode through the hotel's glass doors and into the foyer.

Leaving Aslin to watch her go.

# Chapter Six

Fifty laps of the hotel's swimming pool hadn't helped her. Working out in the hotel's twenty-four-hour gym hadn't either. Masturbating in the shower had achieved fuck all and consuming ice-cream sundaes smothered in hot chocolate fudge sauce from room service while watching in-house movies back to back did little but make her feel guilty for charging so much to Chris's hotel bill.

It didn't matter what Rowan tried through the agonizingly long hours after Aslin left to when the sun broke the eastern horizon—six hours that felt like forever—she couldn't stop wishing she hadn't told him to go.

Now here she was after maybe two hours of restless sleep, sitting on the spacious balcony of Chris's suite feeling drained. Coffee in hand, she watched the morning's golden light flow over Sydney Harbour and the Opera House, turning a simple thing like morning into a stunning spectacle. The sight pissed her off to no end. All she could do every time she looked at it was wish the Brit was here with her so she could smile at him and share the moment.

And then ask him to take her inside and fuck her brains out.

She lifted what was left of her croissant—her third of the morning, this one slathered with strawberry jelly and cream—and popped it into her mouth. If she hadn't, she would have let out a very disgusted snort.

Oh yeah, she was definitely well on her way to solving the Aslin Rhodes problem, wasn't she? Ice cream, movies, exercise and masturbation. The perfect tools needed to decide what to do about him.

She sighed.

Somewhere around four a.m., she'd decided she was going to sleep with him. After she got that out of her system, she was going to see if she could spend more than fifteen minutes in his company without thinking about sex.

Now however, in the light of day, she wasn't sure if that was a wise move.

For starters, what if he was a hopeless lover?

Rowan *did* snort this time. And then coughed around the remains of her croissant she'd yet to swallow.

Huh. It wasn't possible. With the way he kissed? With the arrogance of his touch? The mastery of her pleasure?

A shiver rippled through her. A tight, hot, delicious ripple. She had no doubt whatsoever that Aslin Rhodes would be an amazing lover. What she did doubt was her ability to walk away when it was over. Because a British bodyguard, or whatever he was now, wasn't exactly part of her plans for her future. Looking after her brother was her plan for the future. Making sure people didn't take advantage of his far-too-easygoing nature.

Aslin Rhodes did not fit into that plan at all.

*Which is why you haven't stop thinking about him, right?*

With another snort, she pushed herself to her feet and turned from the breathtaking vista of the harbour and its architecturally weird opera house. She needed to call the hospital, find out when Chris was going to be discharged and order a taxi so she could get there before hand. Then she'd have another shower, dress and ring Nigel McQueen and let him know she was collecting her brother.

She didn't have the time to sit and ponder her inconvenient pre-occupation with Aslin Rhodes. Maybe if she was lucky when she next saw the British soldier-cum-bodyguard-cum-whatever he was now, she'd be over him. After all, it wasn't like she'd never had a man make her moan with pleasure before.

Just not on the back of a Ducati. In plain view of anyone who might come along.

Her pussy contracted in an almost painful throb.

Letting out a huff, Rowan crossed to one of the suite's many phones and had hotel reception connect her to Sydney Royal North Shore Private Hospital. Ten minutes later, having been told by the nurse that she could not divulge any information about Chris Huntley over the phone no matter how many times Rowan insisted she was Chris's sister, she walked into the opulent bathroom, stripped off her PJs and stepped into the shower.

Only to have the suite's many phones burst into ringing life the second the warm water started streaming over her naked body.

"Damn it." She killed the water, wrapped the fluffiest towel in the world around her torso and hurried to the closest phone. "Hello?"

"I'm waiting in the lobby." Aslin's deep voice caressed her senses through the connection, his British accent making her sex throb again. And her nipples pinch tight.

Her heart leapt into her throat. Her lips parted in a silent gasp. She gripped the hand piece, her knuckles popping.

There was a soft chuckle, most likely at Rowan's complete failure to respond to Aslin's statement. "Don't forget my helmet."

He disconnected before she could say anything. Which really pissed her off.

Damn him. Who the fuck did he think he was?

*The guy who made you whimper and beg to be fucked on the back of a Ducati last night after only knowing you for twelve hours, that's who.*

Still, she wasn't going to play his game. Damn him.

Returning to the shower, she washed her hair. Twice. And then conditioned it. And then snared Chris's razor—conveniently perched on the soap rack—and shaved her legs and under her arms. Then she stood under the warm water, palms to the marble wall, head down, eyes closed, lips parted and counted to one hundred. Twice.

*You're playing with fire, woman.*

The thought made her heartbeat quicken. Her pussy contracted. She imagined Aslin kicking the door to the suite open, his nostrils flaring, his expression promising pain and pleasure.

She pictured him storming across the lush carpet to the bathroom. Saw him closing the distance between the door and the shower with long, steady strides. Felt his hand circle her wrist as he pulled her from the water and yanked her against his chest. Felt his erection grind against her belly.

Her head swum at the delirious fantasy. Her breath grew

shallow. Ragged.

She opened her eyes and raised her head.

Just as the shower cubicle's steam-fogged glass door opened.

She gasped, staring at the man standing on the other side, her pulse detonating in her throat.

"You do know Sydney is experiencing a drought at the moment?" Aslin's dark brown eyes revealed nothing. "A thirty-five-minute shower is a might excessive, even if you are trying to avoid me."

Rowan gazed at him. Her breasts ached. She knew she should smack the shit out of him. She knew she should at least tell him to fuck off. Instead, she stared at him, her nipples way too hard, her pussy prickling with eager want.

"How did you…" She stopped.

The smallest of smiles pulled at one side of Aslin's mouth. "Nick stayed here whenever he was in Australia. He and his wife spent their wedding night here."

Rowan drew a deep breath, pushing herself from the wall. The water continued to stream over her body. Down between her swollen breasts, over her belly, between her thighs, over the seam of her sex… "So what? You know the manager?"

Aslin inclined his head. Not once did his stare waver from her face.

"And he just let you come on up?"

"Yes."

"Wasn't that nice of him."

Another single nod of his head.

She swallowed. Straightened her spine. Tilted her chin. "And now you're here, what do you plan to do?"

His nostrils flared. His jaw bunched.

*Grab my wrist. Grab my wrist and yank me to your body. Kiss me. Fuck me. Please. Please do that. Oh God, please...*

"Tell you to bloody well hurry up." His voice was a rumble, like distant thunder.

She caught her bottom lip with her teeth. And bit back a groan of protest when he turned and walked from the bathroom.

Her heart hammered. Her sex pulsed and throbbed and squeezed a cock that wasn't there.

She stared hard at the closed bathroom door, willing him to walk through it. Willing him to take away any choice she had.

But he didn't.

Throat thick, disgust licking through her, she snapped off the water and stepped out of the shower stall.

She dried herself with savage force, the world's fluffiest towel an instrument of punishment in her hands as she rubbed it against her skin like a frenzied house painter sanding the walls.

When she knew drying herself had dragged into hiding out in the bathroom, she wrapped the towel around her chest, raked her fingers through her damp hair and exited the room.

Aslin stood on the balcony, his back to the suite. His legs were braced apart, his hands planted on the steel railing.

Rowan studied his wide back, her gaze charting a journey over the sculpted strength of his shoulders, his lats, down to the bunched perfection of his gluteus maximus.

Day-um, he had a gorgeous ass.

"You've got ten minutes, Rowan." She flinched at the low statement thrown at her over his right shoulder without looking at her.

"For what?" she asked, for some reason feeling the need to clutch the towel more tightly to her breast.

"To get dressed before I come in there and do what we both want me to do."

Rowan's heart punched up into her tight throat again. Damn it, she'd never met a man who flustered her so quickly and easily.

She toyed with the idea of letting fate take over. Of keeping her feet in place and dropping the towel to the floor.

What got her moving was Aslin's growling, "And I won't be gentle."

She all but ran for the suite's bedroom and her overnight bag.

Five minutes later, dressed in cut-off denim shorts, a retro Bruce Lee T-shirt and her favourite cowboy boots, her heart far too fast, her expression as calm as she could force it to be, she walked back into the suite's living room.

Aslin still stood on the balcony, his back to her. He was talking on a phone, his voice nothing but a low rumble of indecipherable sounds rolling with that sexy British accent of his. Rowan couldn't make out the words, but she could tell from his body language he wasn't happy. At all.

"Okay," he suddenly said, louder. He turned to toward her, the rising sun casting him in silhouetting shadows that hid his face from her. "I've got to go. Let me know what you find out."

He didn't seem to wait for whomever he was talking with to answer. Sliding his cell phone into his back pocket, he crossed the balcony threshold and strode over to her, his expression unreadable.

"You're really going to wear shorts on the back of a motorbike?"

Rowan tilted her chin. "You want me to take them off?"

A dark fire flickered in his eyes. "I want to rip them off, Rowan." His matter-of-fact response made her pulse thump fast and her palms prickle. "Along with the rest of your clothes. I want you naked and coated in sweat as I bring you to the wildest orgasm of your life. But your brother is waiting, and he refuses to start filming until you're on set."

At the mention of Chris's name, Rowan's heart slammed into her throat. Oh God, here she was flirting with a man that left her utterly discombobulated and her brother was still in hospital?

She swallowed, guilt and shame heating her cheeks. "How do we pick him up on your bike? Isn't that going to be a physical impossibility?"

Aslin scooped up his helmet from where she'd left it on the coffee table the night before and handed it to her. "He was discharged at six this morning and Nigel asked if I would collect him. I dropped him off at the barracks before coming here."

A finger of irritation stroked down Rowan's spine. Aslin had collected her brother? Aslin? A man Chris had known for less than a day?

She narrowed her eyes. "Of course you did. That being your purpose in life and all. To look after celebrities and be at their beck and call?"

The moment the insult was past her lips Rowan regretted it. It was petulant and childish.

Aslin's stare never left her face. Nor did his ambiguous expression change. "Rowan, at this point in time, my purpose in life is to get you to the set of *Dead Even*. But if you insist on standing here trying to antagonize me, it will very quickly become to teach you a lesson." He bent at the waist—just enough to make her shift her feet to maintain her glare on his face. "And trust me, I have no problems telling Nigel McQueen and your brother filming was delayed because you provoked me into throwing you on the bed and fucking you senseless. Is that what you're hoping to achieve?"

His calmly delivered words slammed into her like a fist. Her breath caught in her throat and her pussy squeezed tight with urgent need. She drew in a steadying breath, wishing her nipples would stop pinching into hard peaks. He was correct of course. She *was* antagonizing him. He'd thrown her carefully controlled world into chaos since the second she'd met him, and she had no freaking clue how to deal with that.

She either wanted to fuck him or beat the shit out of him. Sometimes both at the same time.

It was messing with her head.

Wrapping her fingers around his helmet where he still held it out between them, she all but snatched it from his grip. "I'm not changing out of my shorts," she muttered.

The edges of Aslin's lips curled. A little. "I didn't think you would."

She stared at him, wishing she could think of something to say. Something smart and full of sass. Hell, even something funny. But Chris had got all the funny in their family. She had got the...

*What? Ability to beat someone in a fight?*

It was a bleak thought, one she couldn't deny. Since her parents' murder, she'd honed herself into a fighting machine. She didn't need sass or wit. She had her fists and her feet. She made her living being the best fighter on the circuits. On the mat, in a dojo, there was no need for snappy comebacks or droll comments. On the mat there was just punishing pain and victory.

A thick lump filled her throat and she turned away from Aslin.

"C'mon," she snarled, storming for the door. "I want to see my brother."

If Aslin noticed her abrupt shift in mood, he didn't comment. She almost wished he would. If he did, if he tried to cajole it out of her in the elevator ride down to the hotel foyer, it would give her an excuse to slam him against the wall and tell him to back the fuck off. Instead, he stood beside her, silent. His towering presence made her feel small and woefully vulnerable even as his undeniable maleness made her ache for his touch and wish he'd carried out his threat and stripped her bare back up in Chris's suite.

Oh God, she was messed up.

She refused to cling to him on his bike. It was tricky. For one thing, they were moving through the Sydney streets during rush hour traffic. Aslin was constantly accelerating and braking, the G-forces throwing her backward and forward on the pillion passenger seat. For another, he smelled so damn good. This close, with her breasts brushing at his broad back, she breathed in the subtleness of his scent—sandalwood soap, leather and something else. Something perfect, intoxicating, addictive and uniquely him.

Even with the helmet's visor down, she could smell him.

It infuriated her.

It aroused her.

When they finally drove through the gate at the film site, pausing briefly as Aslin flashed their security passes at the waiting guard, she was damn near giddy with sucking in breath after deep breath.

He'd barely brought the bike to a halt in front of Chris's

trailer when she threw her leg over the back and hurried for the open door of her brother's on-site abode.

She tried to tell herself it was anxious impatience to see Chris that made her behave so ridiculously.

Aslin's laugh behind her—low and far too knowing—told her she wasn't fooling anyone.

She drove her nails into her palms and vaulted up into the trailer, determined to ignore the annoying Brit. Only to discover Chris wasn't there.

"He's on set, Rowan." Aslin's deep voice played over her senses, his breath warm on the side of her neck as he entered the trailer after her. "On the other side of the site in the old convict dormitories. No doubt waiting for us."

She spun to glare up at him, her heart racing too damn fast for her liking. "Then why did we come here?"

"So I could do this."

Before she could do anything—and with reflexes as fast as hers, she should have been able to do *something*—his hands came up to cup her face and he brushed his lips over hers.

She froze, the gentle beauty of the simple kiss stealing any ability in her to move.

When he straightened, her breath caught at the raw desire in his eyes. There was nothing arrogant, dominating, threatening or confusing about it. Just pure desire.

Her belly knotted. Her sex grew thick with wet need.

"I know I could take you here and now, Rowan," he murmured, tracing her bottom lip with the pad of his thumb in a slow stroke. "I can feel your need in your body, see it in your face, but I won't. I'll wait. Fuck knows how I'll find the control, but I'll wait. Until you tell me to take you."

She gazed up at him, unable to draw breath.

"And when you do—" the desire in his stare turned molten, "—I'll unleash my control and nothing will stop me. Do you understand?"

She nodded. A single dip of her head.

Aslin smiled. "Good. Now let's go find your brother."

He stepped aside, holding out his arm toward the open door.

The pit of Rowan's belly churned. For a split second, she wanted to say "to hell with my brother", but the moment the thought formed in her mind—like the softest of whispers— prickling guilt and self-disgust rushed through her. She turned and hurried for the door, practically leaping down the steps to ground.

Only to bump into a woman with dyed-red hair wearing a skin-tight *Chris Huntley* T-shirt.

Rowan stumbled back, her cheeks flushing with heat as she smiled an apology at the older woman. "I'm sorry. I should look where I'm—"

"How did you get past security?"

Rowan jumped at Aslin's growl. As did the woman. The blood drained from her makeup-caked face. Her stare snapped up to the Brit where he stood in the trailer's open doorway. "Damn it," she muttered, a second before she spun on her heel and bolted.

Rowan blinked. "What the fuck?"

She turned to look at Aslin, just in time to see him launch himself from the top step. He sprinted past her, a chilling expression on his face, his jaw set.

The woman ran fast. Aslin ran faster. If the situation hadn't been so bizarre, Rowan would have been impressed by his phenomenal speed and grace. He caught up with the fleeing woman in no time at all, snaring her arm with one hand and yanking her to a halt.

"Let go of me you fucking Pom!" the woman screeched, lashing out at Aslin with her free arm.

Rowan blinked again. Pom? That was the second time she'd heard Aslin called a drink. What the hell did it mean?

*Don't you think the more important question is why did she run when she saw him? Or even, who the hell she is?*

"Ah, you know I can't do that, love," Aslin's chuckled voice came to Rowan, his humoured tone surprising her. "Now stop being silly before I have to hurt you."

The woman screeched some more, louder this time, her legs joining in her free arm's wild attempts to do Aslin damage. It wasn't working. The Brit was too tall, too large for her to even come close with any of her frenzied blows.

Film crew was coming from everywhere to watch the show. Most gave Rowan curious looks before turning back to Aslin and the incensed, flailing woman. Some, Rowan could hear, started placing bets on how long it would take before Aslin knocked her out.

"Fucking Pom," she continued to wail, her face twisted into a murderous glare. "Lemme go, you fucking Pom."

"Insulting my nationality is only going to make it worse, love." Aslin's voice turned to a purr. To Rowan's ears it sounded like his British accent grew thicker. More pronounced. "Now tell me how you got in—"

*"Rhodes!"*

Rowan jumped at the sound of her brother's shout. She turned away from Aslin and the struggling woman, watching Chris run toward them both, his personal assistant stumbling to keep up behind him.

Her stomach dropped. He looked furious.

"It's okay, Chris," Aslin said, dragging the woman behind

him, even as she squealed so loud it hurt Rowan's ears. "I've got it under—"

"When I asked you to look after my sister," Chris's shout cut over Aslin's calm statement and drowned out the rabid fan's cries, his speed increasing the closer he got to Aslin, "I didn't mean fuck her on the back of your bike for the whole world to see!"

A collective gasp went through the gathering crowd. All stares snapped to Rowan. All of them. Including Aslin's.

Which meant it was only Rowan who saw Chris smash his balled fist hard into Aslin's jaw.

Only Rowan who watched Aslin's entire body tense as he recoiled from the blow a heartbeat before he fixed his focus back to her brother.

Only Rowan who saw his face turn to a mask of cold, deadly fury.

And then all hell broke loose as Chris tried to punch him again.

# Chapter Seven

*This is what happens when you get mixed up with the Hollywood crowd, boyo.*

The surreal thought tickled through Aslin's rage…a second before he clamped his fingers around Chris Huntley's fist, capturing it mid-swing on its second attempt to smash into his jaw.

"Fucker!" the actor shouted. "You fucked my sister on a bike, you fucker!"

Sharp pain detonated in Aslin's shoulder, and it was only a quick look to his right that told him the woman from the café yesterday had sunk her teeth into his flesh. He shrugged her off just as she slammed a foot at his shin.

Fresh pain stabbed into his leg.

"I fucking trusted you, man!" Chris was shouting in his face, desperately trying to yank his hand free of Aslin's hold. "I trusted you."

Aslin turned back to the incensed actor, his blood roaring in his ears. Christ, what a soddin' balls up.

"Chris," Rowan's cry rose above the ruckus. She wormed her way between them with determined strength, her hand pressing flat to Aslin's chest, her thigh wedging against his groin. "Stop it. Stop it right now."

Chris didn't stop. He glared up at Aslin, hate in his eyes. "I trusted you, man."

Another bite in his shoulder made Aslin release the woman in his right grip. Someone else would have to deal with her. Chris was more important.

He heard a scuffle of feet, a loud *oof*, someone mutter, "freaking bitch" and more feet pounding the concrete, but he didn't tear his focus from the angry young actor still trying to get at him.

"Chris, I didn't make love to Rowan."

"He didn't, squirt." Rowan shook her head, pushing hard on Chris's chest. "Honest."

Chris dropped his glare to her, his brow furrowing. "Then explain the photos plastered all over the net. It sure as hell looks like he was about to get to third fucking base."

Hot anger punched into Aslin's gut. He ground his teeth. Holston.

Rowan flicked him a quick look, realization flaring in her eyes.

Aslin lifted his stare to her brother's face. "Chris, I know what it looks like, but you need to let me—"

His phone rang, the sound of the "Funeral March" telling him his boss was calling.

*Sod it. Just what I need. An angry Nick on my arse.*

"What the *fuck* is going on?"

It was Nigel McQueen's shout that made them all flinch. Chris stumbled back a step, Aslin releasing his fist as he did so. To Aslin, the actor looked shell-shocked. Guttered. "Rhodes..." Chris began, shaking his head even as he continued to glare at Aslin. "The fucking prick—"

"Enough, Chris," Rowan snapped. She shoved at his chest, straightening between them, her back to Aslin. "That's enough. I can have sex with whomever I want, whenever I want. Got it?"

The film's director frowned at her. "Who are you having sex with, Rowan?"

In Aslin's pocket, his phone fell silent, Nick no doubt giving up.

*Thank effing God for that.*

"Aslin," Rowan shot back. "I mean, I'm not having sex with Aslin. But I...we almost...Jesus. This is no one's business but mine and Aslin's."

Movement from the corner of Aslin's eye made him turn. He watched Chris's assistant hurry over to Nigel, iPad in hand. Tilly tugged at Nigel's sleeve, holding the tablet out to him to show what was on it.

Nigel's eyebrows shot up, his attention fixed on the screen. "Nice bike."

Aslin drew in a slow breath, returning his focus to Chris. "Thanks."

The actor snarled, his stare dropping to Rowan. "You know what's funny about this, sis?"

"What, Chris?"

Aslin's gut clenched at the anguish he heard in Rowan's

voice.

Chris's glare turned black. "You spend all your time lecturing me about behaving like a real person, about not doing stupid things just because I'm a celebrity, and you go and let a celebrity bodyguard feel you up and dry hump you in a hospital car park while I'm in said hospital on a freaking drip." He flicked Aslin a scowl. "How fucking hilarious is that? Might ask the writers to incorporate it into an episode of *Twice Too Many* next season."

With a final look at Aslin, hurt betrayal etching his face, he stormed into his trailer and slammed the door shut.

A prickling sensation told Aslin everyone in the crowd was now looking at him. He refused to look at any of them. Instead, he waited for Rowan. What happened next was her call. He knew what he wanted to do—tell everyone to mind their own sodding business, but this wasn't his world. This was the movie industry, and the movie industry was a world unto itself. He knew the rock industry. He knew the world of war. What happened next had to be Rowan's play, for her brother's sake. And hers.

She stood motionless for a long moment. Nigel stood before her, the iPad handed to him by Tilly showing everyone who cared to look the images Holston had captured of Aslin and Rowan in the hospital parking lot.

"Rowan?" the director's voice was low. Curious.

She let out a ragged breath. "Fuck." With a shake of her head, she turned, glanced up at Aslin and then walked over to Chris's trailer, stopping briefly to say something to Tilly at the base of the steps before climbing to the door.

No one said anything as she knocked once, called Chris's

name and then slipped inside.

That prickling sensation razed over Aslin again. He didn't move. Kept his stare on Nigel McQueen. He'd cut his teeth on the slums of London, fought for his life in Iraq and Afghanistan and spent a decade and a half guarding Nick Blackthorne from crazy fans. The speculative attention of curious film folk didn't perturb him in the slightest.

*What Rowan thinks of you, though...what Chris does...*

He ground his teeth.

Nigel frowned. "Why was the paparazzo following you?"

Aslin bit back a sigh. "Holston and I have history. He's been tailing Nick for as long as Nick's been in the public eye. It didn't take Holston long to realize ninety percent of the time, wherever I was, Nick was too. I suspect he was lurking in the emergency department's waiting room along with the other paparazzi and saw me arrive with Rowan. Nick Blackthorne's bodyguard and Chris Huntley's sister would be too much to resist for scum like him." He paused. "Unfortunately, he saw more than he should have."

Nigel's frown deepened. "Look, Mr. Rhodes." He stepped toward Aslin, passing the iPad to his assistant as he did so. "I know you can probably snap me in two with your bare hands, but I just want to say I really like Rowan. I've known her for a while, ever since she was my twin daughters' Taekwondo instructor. She loves her brother more than life and will do everything in her power to keep him safe. Bringing you in was meant to be good for him. I had it on Nick Blackthorne's word you were going to be good for him, and I think you are, but after this..." He let out a slow breath. "I'm prepared to let you stay on if she is.

I like her, my girls like her, hell, even my wife likes her, but she's not as tough as she pretends to be. And I may only be a film director, but I would do everything in my power to make sure she doesn't get hurt."

He paused, but Aslin didn't fill the silence with anything apart from an unwavering gaze.

"Do you understand?"

Aslin inclined his head.

Nigel let out another breath. "Excellent. Now, I want to talk to you about the next scene we're shooting today. Chris's character is going to be ambushed amongst all those hammocks in the convict dormitory. Ricco had choreographed the scene to have the hammock fall down and tangle around Vin's legs, allowing Chris to apprehend him, but I want to go for something more brutal. Bloody. Can you help me work on that?"

Aslin studied the director for a long moment. Bloody. Brutal. Words he understood very well. He nodded. "I can do that."

Nigel flashed whiter-than-white teeth at him in a wide smile. "Good, good. Tilly?" He shouted over Aslin's shoulder, "Can you tell Chris and Rowan we'll be on set when they get out?" And without waiting for the young woman to respond, he started walking away from Chris's trailer. "By the way, who was the woman you were holding when I first got here? The one that seemed to enjoy biting you?"

Aslin's nerve endings crackled at the mention of the zealous fan. He cast a steady look around the area, wondering if she'd gotten away. "A fan," he said, turning back to Nigel. "A determined one. She was trying to gain access to Chris.

Apparently she was thrown off the site yesterday after she was caught pretending to be with catering. Whoever is in charge of security needs to have their arse kicked."

Nigel clicked his fingers at his assistant walking a few paces behind them. In a hurried step, the young man caught up with them. "I want to talk to Miller," Nigel snapped. "Find him."

Aslin continued to walk beside Nigel, forcing his feet to move one in front of the other. He wanted to go back to the trailer. He wanted to apologise to Chris, to Rowan. For all his mightier-than-thou arrogant caveman-thumping behavior to Rowan, he didn't like to see either her or her brother upset, especially given he was responsible for that pain.

Hadn't he learnt anything from all his time trying to protect Nick?

*You've never been so attracted to a woman before, boyo. Never felt such raw, overwhelming desire. What you feel for Rowan has thrown you for a loop. You need to control it before you fuck it up.*

Thirty minutes later, during which Aslin instructed Nigel how the fight scene should play out—with the film's antagonist watching the whole time—Chris walked back onto set. Followed by his assistant. And Rowan.

Aslin's heart slammed into his throat.

He swallowed, nerves exploding in his gut like a nuke full of butterflies.

*Nerves? Christ, you really are falling fast, aren't you?*

When Chris walked over to him, he remained motionless. It was damn near impossible, but he did.

The actor stopped a foot away, his blue stare challenging. Direct. He may have started his career as a sitcom star, but he'd obviously spent a considerable amount of time working out in preparation for this role. He was ripped and sculpted. Anger no doubt flooded his muscles with adrenaline. His fingers curled into a ball at his sides. His legs seemed to tremble with charged energy.

He studied Aslin, unmoving. Silent.

Around them, the set fell to a hush. Even the ubiquitous soundtrack of hammer on nail Aslin had noticed on his first day seemed to stop, as if what was playing out under the cinematographer's lighting was more important than the building of artificial surrounds.

To the left of Chris, Rowan walked into Aslin's line of sight. She gave him an unreadable look, her teeth worrying her bottom lip.

Aslin's throat tightened. Damn, he wanted to kiss that lip. Bite it. Suck it. Worship it.

Returning his gaze to Chris, he gave the man a brief nod. "You've got an impressive right hook on you, Chris."

The actor narrowed his eyes.

Aslin raised an eyebrow. "Want me to show you how to make it better?"

"Depends." Chris's voice was flat. "Are you the punching bag?"

"I can be. Do you want to hit me again?"

"Are you going to touch my sister again like you did on the bike?"

To Chris's left, Rowan let out a soft groan.

Aslin's heart thumped hard. He kept his stare on her

brother's face, all too aware that everyone hung on the next words to come out of his mouth. "I plan to," he said. "But only if she lets me. And I won't do it in public."

Chris's nostrils flared. His jaw bunched. His Adam's apple jumped up and down his throat.

Aslin saw the punch coming before Chris even lashed out. The actor's body telegraphed the intent a second before his fist cut through the space between them. Aslin didn't dodge it. He didn't block it.

He took the punch, rolling his head to the side as Chris's knuckles smashed into his jaw.

"Fuck." Chris staggered to the side, shaking his hand as he opened and closed his fingers. "That hurts."

"Chris." Rowan's murmur echoed through the silent dormitory like a shout. "You are overreacting. It was more than sex on a...a bike." Her cheeks turned pink.

"You're blushing?" Chris said, his obvious shock piquing Aslin's interest. "Jesus, sis, you never blush. Ever." The actor turned to Aslin, his stare intense, contemplative, before he pinned Rowan with a narrow-eyed look. "Is it serious?"

"I..." Rowan began, her cheeks—Aslin was delighted to see—growing pinker.

"As far as I'm concerned it is," he said, letting his intent fill each word.

"It doesn't matter if it is or not, Chris." Rowan flicked Aslin an ambiguous frown. "You can't just go around punching people because—"

"They kiss my sister?" Chris interrupted. "I can if they're just trying to get in your pants. But if they're *serious*..." He let the rest of the sentence go unfinished, grinning at Aslin.

"Oh, Chris." Rowan shook her head. "Really? This is you being a protective brother, is it?"

Chris's lips twitched. "Yeah, it is. Aren't you lucky? Now shut up and stop bothering me. I got a scene to film. You can kiss your boyfriend better when we're done."

"He's not my—"

But whatever Rowan was going to say, the surrounding onlookers seemed to believe the show was all over. Like that, noise returned to the set. As if someone flicked a switch, all the activity Aslin had noted since first stepping foot on *Dead Even's* set yesterday—people shouting commands, sound equipment being moved, hammers whacking nails, trolleys and cameras being pushed from one spot to the next—instantly erupted into a cacophony of organized chaos again.

From out of nowhere, Nigel appeared at Chris's side, as did a pink-haired woman who began brushing the actor's face with a large make-up brush, another woman who attacked his hair with goop-covered fingers, and a man who hovered about holding out a small black device Aslin recognised as a light metre.

Aslin looked at everyone, unable to keep the bewilderment from his face. It was all so weird. So surreal. By the time Nigel had finished telling Chris what he wanted him to do, the actor looked like he'd been through hell and back, his hair a disheveled mess, his face smudged with what Aslin assumed was meant to be dirt and sweat.

"Okay, Chris." Nigel took a step back. "Are you ready?"

Chris's gaze found Aslin. A tension flickered in his eyes, and Aslin knew what had started with a punch to the jaw wasn't finished yet. But, with one final adjustment to his hair by the woman with the goop-slicked fingers, the actor rolled his shoulders and neck and then gave the director a sharp nod. "Ready."

"Ready, Vin?" Nigel called over his shoulder, hurrying back to a stool as the film's bad guy ambled into the stark white glare of the trolley lights.

Aslin took his own step backward, dodging a rapidly moving camera operator as he sought a place out of the road. He stopped at the chair marked with Chris's name, folding his arms across his chest just as Nigel raised a megaphone to his mouth and yelled, "Action."

It was the subtle kiss of her heat on his body that told him Rowan stood beside him. Her heat, the delicate scent of her perfume… He stiffened, wanting like hell to turn to her. To smooth his hands over her face, cup her jaw and kiss her. To say sorry for what had taken place. Instead, he stood still and watched her brother beat the shit out of Vin Diesel as a traitorous CIA agent, surrounded by hammocks the film's props department had created to replicate the historical ones normally hanging in the convict dormitory.

Nigel called cut often, each time asking Aslin to comment on the scene's action, more than once getting him to check what was captured on playback. Every time he did, Aslin would step away from Rowan, leaving her sitting in Chris's chair. Every time he turned back to her, his advice on the fight sequence given, he would find her smiling at him.

It was a wholly wonderful experience, made all the more special by the fact he was enjoying every second. Telling Nigel how the fight would unfold, having Chris and Vin ask questions and listen to his answer, watching the actors take it all in and put it into play…it was rejuvenating. Exhilarating. Hell, he'd go so far as to say addictive.

Three hours later, when Nigel called an end to the scene, Aslin was surprised to discover he was disappointed.

Until Rowan stood from her brother's chair and grinned at him.

"Was that fun?"

He chuckled. "How did I do?"

"Very well." She threw Nigel a sideward look. "I think you may be retained as Nigel's permanent super-soldier go-to guy. Do you think Nick Blackthorne would be okay with that?"

At the mention of his boss, Aslin laughed. "I suspect the rock star is getting sick of me stalking his shadow. Besides, there aren't that many crazed fans in Murriundah, and those that are there are crazed fans for the Murriundah Under 12s Soccer team."

A stillness fell over Rowan for a moment—in her shoulders, her face—and then just as quickly, her lips curled with an easy smile. "So if there's a sequel you'd be open to the consultancy job?"

Aslin studied her. The thought of being with Rowan for the filming of another movie after this made his mouth dry. And his groin tight.

Not just another movie, but longer than that. Maybe even…

"It's a possibility."

"What if it filmed in the US?"

He swallowed. "Still a possibility."

Rowan's lips parted.

"What did you say to Chris in his trailer?"

She let out a ragged breath at his question. "I told him I like you."

Aslin raised his eyebrows. He kept his expression calm. Inside, his gut was knotting. His palms prickled. His balls throbbed. "Like me?"

Rowan rolled her eyes. "Yes, *like* you. You confuse the shit out of me, Rhodes. You scare me too, which I absolutely hate. Nothing scares me, but you do and that pisses me off. I wasn't planning on you coming into my life, but here you are and now I don't really know what to do with you." She turned away, her teeth catching her bottom lip. "Apart from the obvious, and look what happened the last time we did that. Photographed by a fucktard paparazzo for the whole world to see."

"You have to admit—" Aslin risked leaning a little closer to her, her tantalizing scent threading into his breath, "—he really captured your good side."

Rowan's laughter turned the throb in his balls to a heavy pulse. His cock stiffened. Christ, he could spend the rest of his life listening to that laugh.

"What?" She snorted. "My foot?"

Aslin barely resisted the urge to smooth his palms around her hips and pull her to his body. "It's a bloody brilliant foot. I know, I've felt it, remember?"

She cocked an eyebrow at him, the grin back on her lips. "I never forget a man whose ass I've kicked. Ever."

The sound of a throat clearing to their immediate left made Aslin stiffen. He turned, finding Chris—hair slicked back, face free of smudge and sweat, clothes free of rips and tatters—standing beside them. "Nigel's called lunch. Wanna get some?"

*No.*

The word came close to passing Aslin's lips. He bit it back. Just. As much as he wanted to throw Rowan over his shoulder and carry her off somewhere, he had nowhere to carry her off to. The trailer he'd been assigned still hadn't arrived, his hotel was too far away and he'd promised Chris he wouldn't touch his sister in public. Which was damn inconvenient, given how much he wanted to touch her.

Touch her. Kiss her. Hold her.

"Jeff is waiting for us in the car," Chris went on, looking back and forth between Aslin and Rowan. "Thought we might try that restaurant near the Opera House the writer keeps raving on about." An ambiguous tension twisted his mouth. Aslin couldn't decide if it was a smile, or a grimace. He guessed the answer would come later when Chris made up his mind about the whole situation.

"Sounds good." Rowan nodded. Aslin's chest tightened at the note of impatient annoyance in her voice.

Chris heard it as well, if the way he rolled his eyes at his sister was anything to judge by. "If you were anyone but my sister, I'd tell you to get a room." He frowned, shooting Aslin a sideward glance. "But my knuckles still hurt from punching Rhodes in the jaw, so just pretend for an hour you don't want to fuck each other's brains out, okay?"

Rowan threw her own frown back at him. "Shut the fuck up, Chris."

"Mr. Huntley?"

Tilly appeared at Chris's elbow, her young face wide

with an expectant smile. Behind her stood her boyfriend, his expression unreadable. Aslin narrowed his eyes. The man gave off a sullen air.

Chris grinned. "Warren, dude." He bumped fists with Tilly's boyfriend. "How goes the key-grip job?"

Draping his arm around Tilly's shoulder, Warren smiled. "Not bad, bro. Not bad. Not as good as hanging out with you all the time." Aslin didn't miss the quick glance he gave Rowan. "But not bad. Meant I got to meet this lovely lady here." He squeezed Tilly's shoulder and dropped a kiss on the side of her mouth before looking back at Chris. "So we doing lunch? I'm freaking starving."

A soft noise drew Aslin's attention to Rowan. She was frowning, her arms crossed over her breasts, her lips twisted into a thin line.

*That's not a happy woman.*

The memory of her distaste for the key grip came back to him.

"Sorry, dude," Chris's rejection, spoken with a soft chuckle, made Aslin look back at Tilly's boyfriend. "Not this time. I haven't really had the chance to catch up with Rowie yet."

Warren laughed. "Sure, sure. Understand." He hugged Tilly tighter with his arm. "I'll take this little lady out to the catering truck and buy her something nice. Catch you later."

Chris nodded. "Hell, yeah."

"Later." After another fist bump with Chris, and a quick glance at Rowan, the key grip turned and walked away, almost dragging Tilly with him.

"Wow," Rowan's laugh sent a lick of tight heat into the

pit of Aslin's stomach. "I'm impressed."

"Shut up, sis." Chris swiped his hand at her chin. "I only said no 'cause I don't want to hear you carrying on about my entourage. You know those guys weren't all that bad. We had a lot of fun."

Rowan pulled a face. "I remember. Most especially the times I had to come pull your stupid ass from one party or another when you were all too drunk to even know your names."

Chris pulled a face in return. "Yeah, okay. I'll give you that." He grinned at Aslin. "I was a little shit when I was younger."

Rowan barked out a dry laugh. "A little?"

"Shut up, shut up." Chris reached out and gave her a quick hug, releasing her just as quickly. "Let's go. Before I change my mind and call Warren back."

# Chapter Eight

Lunch turned out to be an interesting affair. Aslin spent most of it watching Rowan and Chris trade insults back and forth, their smiles wide and their eyes shining with joy. It was obvious the siblings had a deep love for each other, a love that extended to Rowan being very prickly and on edge when more than one diner at the restaurant approached their table and asked Chris for his autograph. Aslin sat back observing it all. It was unusual for him to be in a social environment with a celebrity without being employed to guard them, and he was perplexed by the situation. The second they entered the restaurant, he'd scoped out all exit points, noted who was sitting at the surrounding tables and how many staff were visible. He couldn't stop himself positioning Chris with his back to the main entry, which meant anyone outside would be unable to see the actor's face and gave Aslin a clear view of anyone who came in from the street.

The other thing he couldn't help but notice was how often Rowan studied him. When she wasn't giving her brother grief about his ordered meal, or teasing him about how woeful his kicks and punches were on set, she was watching Aslin with an expression he could only call speculative.

Surprisingly, he liked her inspection. Never one to enjoy or endure any protracted scrutiny, he found Rowan's gaze on him more than pleasing. It meant she was thinking about all of him. He could see it in the way she chewed on her bottom lip. They'd been king-hit by their overwhelming sexual attraction to each other, but in this moment, sitting eating in a restaurant with one of the world's most famous actors, they were just two people enjoying each other's company. And getting to know each other in the process.

"Did you know that, Aslin?"

Aslin blinked, caught completely off-guard by Chris's question.

"Sorry?" He turned to the actor, unable to miss the way the lad was grinning at him.

"Caught you."

Aslin frowned. "Caught me what?"

Chris laughed. "Caught you staring at my sister."

"Oh for God's sake, squirt." Rowan snorted. "Grow up."

Chris chuckled before looking at Aslin again. "Did you know Rowan was in the very first episode of *Twice Too Many*?"

Aslin's eyebrows shot up. He turned to Rowan, loving the way a faint pink tinge painted her cheeks. "Really?"

"Yep." Chris nodded. "She was 'Woman with dog', the woman my character had an argument with about the dog shit I'd just slipped on."

Aslin gave Rowan a curious look.

Rowan rolled her eyes. "I said four words. 'It wasn't *my* dog'. The director pulled me aside and told me I had no acting talent to speak of."

Chris's laughter reverberated around the restaurant. More than one diner lifted their attention from their meal. "He was right. Sorry, Rowie, but you can't act to save yourself."

"Gee, thanks, brother mine."

Chris grinned. "You're welcome. Me on the other hand—"

"Can't fight your way out of a wet paper bag," Rowan cut him off with a smirk.

"In Chris's defense," Aslin said, giving them both a serious gaze, "wet paper is actually harder to puncture and tear through than dry paper."

Chris frowned at him. "Really?"

Aslin shook his head. "No. Sorry."

Chris let out a snort. "Geez, where's my entourage when I need it?"

"*Not* draining your bank account," Rowan shot back. "Now eat your salad."

Aslin laughed. He couldn't help himself. He'd never felt so relaxed. So…so…content. It was a genuinely unexpected feeling. One he could get used to.

*And how is that going to happen? Are you telling Nick you're quitting? Or will you become Chris's guard purely so you can be with Rowan? What exactly do you think is going to happen, boyo?*

He didn't know. But he wasn't going to think about it now. He was going to enjoy his lunch, enjoy Chris's easy company, and enjoy every second spent with Rowan. After, when the day was finished and he had Rowan all to himself, then he'd explore the new emotion boiling through him. Then, when he was buried balls deep in her tight wetness, he would think about where exactly he wanted this unexpected direction of his life to take him. Then he would—

"…the film so far?"

He blinked, once again caught out by Chris.

The actor laughed. "Oh, dude, please don't tell me you were thinking about my sister again. My hand hasn't recovered yet."

"Seriously, Chris." Rowan's tone took on a warning note. "Shut up."

"No, really." Chris lifted his right hand and flexed his fingers, studying them with a melodramatic pout. "I don't know if I'll be able to hold a pen for days."

"When the freaking hell do you ever need to hold a pen?"

"When I sign contracts. Sign autographs. C'mon, you've seen how bad I was at signing the ones I did in here. Some sympathy would be nice."

"Chris," Rowan dragged out his name. "Enough."

Chris laughed. "Okay. Okay. But honestly, give me a week or two before you pair go making out in public again, please? My hand won't be able to survive if you keep doing it too often."

"Another word," Rowan snapped, poking her fork— tines first—at him, "and I'll stab you with this. Does your face insurance cover eating-utensil injury?"

The rest of the meal was spent in casual conversation, the film the main topic of discussion. Chris was very happy with the way it was going. He talked often about the opportunity to show the world he was more than a fast joke and a tight butt. Rowan pointed out she'd been telling him that for years, and then commented his butt wasn't as good as he thought it was. By the time their empty plates were taken away and the head chef came out to accept Chris's compliments, Aslin knew so much more about the two people beside him than they realised.

Chris hid his insecurities behind his jokes and humour, Rowan hid hers behind a shield of maternal strength and mother-bear protectiveness.

But what was there to be insecure about? Aslin pondered the question as he watched Chris rise from the table to meet the owner of the restaurant. He knew little about the actor's background and had never watched an episode of his sitcom. And as for Rowan...

"He's not as silly as he pretends to be."

Aslin turned to Rowan, finding her studying her brother as he chatted with the owner.

"I gathered that."

She turned her gaze to Aslin. "He's just...lost. I don't think he's really let himself be who he is yet. After what happened to Mom and Dad..." She shrugged. "Well, that kind of thing messes you up, of course."

"What happened to your mum and dad?"

Rowan stiffened. "You don't know?"

He shook his head.

Returning her attention to her brother, who was now laughing with the chef, their waiter *and* the restaurant owner, Rowan let out a long sigh. She folded her arms across her body, tucking her hands under her armpits. It was the most guarded position Aslin had seen her take, the action of someone vulnerable and worried. "I thought everyone in the industry knew. Hell, since the day Chris first appeared on TV everyone in the world knew. Or maybe it just felt that way to me?"

"What happened?"

She let out another sigh, this one shaky. "When we were younger our parents were killed in a burglary in progress. Chris and I watched it happen. He was only sixteen." She stopped. Her jaw bunched and she looked away.

Aslin waited. He knew there was more in her heart. Whether she wanted to share it now was a different matter.

"We came home while it was happening," she continued, her voice soft. "We'd all been to the movies. There were three of them in the house. They knocked Mom out with Dad's baseball bat as she walked through the door and beat the shit out of Dad before Chris or I could do a thing. Then they tied us to a chair and…attacked Mom while she was still unconscious, beat her with the bat when she came to, laughing the whole time. When they got tired of that, when she was unconscious again, they untied me…"

Aslin's gut rolled. Cold fury turned the blood in his veins to ice. He didn't say a word.

"Someone must have called the cops though, one of our neighbours maybe, because before they could do…what they were going to do to me…the sirens came and they took off."

She looked back at her brother, now standing at the counter, signing for the bill. Or maybe an autograph. From where Aslin stood at the door with Rowan, he couldn't tell. It didn't matter. Not when the horror in Rowan's emotionless voice kept him rooted to the spot. Not with the dead rage thrumming through his body.

"Mom died in my arms. Chris sat tied to the chair watching it all. They never caught the bastards that did it."

She swallowed. Aslin could see her throat work. And then she turned and looked up at him with eyes that shone with a bone-deep grief he knew he could never truly fathom. A grief he wanted to take away from her. "So he hides behind the laughter. It protects him."

"And what protects you?"

She caught her bottom lip with her teeth at Aslin's low question. "I don't need protecting."

He wanted to tell her she was wrong. He wanted to take her in his arms and hold her until every moment of pain and agony and fear in her soul was gone.

Instead, he tucked his finger under her chin and lifted her gaze to his face.

"Please don't," she whispered. A second later, she rose onto tip toe and placed her lips on his.

The kiss was simple and gentle and over before Aslin could slide his arms around her body. But it was enough. Enough for him to know he was never letting this woman go. Whether she liked it or not, he was protecting her for the rest of her life.

"I love this place." Chris suddenly appeared at their side, his grin wide. "Where else in the world can you order the country's national emblem for lunch?"

Rowan pulled away from Aslin, her cheeks pink, her gaze shifting from Aslin's. "I still can't believe you ate kangaroo. Have you no heart."

"I did eat kangaroo." Chris rubbed at his stomach as they walked from the restaurant out on the esplanade. "And it was delicious. Grilled to perfection." He nudged his sister with his shoulder. "You know what makes the whole thing ironic though, sis?"

Rowan cast him a dubious look.

"I'm getting my photo taken tomorrow at the zoo *with* a kangaroo. A live one."

Rowan let out a groan. "Oh God, you're going to burn in Hell. You know that, r—"

"*Chris Huntley!*" A high-pitched squeal cut her short. "Look, it's Chris Huntley!"

Chris burst out laughing. Rowan groaned again, and Aslin prepared himself for the group of teenage girls—all dressed in school uniform—frozen to the spot a few feet away, their enrapt stares locked on the actor.

Fifteen minutes later, during which Chris signed everything thrust at him by the girls, along with posing for so many photos Aslin lost track, Rowan gave Aslin a quick glance.

"This is all your fault," she muttered, her arms folded over her breasts.

He cocked an eyebrow at her.

"He feels safe with you around. It's the only reason I can come up with for his behaviour. Normally he tries to avoid this kind of thing. He'd never admit it, but it makes him nervous."

Aslin looked back at the young man surrounded by giggling teenage girls and tried to imagine what it would be like to exist as a sitcom star in a world filled with such personal horror. He couldn't do it.

"Thank you for that," Rowan murmured. She frowned up at him. "I think."

The sound of a car horn behind them made them both jump. Aslin bit back a growl. He'd never been so disconnected to his surroundings as he'd been today. If he didn't know any better, he'd say he was thoroughly distracted.

*Huh. That's an understatement, boyo.*

"Nigel wants Chris back on set, Rowan," Jeff called from the open driver's side window of the SUV they'd arrived in. "Said there's been a problem with the dormitory scene and he needs to reshoot something."

It took Aslin roughly five minutes to extract Chris from the school girls, who all giggled and blushed their way through goodbyes and thank yous to the actor.

"That was fun." Chris grinned in the backseat, fifteen minutes later. "Let's do it again tomorrow."

Aslin couldn't help but smile. It *had been* fun. And he

was enjoying himself so much more than he expected. Even when he received a call from Nick—the singer wondering what the hell he'd been thinking letting Holston catch him "with a handful"—Aslin couldn't stop the warm happiness making itself at home in his chest.

"Where the fuck have you been?" Nigel demanded the moment they walked onto the film set.

"Eating," Chris shot back. "Got a problem with that, take it up with Aslin."

The director threw up his hands. "I think I liked it better when you were in awe of him. Or trying to break your hand on his jaw. Can we start now?"

Grinning, Chris tossed his wallet and phone at Rowan. "Take care of that for me, sis?"

Aslin watched her snatch the items from the air, even as she pulled a face at her brother. "*I* liked you better when you were a snot-nosed kid."

"Yeah, yeah." Chris smirked. "Now shut up and let me do my thing."

"God, you're pathetic." Rowan turned and crossed to Chris's chair and dropped into it with a chuckle. "Remind me to beat the crap out of you later."

As before, people came running from everywhere, flooding the set with sound and movement. It was such a different soundtrack to what Aslin was used to. He stood back, watching it all. Taking it all in. Listening to it all.

Which was the only reason he heard the splintering wood behind him. The only reason he spun in time to see the large beam erected across the back of the dormitory set crack.

The only reason he was able to slam into Rowan before the beam split in two and smashed to the ground, crushing Chris's chair.

# Chapter Nine

"Why the fuck won't anyone listen to me?" Rowan ground her teeth. She squeezed the ice pack in her hand, damn near close to throwing it across the dormitory. "I'm fine." She looked up from where she sat in Nigel's chair, now up-righted after being knocked over by the falling beam.

Everyone looking at her wore worried frowns. Chris hovered over her like a nervous mother hen. "Sis," he began.

"Really—" she raised her hand and offered him the ice pack, "—I'm fine."

His frown deepened before he turned to Aslin. "I don't believe her."

The Brit stood silent directly in front of Rowan, his eyes flinty. What he was angry about, Rowan couldn't fathom.

Behind her, film crew swarmed like frantic bees over the wreckage. She could hear their hushed voices and hissed expletives as they inspected the mess. She heard Warren bark an order at one of the grips, something about, "doing it right the first time, dickwad."

"Put the ice pack on your head, Rowie," Chris told her, refusing to take it. "Jesus, I can see the crack in the ground where your head hit it."

Beside Chris, equally as worried judging by the furrows in his brow, Nigel let out a strangled chuckle.

Rowan glared at them both. "I already told you. My head didn't hit the ground. It hit Aslin's shoulder or biceps or something."

At the mention of Aslin's name, Chris grabbed the still-silent man's left hand and shook it. Fast. "You saved my sister, dude. Jesus, you saved my sister."

Aslin didn't say a word. He studied Chris for a second before moving his unwavering inspection to the crew and wreckage behind Rowan.

Rowan's stomach rolled. She'd never seen such an intense expression. Like he was dissecting everything with his gaze.

"I still want to know how it happened." Nigel frowned some more. "McCreedy!" His shout rose over the commotion. "Get over here."

The gathering crew shuffled aside, making room for the key grip. Except for Aslin, Rowan noticed. Aslin didn't move an inch.

"Tell me what's going on," Nigel demanded. The pinning glare that had cemented his reputation as a formidable director locked on Warren. "Your guys checked the support structure this morning, right?"

Warren nodded. "All I can figure out is there was a hairline split in the wood, Mr. McQueen. I checked everything myself during lunch, and it was all sound." He scratched at his cheek and Rowan scrunched up her face at the rank B.O. that assaulted her nose. "The lighting crew was working around the same area yesterday." He shrugged.

"Maybe—"

"There was that freaky woman with the red hair in here too," Tilly piped up. "The one Mr. Rhodes caught trying to get into Mr. Huntley's trailer."

Chris's eyebrow shot up. "What woman?"

Nigel dragged his hands through his hair. "Damn it. What the fuck is security doing?"

"Are you gonna call the cops?" Warren asked.

Rowan let out an exasperated breath. "Don't you think the question should be who's trying to hurt Chris?"

"Me?" Chris snorted. "Who the fuck wants to hurt me?"

Nigel's face drained of blood. "Christ, do you think..."

Rowan's pulse pounded fast in her throat. "Yes, I do think. First the steps on his trailer were deliberately tampered with, and now the beam above his chair falls down?" She gave the director a pointed look. "It doesn't take a genius to—"

"Chris is right," Warren cut her off. "Who would wanna hurt him?"

Rowan snapped her glare to his face. "A crazed fan? A pissed-off friend?"

"Okay, Rowie." Chris stepped forward and directed her hand—still gripping the ice pack—to the back of her head. "That's enough."

"My head doesn't *hurt*!"

Silenced slammed over the set at her shout. Everyone stared at her. Everyone.

"Let's go, Rowan."

It was Aslin's voice that broke the shocked silence. Calm, but commanding.

She glared up at him, the sight of his unwavering focus on her face sparking jolts of anger in her gut. "Where? Away? So whoever it is who is trying to get at my brother can make another attempt?"

"Rowie—"

"Now, Rowan," Aslin spoke again, as if she hadn't uttered a word. He leant forward, wrapped her free hand in a firm grip and pulled her to her feet.

The crowd parted like a wave. Which irritated Rowan more. Since when had Aslin Rhodes become the damn commanding officer of the film set?

"Let me go, Rhodes."

"Shut it, Hemsworth." He turned and began walking away, pulling her behind him.

For a split second, the urge to throw herself into a reverse spinning kick and slam her heel into his shoulder stole through her. She curled her fingers into tight fists and tensed.

A heartbeat before Aslin turned to stare straight into her eyes. "I wouldn't."

Rowan's mouth dried at the barely contained menace in his gaze.

Without waiting for her to respond, he turned and continued walking from the set. He didn't stop, or talk to anyone—including her—until they reached the door of a trailer located next to Chris's.

Rowan frowned. "Whose trailer is this?"

"Mine."

His answer was a low growl. He pulled a key from his hip pocket, unlocked the door and pulled it open.

"Yours? Since when do you have a trailer?"

He shot her a look over his shoulder. "Since one p.m. today."

And with that terse answer, he crossed the threshold, dragging her behind him.

The interior wasn't as luxurious or extravagant as Chris's, nor was there anything to indicate Aslin had spent any time in it. Tiny specks of dust danced on the air, picked out by the sun streaming through the narrow windows lining the walls. Rowan took it all in. "Homey," she muttered.

"It needs a woman's touch."

She snorted at Aslin's unexpected dry comeback, rubbing her wrist when he released it.

"Sit."

His one-word command made her spine stiffen. "I'm not a—"

Piercing brown eyes locked on her face. "Sit, Rowan. Now."

She plopped onto the edge of the nearest seat.

"Good. Now put the ice pack on the back of your head and listen to me."

She scowled at his order. "Aslin, we should be back on set. Chris—"

"Is fine." He pulled the door closed and leant against the bench beside it, folding his arms across his massive chest. "After the incident with the red-head yesterday I spoke to the head of security this morning and arranged a bodyguard. Someone I worked with often when Nick did high-risk public appearances in Sydney. Your brother won't even know Liev's here, but he'll be protected. The more pressing matter *I'm* concerned with is who is trying to harm *you*."

Rowan's mouth fell open. "Are you serious?"

Aslin's eye narrowed. "I know you're in shock from the accident, but I have to be blunt, and for that I'm sorry."

"In shock?" Rowan shook her head. "I'm not in shock. I'm furious. Someone is targeting my brother and you drag me away?"

"I told you, he's now well protected. And in my opinion, he isn't the target."

"Why would I be the target?"

Aslin levered off the wall and destroyed the small space between them in two strides. He lowered into a deep crouch, drawing his gaze level with hers. "Think about it, Rowan. Chris didn't sit in that chair once for the duration of the shoot. Not once. You were in it all morning. And again when Nigel called Chris back. And your bag was outside his trailer next to the steps. We both know they were tampered with, and I suspect it was by someone hoping you'd come out to retrieve your bag."

A cold fist sank into Rowan's chest and squeezed her heart. She stared at Aslin, her lips tingling. "You're insane."

His nostrils flared, the only reaction to her incredulous accusation. "No. I'm worried."

"About me? Forget it. You don't have to be. For two reasons. One, your theory is loco, and two, I. Can. Take. Care. Of. Myself."

Aslin's jaw bunched. "So you're ignoring the evidence?"

Rowan threw up her hands. The ice pack in her grip was no longer chilly and she squeezed it tight in an effort not to toss it at the irritating Brit. "I am. Because it's ridiculous. Now call off your muscle and let me go back to my brother."

"I can't do that, Rowan."

She cocked an eyebrow. "Why not? Are you going to give me some macho bullshit reason about me being weak and defenseless and needing someone like you to look after me?"

He shook his head. "No, I can't do that because of this."

He snared the hair at the nape of her neck and crushed her lips with his.

She froze. For exactly two heartbeats. And then she slammed her palms into his chest and shoved him backward.

He didn't land on his ass like she'd hoped. Instead, he recovered with nimble grace to stare down at her.

She looked up at him, her pulse wild, her belly churning. Her lips throbbed from his kiss, as did the junction of her thighs. A wicked, greedy, constricting heat that told her just how quickly and powerfully her body reacted to his. "S-so, you can't let me go back to Chris because you want to kiss me? Where's your control, Rhodes?"

"Rowan." Her name was a low growl on his lips. His jaw bunched at her taunt. "I think someone is trying to hurt you."

"And that's why you kissed me?"

He let out a ragged breath and ploughed his fingers through his hair. "Fuck, woman. You're infuriating. I kissed you because what happened back on set scared the sodding shit out of me. You could have been killed."

Scared.

The single word tore at Rowan's senses. She stared at him, her throat so tight she could barely draw breath. She'd only known Aslin for a short time, but she had little doubt nothing scared him.

Until now.

She shook her head. "I can't believe someone is trying to hurt me."

"And I can't believe you refuse to even consider it."

"Why would I? I haven't done anything."

"Except guide Chris, look out for him when others would take advantage of him?"

Rowan snorted. "And you think that's it? Not the crazy fan you caught this morning trying to get to him?"

"It's a theory."

"It's a stupid one."

Aslin crossed his massive arms over his massive chest. "I hope so. But my gut tells me otherwise."

"Then your gut has shit for brains."

"Thank you, John Cusack."

Rowan blinked. "How did you know I was quoting a movie?"

It was Aslin's turn to snort. "I don't live in a vacuum, Rowan. I do have a life you know."

"Really? And here I was thinking you just follow a rock star around all the time."

The corners of his lips twitched. "It pays well. Now I think I might just follow you around all the time."

She snarled. "Just try it, buster."

He cocked an eyebrow. "I've got to do something. You're too sodding stubborn to listen to reason. At least if I'm tailing you I can protect you from—"

She didn't let him finish. She leapt from her seat and slammed her shoulder into his gut. He let out a strangled *oof*, his back smashing into the door behind him.

The vibration shook all the way through him into Rowan's body. She jerked back, preparing to smack her fist into his jaw. Fury roared through her. Hot and encompassing.

"I don't need to be *protected*," she snapped, glaring at him. "I'm not defenseless. I'm not weak."

Aslin straightened, and it was as if she'd never barged into him. "No, you're not weak or defenseless, Rowan. But I'll be damned if I'll be that scared again."

She ground her teeth, her nails driving into her palms. "Then fuck off. Find someone else to play super-soldier around."

Black fire flared in his dark eyes. "I don't want someone else."

"Well, you can't have me."

"Bullshit."

The word sliced through the trailer's air a second before Aslin snatched her wrist from her side and yanked her to his chest.

His mouth captured hers, savage and brutal. His tongue swiped over her lips, her teeth, stroking her tongue with dominating purpose. The effect on her body was instantaneous. She whimpered. Liquid heat flowed through her core, pooling in her sex. Her nipples hardened until they were twin points of aching need.

He deepened the kiss, taking possession of her mouth and pleasure. She couldn't fight it, couldn't fight him. She didn't want to. Not anymore. Hell could rise up and damn them all, but Rowan wouldn't care. As long as she was in Aslin's strong arms, being kissed by him, worshipped by him.

She pressed her palms to his chest—the very place she'd shoved him only a moment ago—and splayed her fingers. The rapid sledgehammer beat of his heart under her hand sent fresh heat to her pussy. The rock-hard tips of his nipples stole her breath. She dragged a thumb over one of them, curious to see what he would do.

"Oh fuck, yes," he ground out against her mouth, cupping her ass with his hands to haul her hips to his.

The thick, rigid pole of his erection rammed into the curve of her sex. Undeniable. She whimpered her approval and teased his nipple again.

He hissed in a breath, thrusting his hips forward.

Rowan's pulse quickened. She slid her hands down his torso and her head swam at the sculpted shaped of his abs under her fingers. They were so hard, so defined. The man was the epitome of physical perfection. And she was going to fuck him.

The realization slammed into her like a jolt of exquisite electricity. Her breath caught in her throat, and then she yanked his shirt free of his jeans and slipped her fingers under the hemline.

Oh boy.

His flesh was warm and smooth. His belly hitched at her touch. A raw groan tore from him, his hands squeezing her butt with cruel pressure as she sought out his nipples.

Fine hair dusted the massive expanse of his chest, tickling her fingers, exciting her need. It was rare to find a man with a hairy chest in Hollywood nowadays, and even the professional martial artists she occasionally dated had all fallen under the deluded opinion waxing and manscaping was the only way to go.

She moaned, loving the way the wiry hair felt under her fingertips.

Real. So real. There was nothing fake about him.

Nothing.

She captured a nipple between two fingers and pinched.

His mouth jerked away from hers, another harsh hiss escaping him.

Ducking her head to his chest, she bunched up his shirt, closed her lips around the nipple she'd just squeezed and sucked.

Aslin raked his hands up her back. His hips bucked forward, driving his jeans-trapped shaft against her mound. He groaned, digging his fingers into her shoulders. "Christ, Rowan…"

A shudder wracked his body. He snatched her chin with a strong grip, forcing her upright. His nostrils flared. His Adam's apple slid up and down his throat. "Don't start something you won't let me finish, Rowan." His voice was a hoarse whisper. "I promised I wouldn't touch you like this again until you told me to. I also promised once you did, I would unleash my control and—"

"Fuck me, Rhodes," she cut him off, her heart wild, her breath nothing but shallow pants. "N—"

The word *now* never passed her lips. He captured it with his kiss, his tongue silencing her with hungry possession just as he grabbed her ass and spun around.

He slammed her against the door, his knee wedging between her thighs, his hands reaching for the hemline of her shirt. He pulled it up over her head, stripping her of its paltry protection without pausing for a beat. She gasped, liquid want flooding her pussy.

"Christ, Rowan." His murmur filled the trailer. "You are beautiful."

He covered her breasts with his hands, rasping his thumbs over the distended points of her nipples. The satin of her bra emphasized the caress and she shivered, gazing up into his face as she reached for his belt buckle.

His stare melded with hers for a split moment, a low groan rumbling in his chest, and then his hands covered her shoulders and he was sliding her bra straps down her arms.

Her breasts fell free immediately. Her nipples—already puckered—grew tighter. Aslin's nostrils flared at their erect state. He watched his fingers trace the aureole, his knee pressing harder to the junction of her thighs as he did so. She whimpered, arching her back to his gentle exploration.

It was ecstasy. It was wonderful. But she didn't want him gentle. She wanted him forceful.

"What are you waiting for?" she whispered.

His stare jerked up to her eyes, and she couldn't miss the strained tension around his nostrils, the edges of his mouth.

"I don't want to hurt you," he answered. "I want you so much I'm afraid I will if I don't try and—"

"I'm yours, Aslin." She slid the backs of her hands up the door to above her head, lifting her breasts upward as she rubbed her pussy on the top of his knee. "Take me. Fuck me. Please."

The words had barely left her lips when he captured her right breast with one hand. He kneaded the heavy curve of her flesh with rising pressure, his knee grinding to her clit equally hard. She let out a hitching cry, closing her eyes to the base pleasure radiating through her.

The sound of him lowering her zipper set her heart racing, as did the tug on her fly. She sucked in her belly, her sex filling with fresh moisture. He pulled at her shorts, parting them wide. And then he slipped his fingers between her spread legs, over the curve of her mons, to the folds of her pussy.

He fingered her clit, rolling the button with frenzied pressure before dipping into her wet heat.

She cried out, the sound loud in the silent trailer. He growled against the side of her throat, the hand on her breast squeezing tighter. She writhed against him, wanting to feel his fingers deeper in her heat.

He complied to her unspoken request, driving up into her sex with savage force. Shards of wicked pleasure shot through her and she dropped her hands to his shoulders, scraping her nails across their breadth.

Her orgasm hit her. So fast, so wild, she couldn't breathe. Her juices gushed from her pussy.

"Fuck, yes." Aslin's groan heated her ear. "I can feel you squeezing my fingers. So tight. So wet…"

She moaned, the pulses of her climax growing faster. Building. Mounting. And then another one claimed her, more intense than the first. More absolute.

"So perfect." His lips scored a line over her jaw, her chin. His teeth nipped at her lips. "So mine."

He withdrew his fingers from her sex enough to torture her clit again. She bucked, the sheer rapture of her duel orgasm making the swollen button almost too sensitive to touch.

"Aslin," she panted, "I…"

Whatever she was going to say next was lost to his plundering kiss. Concentrated pleasure poured through her veins. His control was deserting him. She could feel it in the urgent greed of his touch. A low groan tore from his chest and his hand yanked free of her sex. He broke away from the kiss, cupped her jaw in his palm and dragged his thumb over her lips before slipping it into her mouth.

She tasted her cream—musky and salty at once.

"Taste your pleasure, Rowan," he commanded before reclaiming her lips with his. His tongue mated with hers, untamed and feral. She whimpered, grinding her sodden pussy to his knee even as she reached for his fly.

He tore his mouth from her lips, grabbed the waistline of her undone shorts and shoved them down her hips.

The air-conditioned air of the trailer wrapped around her newly exposed flesh, streamed between her newly revealed pussy lips. She gasped, and then again when Aslin dropped to his knees and swiped his tongue over her clit. He hooked his hands high on her inner thighs and shoved her legs wide.

She leant her shoulders back into the door, every nerve-ending sizzling with scalding, mounting need as he fucked her pussy with his tongue. Another climax built within her walls, a radiating tension that shot up her spine and deep into her core. "Oh, yes, yes," she moaned, rolling her head side to side. "Yes."

He smoothed his hand down the back of her left leg, and with a sudden yank, her calf was on his shoulder. He buried his tongue into her spread seam, his nose in her trimmed pubic hair. She fisted her hands in his hair, her third orgasm slamming into her.

God, she'd never had so many so quickly. How would she survive when he drove his cock into her?

The delirious thought fired off new throbbing pressure in her core. A keening sound filled the trailer, and it was only when Aslin ground out, "I love the sound you make when you come," that Rowan realized it was her.

She was drowning in pleasure. It engulfed her. Every time Aslin's tongue painted her folds, her clit, she shuddered and clung to him. Her breath left her in ragged pants. Her nipples ached. Her belly knotted.

And still she wanted more. She needed more. It wasn't enough. She wanted —

Without warning, Aslin rose to his feet. He took a step backward, just one, his gaze holding her prisoner.

She watched him, her lips parted, her breasts heaving.

Wordlessly, he unthreaded his belt, popped his button and lowered his fly. His cock pushed free of his jeans, thick and long and venous. Its bulbous head was a deep blood-purple. Beads of precome anointed its crown, seeping from the tiny slit there.

Rowan's heart slammed into her throat.

"C-con...condom," she stammered.

Still wordless, his jaw bunching, he reached into his back pocket, pulled out his wallet and withdrew a small square packet from inside in.

If it was possible, Rowan's heart beat faster.

She stared at him. At the condom in his fingers. At the massive erection jutting upright from his jeans. Oh God, how was she to take him all?

As if he saw her fear, he drew a long breath as he slowly sheathed his cock with the protective shield. "I will try to be gentle, Rowan. I pr —"

She shook her head. "Don't."

The single word was all it took. She saw his eyes dilate. Saw his Adam's apple jerk up and down, and then he was pinning her to the door, his right hand hooking under her left knee, yanking her foot from the floor.

Parting her moisture-slickened sex.

He penetrated her in one powerful thrust. Buried himself in her heat. She cried out, the fire of his exquisite invasion detonating a wave of pleasure so close to pain for a giddy moment black stars swirled in her vision.

She drove her nails into his shoulders as she was impaled on his cock.

"Rowan…" he rasped, his eyes wide, horror etching his face. "Fuck, I'm sorry, love. I didn't want to hurt you. I'll stop. I'll—"

"Don't you dare," she cut him off, even as she bent her leg more around his elbow and squeezed her inner muscles tight on his buried length. "Or I'll be forced to beat the shit out of you. Got it?"

His nostrils flared. "Got it."

With that, he thrust up into her. Again and again and again, until nothing mattered in Rowan's world except the pleasure he wrought on her body. And her complete surrender to it.

And when he came, she came with him.

As she knew she would.

Minutes, maybe hours later—Rowan didn't know—they leant motionless against the door, their ragged breaths the only sound to be heard. The fading pulses of Rowan's orgasm throbbed through her, each one squeezing Aslin's cock still embedded in her sex.

They stared into each other's eyes, their hips pressed together, her leg hooked over his arm. "Holy shit," she murmured. "That was…that was…"

The door opened behind her and before either she or Aslin could prevent it, she tumbled backward. Crashing into a hard, firm body.

"Damn, sis." Chris's laughing voice flooded Rowan's cheeks with embarrassed heat as Aslin leapt out of his trailer and scooped her off her brother. "This is going to fuck me up for life. On the plus side, I see your head is feeling better."

# Chapter Ten

Saving Chris from a horny kangaroo was probably the most surreal thing Aslin had ever done. Thank God, the media had departed by the time the marsupial decided the man scratching its fur was its type, locked its front legs around his hips and began to mount him.

Aslin had never seen so many frantic, embarrassed zoo staff run so quickly to save the shocked American actor. Nor had he heard Rowan laugh with such unabashed mirth. She stood to the side of the enclosure, arms wrapped around her belly, tears streaming down her cheeks as Chris yelped in surprise. The kangaroo keepers battled the determined animal and the zoo manager barked horrified commands.

It wasn't until the kangaroo levered back onto its thick, powerful tail in an attempt to reposition Chris, that Aslin realized the staff weren't having much luck controlling the situation.

In three strides, he crossed the lush grass, elbowed his way between the roo's chest and the actor and—with a shove he knew wasn't gentle—dislodged the rather unfortunate embrace.

"Holy shit." Chris stumbled sideways, his face an incredulous grin. "That's taking my animal magnetism to a whole different level."

From the sidelines, Rowan's laughter grew louder.

"I'm so sorry, Mr. Huntley." The zoo manager wrung his hands together, disbelief turning the apology to a strangled squeak. "I don't understand—"

Chris laughed, holding up a hand to the mortified man. "Nah, it's okay. I'm good."

"That's what the kangaroo was thinking as well," Rowan called.

Aslin turned and gave her a look, fighting his own laugh. The roo keepers were standing beside Rowan, holding the animal by a leash as she and Tilly petted its muscled back. Whatever had aroused its interest in Chris had seemingly passed and the animal was now happy to munch on the grass under its paws without any interest in the humans around it.

Ten minutes later, with Tilly clutching an almost life-size kangaroo soft toy—a gift from the zoo to Chris—they made their way to the harbour jetty and climbed aboard the luxurious motor yacht arranged by the studio.

"Well—" the actor smirked, lounging on the cockpit's leather bench seat, "—that was one for the books. Thank God your paparazzi friend wasn't there to capture it all, Rowan, or my reputation would be in serious danger."

Beside Aslin, Rowan snorted. "You know, squirt, there's a part of me that kinda wishes that had happened."

Chris grinned. "Ah, shut up, sis. Or I'll tell everyone on set what happened yesterday."

Tilly lifted her face from the side of the plush kangaroo. "What happened yesterday?"

Rowan glared at her brother. "Nothing."

Aslin forced his grin to stay away. He couldn't however, stop his groin stirring. Even the thoroughly embarrassing arrival of Chris at his trailer and Rowan's subsequent backward tumble through the door couldn't taint the memory of making love to her for the first time. It was too potent. That they'd spent the night together only added to the powerful response in his body.

They'd travelled back to Aslin's hotel room after filming finished for the day, hung the *Do Not Disturb* sign from the door knob and proceeded to get to know each other on a purely carnal level. He'd never come so many times in one night as he had last night. Thank sodding God, he was in peak physical condition or he'd be completely buggered now.

He'd just started to fall asleep when the morning sun began bathing his modest room in a warm golden glow. Opening his eyes, a smile had stretched his lips. Rowan still snuggled against him, her cheek resting on his chest, her thigh draped over his legs.

He'd let her stay that way, his gaze tracking the sunlight as it moved across the ceiling, as the realization he never wanted to share a bed with anyone else but her again crashed into him.

The notion of having sex with anyone else but Rowan had made his gut churn.

The thought of Rowan having sex with anyone else but him didn't just make his gut churn, it made him…angry.

He'd stared at the ceiling, his heart thumping wildly in his chest, Rowan's heat seeping into his body, his morning hard-on a steel rod of eager need, and bit back a shaky breath.

Falling in love with an American hadn't been part of his

plan when he'd left Murriundah. What the fuck did he do about it?

Now, standing on the motor yacht, the husky timbre of Rowan's voice playing with his senses as she and Tilly and Chris talked amongst themselves, he still didn't have an answer.

Nor did he have an answer about who was trying to hurt her.

He didn't know what pissed him off more.

"Four more days of shooting before we pack up and move to Berlin."

The sudden silence told Aslin he'd missed something important. He pulled his focus back to the three Americans sitting in the cockpit. "Sorry?"

Chris chuckled. "I said Nigel estimates we've only got four more days of shooting in Sydney left. If it all goes well, we'll be flying to Berlin on Saturday."

A cold tension stole through Aslin's muscles. He flicked Rowan a quick look, doing his damnedest to keep his expression relaxed. Berlin?

Rowan wasn't looking at him. She was studying the water around them, her shoulders square, her eyes hidden by black Ray Bans.

"What about you, Ms. Hemsworth?" Tilly frowned at Rowan's profile. "Are you going to Berlin? Don't you have a tournament in New Delhi to fight in next week?"

"Ah, shit, that's right, sis." Chris turned to his sister, his frown mirroring Tilly's. "When do you fly out for that?" He waited for a second before sliding his gaze to Aslin. "Or are you *not* flying anywhere?"

Whatever answer Rowan was going to provide was halted by a group of women squealing Chris's name from a yacht sailing past them. *If* she was going to answer at all. By the way she continued to stare out over the boat's aft, her spine stiff, her jaw bunched, Aslin highly doubted a word was going to pass her lips.

He studied her, the thrum of the boat's motor adding to the churning sensation in his gut.

Berlin. New Delhi.

She hadn't mentioned New Delhi last night. Come to think of it, they'd hardly talked about anything last night. They'd fucked. Showered. Fucked some more. Ordered room service. Ignored the food as they went at it again. Picked at the cold burgers and chips while searching for something on the hotel movie service to watch before giving up any pretense of being restrained and fucking like rabbits again. Aslin drove his blunt nails into his palms. When, in amongst all that, had any chance of talking about their future plans popped up?

*Future plans? Christ, boyo. What future plans? Maybe she didn't think to mention it because as far as she's concerned, whatever this thing is between you, it's over when she leaves Sydney?*

A gripping pressure wrapped Aslin's chest and he bit back a curse. He had no grounds for being angry, but he was. Angry he'd let himself reach this state. It had to be because he felt adrift. Uncertain about where his life was heading. That was the only explanation he could think of.

The subject of Rowan's future tournament didn't come up for the rest of the trip around Sydney Harbour. Nor did filming. But the relaxed calm Aslin had experienced since making love to Rowan in his trailer had deserted him.

Back on set, he stood in the wings, watching Chris and Vin Diesel beat it out for the cameras, interjecting when necessary. Chris's fighting technique had improved considerably, a fact the stunt coordinator commented on more than once with begrudging respect. But not even that could elevate Aslin's dark state of mind. He'd gone and fallen for a woman who didn't need him. For that, he had no solution.

When his cell phone started sounding out the "Funeral March", he pulled it from his pocket and walked off set. "What's up, Nick?"

His boss laughed. "Not having a good time, Uncle As?"

"Do you have a crazed stalker after you, Blackthorne? Or can I just hang up now?"

Nick laughed again. "Settle down, Aslin. I just wanted to let you know Lauren, Josh and I are flying out of the country tomorrow. I thought I'd show them the beauty of autumn in New York before Josh has to go back to school."

The tight pressure that gripped Aslin's chest back on the boat wrapped around it again. "Okay, boss. Give me five hours and I'll be home."

"Aslin." Nick's voice was steady. "You're staying put."

Aslin fixed his stare on a group of people—most likely extras, by the military combat uniforms they wore—walking toward the set. His throat grew thick. "Is this it then? Time for me to find another job?"

"No, As. Just time for you to enjoy being Aslin Rhodes, not Nick Blackthorne's nameless bodyguard." Nick paused. "Understand what I'm getting at?"

Aslin swallowed, tracking the approaching extras without really seeing them.

"Besides," Nick went on, "I keep seeing you in the background of the images of Huntley popping up all over the media. Standing there next to your friend from the hospital car park."

"Rowan," Aslin murmured, his chest heavy.

"I know who she is, As. And I don't want to take you

away from her."

Aslin let out a short grunt. "Don't think that's a situation to worry about. She's flying out for Berlin on Sunday. Or maybe New Delhi."

"And you're not going with her?"

Go with her? If she asked him to go with her, would he?

Aslin's pulse smashed hard in his neck. Bloody hell, he would.

"She hasn't asked, boss."

"And you're going to wait for her to do so?"

Aslin ground his teeth at Nick's pointed question.

"Do you remember when I decided Lauren was the only woman I wanted to spend the rest of my life with, Aslin?"

"I do."

"Can you remember how fucked up I was before I found her again?"

"Are you saying I'm fucked up, Nick?"

Nick laughed. "I'm saying don't let the chance of happiness slip away, Rhodes. Grab it, hold it. Hell, strangle it if you have to. But don't let it slip away. Trust me on this, okay?"

Aslin closed his eyes, drew a long, slow breath and released it.

"Now get back to work," Nick ordered, the grin in his voice unmistakable. "I've got to pack for New York. Oh, and we'll be gone for a while, so there's no need to hurry back from Sydney. Take Rowan somewhere perfect and private on that bike of yours. Got it?"

Nick disconnected the call before Aslin could respond.

Studying the group of extras, Aslin let out a breath. Nick was correct. Aslin had watched the singer come close to self-destructing, and it was only when he'd acknowledged Lauren Robbins was his heart and future that he'd found true peace.

Aslin didn't know if Rowan was his heart and his future, but he damn well wanted the chance to find out.

He shoved his phone into his pocket and turned to the film set behind him.

And then spun back around to face the extras.

One of them was wrong.

He narrowed his eyes, staring hard at the group. Picking out the extra that had caught his attention. Tufts of blazing red hair poked out from under a helmet that looked like it came from a costume shop, not a military supply store.

Thick, over-zealous make-up coated the extra's face.

The extra that was the crazed fan hell bent on meeting Chris.

Aslin ground his teeth. "Fuck it."

He ran at the group, letting out a disgusted groan when the woman squealed and took off. She stumbled through the extras, shoving aside those in her way in her bid to escape him.

Aslin increased his speed, keeping his stare locked on her back. Exasperation knotted through his anger. When he was finished dealing with her he was going to have a word with security. How the hell she kept getting on site was inexcusable.

With a yelp, the fleeing fan darted right, her feet skidding on the concrete and an incredulous part of Aslin's mind noticed she was wearing hot-pink running shoes.

*How the bloody hell had she fooled Security in those damn—*

The woman yanked off her toy-shop helmet and hurled it at Aslin. "Fuck off, Pom!" she yelled, scrambling left.

Around them, film crew stopped and stared.

"Go back to England!"

Aslin ground his teeth and pushed more speed into his

legs. He was done being a nice guy.

Crash-tackling her to the ground, he grabbed her wrists before she could scratch him with her nails. "Enough," he snapped, hauling her to her feet.

The crowd cheered, more than one laughing at the woman's wild efforts to break free of Aslin's grip. In amongst her kicking legs and attempts to spit on him, Aslin spied a swarm of burly men dressed in black running toward them.

*About sodding—*

Sharp teeth sank into his shoulder.

With a snarl, he jerked away from the woman's bite. "That's enough."

"Found yourself a girlfriend, Rhodes?"

The broad Australian accent told Aslin that Liev Reynolds was behind him. The chuckle in the part-time bodyguard's voice told him Reynolds thought the situation funny.

"She's a charmer, this one," the Australian pointed out. "Want me to give you a—"

*"Chris!"* the woman shrieked. *"Chris, it's me! Belinda! Chris!"*

At the sound of her name, the men dressed in black let out a collection of curses.

Leiv laughed. "Think they know her?"

Yanking the writhing woman harder against his chest, Aslin shot Chris, who was standing behind Nigel and a collection of crew a few yards away, a quick look. "Do you?" he asked, narrowing his eyes at the closest security guard.

The man nodded, unclipping a set of handcuffs from his belt. "Yeah. She's been a nuisance since filming started. Keeps sending requests for autographs. Begging to meet Mr. Huntley. Don't know how she does it, but she keeps getting on site."

He stepped forward, snared the fan's upper arm and tugged her toward him.

*"Chris!"* She screamed. "It's Belinda! *Chris!"*

Aslin turned to the actor, the stunned expression telling him exactly what he'd suspected—Chris had no idea who the woman was. It was an expression Aslin was more than familiar with. Nick had worn it often when confronted by unhinged, obsessed fanatics.

Returning his attention to the guard, he watched the man click the cuffs around the struggling woman's wrists. "Time to call the cops, honey," the guard snarled.

*"I love you, Chris!"* she cried, stare fixed on the actor as the security team dragged her away. *"Will you sign my—"*

Whatever she wanted signed was muffled, no doubt by the hand of the guard holding her.

Silence fell over the surrounding film crew. For about ten seconds. And then, almost as one, normality resumed. People continued walking to their previous destinations, calls on cell phones were made, conversation continued. The military-dressed extras mingled about, casting uncertain looks between each other until the second unit director hurried over and rounded them up.

"So does this mean I'm not needed anymore, Rhodes?"

Aslin turned his attention to Liev Reynolds, finding the Australian smirking beside him.

"No." He shook his head. "Not yet. Huntley's too easy a target and my gut…" He stopped. His gut was telling him something was wrong. Something that had nothing to do with Belinda.

*Rowan. You still believe someone is trying to hurt Rowan.*

He did. But for some reason he hadn't pushed the subject with her.

*Some reason? Perhaps because you were distracted*

*losing yourself in her body? Making love to her until you could barely move?*

*Fucking her senseless?*

"Rhodes?"

He gave Liev a steady look. "Stay on him, but keep it low. Just in case."

The bodyguard nodded. "Righto. Will let you know if anything feels off."

Without any seeming interest in Chris, who was currently making his way toward them both, the Australian shoved his hands in his jeans pockets and ambled away.

"I tell you," the actor said, a grin splitting his face, "this trip to Oz truly has been wild."

Aslin raised an eyebrow. "I can't imagine life is ever boring for you."

Chris chuckled. "Rowie keeps things pretty normal. Well, as normal as it can get for someone in my line of work."

"Does it annoy you? Her meddling in your affairs? Telling you what you can and can't do?"

Chris burst out laughing. "Not at all. She's right to. I'm a lost cause without her. Before she stepped up to the plate and took charge, I was pissing away all my money on booze, parties and who the fuck knows what else. Poor Tilly had to deal with a lot of shit and vomit back then, I gotta say."

"You know anyone who *would* be irritated by it?"

An unreadable tension pulled at Chris's face. He studied Aslin, eyes narrow, shoulders straightening. "No. Should I?"

The band of pressure that had made itself at home around Aslin's chest grew tight once again. For a second, he considered telling Chris his thoughts. For a second. "No." He shook his head with a smile. "Just wondering if I'm the only one she frustrates to no end."

Better to keep Chris in the dark. A worried brother

would make it impossible to catch whoever it was.

*And that's your plan now? To catch them?*

It was.

A relaxed guffaw bubbled past Chris's lips. "Ah, I figured she was getting under your skin. If it helps, it means she likes you. A lot."

If the band squeezing Aslin's chest grew any tighter, he'd be asphyxiating.

Likes you. A lot.

*What about loves?*

The unspoken question punched into Aslin. He forced his hands into fists as he watched Rowan walk up to Nigel and Tilly a few feet away. His heart quickened.

"So what are your thoughts on coming to Berlin?"

Chris's question slid Aslin's focus back to the actor. "I haven't any yet."

Chris pulled a contemplative face. "What if I ask you about your thoughts on going to New Delhi?"

Aslin ground his teeth.

"Yeah." Chris chuckled. "Figured as much. Want me to ask her to the prom for you?"

Aslin's withering glare didn't stop Chris from laughing again. Nor did Rowan's arrival at Chris's side with Tilly in tow.

Rowan gave her brother a curious frown. "What's so funny?"

"The British super soldier here." Chris threw a nod in Aslin's direction. "He wants to ask you to the prom."

Rowan's frown vanished. "The prom? What the —"

"Do they have the prom in England?" Tilly asked.

Aslin didn't miss the way Rowan's lips twitched. Nor the way Chris drew a slow breath before turning to his personal assistant. "Tilly, can you get me a bottle of coconut water, please? Luke warm. Unopened. Oh, and an apple. I'd prefer a red delicious."

"Sure, Mr. Huntley." The young woman hurried away, the ever-present spring in her step. She was joined by her boyfriend a few steps away, Warren McCreedy flipping Chris a wave before wrapping his arm around her shoulders.

"Now," Chris said, grinning at Aslin. "About the prom—"

Aslin met his smirk with an unwavering stare. "Do you want me to hurt you, Chris?"

The actor held up his hands. "Okay, dude. I get the point. How 'bout I go talk to my director over there about something important while you talk to my sister about—"

Something in Aslin's face sent Chris running.

"What's going on, soldier boy?"

Aslin's heart thumped hard. He leveled his gaze to her face, noting the uncharacteristic uncertainty in her eyes. "Are you going to New Delhi?"

Rowan stiffened. "If I am?"

"I'd like to come with you."

She was quiet for a long moment. "What about the film shoot? Berlin?"

"I'm not interested in Berlin."

Her lips parted at his not-so-subtle answer. She gazed up at him, her eyes battling his, her eyebrows pulling together. "Is this..." She paused. "Can we, you and I...can it work?"

Aslin drew a long, slow breath, refusing to let her stare go. "I fucking well plan on it."

His crude respond made her chuckle. A faint pink tinge painted her cheeks. She looked up at him through lowered lashes. "What if I'm still not one hundred percent certain?"

Aslin lowered his head slightly. His heart was pounding fast. "I can be very convincing."

Rowan tilted her chin. Just enough to bring her lips in line with his. "Then convince me."

He caught his growl of eager approval before it could vibrate through his body. Turning on his heel, he strode toward his trailer. Behind him, Rowan chuckled again, the sound low and decidedly suggestive. In two steps, she was by his side. Two steps after that, her fingers were threaded through his. It was a surreal moment, one Aslin didn't think he'd ever forget. He hadn't held a girl's hand like this since he was a kid—a silly lad of twelve hoping to snog Janine Wellings after walking her home from school.

This was completely different. For starters, he was forty-one. But more importantly, it wasn't just a kiss he was hoping to score when they reached their destination, but a future.

*Ah, boyo, it truly does seem that you're in love.*

A few minutes later, minutes passed in silence both delicious and tense, Aslin's trailer was in front of them.

His pulse quickened, especially when Rowan slipped her fingers from his and slid her arm around his back.

He turned his head to look at her, unable to stop his smile as it stretched his lips.

"Mr. Rhodes?" Someone called behind him and his smile vanished, replaced with an impatient scowl. "Can I have a word?"

Rowan pulled away from him, her eyes sparkling. "I'll wait for you inside."

He nodded, fighting the powerful urge to ignore the man calling him—the head of the film's security—and kiss her witless.

Planting his feet hard to the ground, he watched her walk toward his trailer. She reached for the door, flicking him a quick grin over her shoulder as she twisted the knob.

"Ms. Hemsworth?" he said, his voice loud enough for

her to hear his teasing tone. "Come here."

She cocked an eyebrow at him and tugged on the door. "I think you need to learn some — "

Aslin's trailer exploded in an abrupt detonation of fire, splintering metal and black smoke. Destroying the mobile abode in the space it took Aslin to scream Rowan's name.

In the time it took her body to fling backward from the blast and land on the ground in a boneless, jarring crunch.

# Chapter Eleven

Nothing was in focus. Sound was muffled. Blackness swirled across her vision. A high-pitched ringing drilled into her ears. Her breath balled in her throat, choking her. She couldn't move. Everything was pain. Like she'd been slammed into by a wrecking ball of molten metal.

Pain tore through her lungs. Blistered up her spine.

Engulfed her. Owned her. Tried to tear from her throat in a cry.

"Rowan?"

Aslin's voice. Faint. Almost lost in the ringing.

She tried to open her eyes. To see him. Tried to focus on him through the pain. Tried to claw her way up out of the excruciating agony.

"Rowan, open your eyes and look at me."

The pitch in his voice changed. Grew deeper.

"Look at me, Hemsworth."

She ground her teeth. Fuck, she hurt. All over. She hurt. Why the fuck did she—

"Open your sodding eyes, Hemsworth." She felt something warm and steely hard slip around her fingers. "Now."

She swallowed. Writhed. The ringing grew louder. The pain in her body snarled. Grabbed at her.

Or was it hands? Fast hands? Hands pushing at her neck? Fingers drilling into her—

"Please, Rowan," Aslin's voice slipped into her ear, soft and gentle despite the constant high-pitch sound she heard. "I need you to open your eyes, love."

She tried to open her eyes, but the pain tore at her.

"Look at me, Rowan." The warm steel around her fingers squeezed with gentle force. The pressure on her neck faded. "Look at me."

She forced her eyes open, squinted up at him, swiped her tongue over her lips. The copper taste told her they were bleeding. "Y-you're a…" She winced, the whispered words were like sandpaper in her throat. "You're a bossy son…of a bitch, aren't you, soldier boy?"

The tormented worry etching his face vanished. The gentle grip on her fingers eased…a little. He chuckled, a low sound barely audible over the sirens squealing in the background. "You could call me that."

Rowan hiccupped out a scratchy laugh. "Can I…can I say ouch?"

Aslin's knuckles brushed against her jaw in a delicate kiss. "Only if you want me to call you a big girl's blouse."

Another laugh tore at Rowan's chest, sending shards of pain through her body. "A what?"

He shook his head. "I'll tell you—"

"*Rowie?*" Chris's scream cut him short, her brother almost skidding to his knees at her side. "Jesus, Rowie, what…are you okay?"

His expression told her she wasn't. Stunned horror twisted his face. His stare jerked all over her, no doubt jumping from bloody wound to bloody wound to bloody wound, before he looked at Aslin. "What the fuck happened?"

"An explosive device detonated in my trailer."

The horror on Chris's face evaporated at Aslin's level answer and was replaced with stunned confusion. "What the *fuck* do you mean an explosive device? Did you leave something on? The kettle? The toaster oven?"

The muscles in Aslin's jaw tightened and he shook his head. "I've only been in there once, Chris. Yesterday."

"So how the hell—"

"What the *hell* is going on?" Nigel McQueen's shout cut Chris short. The director appeared at Rowan's side followed by two police officers. "What the fuck is going on?"

Before anyone could do or say a thing, two paramedics were shoving the cops and the director aside. Rowan flinched, hissing in pain as they began to investigate her injuries. She glared at them when they tried to placate her with reassuring words. Words she could barely discern over the ringing in her ears. Damn it, why wouldn't the ringing stop?

Aslin's low chuckle calmed her irritation, as did his fingers threaded through hers. She flicked him a quick look, biting back a groan at the pain the move caused behind her eyes.

"The pain in your head, Rowan," one of the paramedics asked, flashing a narrow light in and out of her eyes, "on a scale of one to ten, ten being the worst, one being—"

"Eight," she answered.

"Are you sure?"

She gave the man a shallow nod, once again suppressing a groan. "I've had a ten a time or two."

Fifteen minutes later, she climbed to her feet.

She had to argue with them, of course. And Chris. No one wanted her to stand up. Nigel, her brother, the paramedics, they all wanted her to stay on her ass.

The paramedics insisted she stay motionless until they fitted a neck brace on her and moved her to the ambulance. Chris insisted she did what they said. Nigel *ordered* her to do what they said. She ignored them all.

Just as she ignored the pain threatening to engulf her again as she pushed herself off the ground.

Holy shit, she hurt.

She straightened, biting back the tight sob tearing at her throat. She wasn't going to just lie around all day waiting to feel better. She was—

"Sis." Chris reached for her, but she shrugged him off. And then stumbled sideways.

Aslin caught her, his expression unreadable. "Okay, you need to go to the hospital."

She protested. Right up until black swirls of dizziness stole her ability to stand. Strong bands of steel wrapped around her back and beneath her knees, and it was only the distinct scent of Aslin's body in her breath that told her he'd scooped her up. The rest of her mind didn't seem to want to register anything but pain.

Pain.

When was the last time she let pain defeat her?

If the answer came, she didn't remember it. Nor did she remember the trip to the hospital, but apparently there was one. Because that was where she woke up, connected to an intravenous drip, her favourite jeans and cowboy boots no longer covering her body, a hospital gown in their place, the ringing in her ears only marginally softer.

She pushed herself—gingerly—up onto her elbows.

"Ouch," she muttered, a sharp shard of pain sinking into her right side.

"Big girl's blouse."

Cocking an eyebrow, she turned toward Aslin's voice.

He stood next to the door, his shoulders pressed to the wall, one ankle crossed over the other. A dark growth of stubble covered his chin and jaw, making him appear far more dangerous than ever.

Or maybe that was the morphine talking?

Rowan caught her bottom lip, shot the clear plastic tube connected to the pump beside her a quick look—*was* that morphine?—and then returned her attention to the silent Brit.

He studied her, his sculpted biceps all the more impressive due to the way his arms crossed his broad chest, his faded denim jeans emphasizing the corded strength of his thighs.

Rowan's belly knotted. Menace oozed from him in waves.

"How do you feel?"

She shifted on the bed and winced.

"That good?"

Before she could answer, a nurse hurried into the room. "How are you feeling, Ms. Hemsworth?" The woman fiddled with the controls, adjusting something on the drip. "Are your ears still ringing?

"A little."

The woman made a note on the chart she'd placed beside Rowan and then stared hard into her eyes. "Can you tell me your level of pain?"

Rowan frowned, letting her body talk to her for a brief moment. "Maybe a four?"

The nurse made a *hmm* sound, nodded, made another

note and then adjusted something else. "What day is it today?"

"Friday," Rowan answered.

"Who is the President of the United States?"

"Obama."

"Are you feeling hungry?"

Rowan turned her frown on Aslin. "How long have I been out of it?"

The corner of his mouth tugged into a small smile. "Forever. I'm going to call you Rip Van Winkle from now on."

"Three hours, Ms. Hemsworth," the nurse answered with a glower at Aslin. "But you've been asleep for most of it, not unconscious. It's good to see you awake and lucid. If for no other reason than the bossy mountain here can stop harassing the doctors."

A soft snort sounded in the back of Rowan's throat. "Told you you were bossy."

Aslin shrugged. "I didn't argue with you."

The nurse clicked her tongue. "No, but you did argue with everyone who came in here. Including Ms. Hemsworth's brother." She smiled at Rowan, checking something above Rowan's left eyebrow. "That's looking very good. I doubt it'll leave a scar."

"A scar?"

The nurse smiled again. "You're very lucky. No stitches required, but you do have a deep cut above your eye and your right eardrum is damaged, I'm afraid. Nothing permanent, but you will be feeling a little groggy for a few days. The doctor will be here in a moment, but until then…" She shot Aslin a look over her shoulder. "I need to check Ms. Hemsworth's other injuries now. Can you please step out?"

Aslin shook his head. "I've seen every inch of Rowan's body, love. I'm not leaving her now."

"Jesus, Rhodes." Rowan's cheeks grew warm, the pit of her belly fluttering at the memory of *how* he'd seen every inch of her body. "Way to behave like a Neanderthal."

In response, Aslin settled his shoulders more firmly against the wall, changed the way his ankles were crossed and gave her a grin.

The nurse *tsked*. "Would you like me to call security, Ms. Hemsworth?"

Rowan chuckled. "No. It's fine."

Casting Aslin a displeased glare, the nurse smoothed a hand behind Rowan's shoulders. "Okay then, I need you to sit up, please?"

Rowan did as the nurse asked, shutting out the shards and slithers of pain stabbing at her body. She ground her teeth, fixing her stare on her knees as the nurse gently lifted the hospital gown from her torso.

A low growl from the other side of the room told Rowan Aslin could see what the woman had revealed. She twisted to the right a little, ignoring the way her body protested at the awkward move, and looked at her side. A deep purple bruise spread over her ribs, an angry red mottled with darker maroon. "Ouch," she murmured.

"You're very lucky, Ms. Hemsworth," the nurse stated, her voice soft and almost disconnected. "Only two broken ribs and no pierced lung. If you weren't in such good physical shape you may be in a whole lot more pain now."

"Which is what I told Chris." Aslin's deep rumble lifted her gaze from her injury.

"Is he here?"

"Outside. With Nigel and Tilly and Warren."

"And two police officers," the nurse finished.

The hair on the back of Rowan's neck prickled. "Why are the cops here?"

The nurse straightened, lowered Rowan's gown and gave her shoulder a gentle squeeze. "I'll be back later. Try to stay quiet and still, Ms. Hemsworth. If the pain gets too severe, press this button. It'll inject a small dose of morphine."

Rowan frowned as the woman hurried from the room, stopping only to whisper something low to Aslin. He nodded once, waited until she slipped through the door and then crossed to where Rowan lay.

"Why are the cops here?"

He folded his arms over his chest, his legs braced, his thigh muscles hard under the denim of his jeans. "Because there is a distinct possibility someone is trying to hurt you."

A sharp breath burst from Rowan. She pulled a face, the ringing in her ears growing louder. "Not this again."

"Yes, this again. If it had been Chris's trailer that exploded, I'd be inclined to agree with you that your brother is the target, but it was my trailer, wasn't it?"

A heavy pressure wrapped around Rowan's chest. "And this is what the police think as well? Someone is trying to kill me?" She stared up at Aslin, wishing to hell she could stand on her feet. She hated being vulnerable like this. Hated it.

Aslin's nostrils flared. "They are investigating the situation."

"Ah, so this is still only *your* theory?"

"It is. Rowan, listen to me. It's not a secret on set you and I are spending...time together. Anyone watching you, studying you, would play the odds my trailer would be your on-set base, given our relationship."

"And you don't think they—whoever *they* are—are trying to hurt you? The woman, the red-headed fan? She hates you. What if she was trying to get at you? Or that paparazzo? It's obvious you two have history. Why don't you think—"

"Holston is a marked man." Aslin's gaze didn't move from her face. "He can't come within fifty kilometres of the set without me being notified, and he knows it. And I'm well versed with fans like the redhead. She's fixated, but I'm not her target."

Rowan's heart slammed faster in her chest. Her head ached. She swallowed, not wanting to believe what Aslin was saying. It made no sense. None at all. "You...you don't think the trailer thing was just an accident?"

He shook his head. "The only time I'd been in there was when we made love. There was nothing switched on or plugged in. And there was nothing in there that could have caused that kind of explosion anyway."

The pressure around Rowan's chest gripped tighter. "Does Chris agree with your theory?"

Aslin's jaw muscles bunched. "I haven't told him. Or Nigel."

"Why not?"

He didn't answer.

She stared at him. Waited. When he didn't say a word, she asked again. "Why not, Rhodes?"

"Because I don't know who is trying to hurt you."

Rowan narrowed her eyes. "And you think it might be my *brother*? His director?"

"It's not Chris." Cold calm radiated from Aslin. He stood beside her like an immovable pillar of controlled menace. "But I've been asking around. Nigel took out a personal insurance policy to convince the studio to sign Chris for the role. If filming shuts down for whatever reason, he gains a sizeable sum—"

"And you believe that? Jesus, Aslin, that kind of gossip

runs rife on film sets. Hell, if you were to believe talk like that the studio that makes *Twice Too Many* have fired Chris five times over, hired a prostitute for him numerous times and paid for him to have a penis extension." She shook her head, glaring at the Brit towering over her. "It's a popular pastime, to see who can make up the biggest pile of horse shit and which pile gets picked up by the celebrity rags and websites first. As far as I know, there's a prize for the winner."

Aslin's gaze didn't waver from her face.

Despite the pain in her body and the ringing in her ears, Rowan pushed herself upright. "Why are you being so stubborn about this?"

He bent at the waist, enough that their stares aligned. "Why are you being so resistant?"

*Because I don't want to be a victim again.*

The words formed in Rowan's mind, a heartbeat before she froze. Icy dread pooled in her belly. Her mouth turned to dust. Her blood roared in her ears, rivaling the ringing there.

She stared up at Aslin, the confession, the very basis for her grueling conditioning of her body, hanging on the tip of her tongue.

*Victim.*

A tornado of memories assaulted her—the wet, fleshy thud of her father's baseball bat slamming into her mother's head, the same sound as the bat hit her father again and again, the men's laughter as he fell to the floor, his blood soaking into the carpet beneath the mess that was once his face... Chris's wails when the men started attacking her mom, his young body thrashing in the chair beside her, his cracking voice screaming at the men to leave his mom alone, the whoops of delight from them as she toppled forward... their feverish eyes as they came for Rowan...

The sound of their zippers sliding open...

The feel of their hands tearing at her shirt, her skirt, her panties…

"I'm not a victim," she growled, fighting down the fear slamming into her. She glared up at Aslin. Hating the terror gnawing at her. Hating the helplessness wanting to eat her. Hating it. Hating it.

Denying it.

"Rowan," he began, and stopped when she slammed the heels of her palms into his chest.

"Go away," she snapped. Pain lacerated through her, hot and excruciating. She welcomed it. It was infinitely better than fear.

And confusion.

He shook his head, his expression calm. That damn British calm he wore so well. "No, Rowan. I'm not going away."

She glared at him, her head throbbing, her ribs aching, her ears ringing. "Why not? Want to play the big strong man? Need someone to protect?"

He shook his head again, fury making the edges of his mouth white. "Soddin' hell, woman, I'm not going away because I love you."

The statement punched into Rowan. She froze. Again.

He stared at her. For a second. And then let out a ragged growl, dragged his hands through his hair and turned away from her bed. "Christ, Rowan, I…"

She didn't say anything. She couldn't.

With another growl, he turned back to face her, his expression haunted. "I've got to go. I need to… I'll be back. Before visiting hours finish."

He turned and strode to the door, yanked it open and crossed the threshold without looking back.

Rowan sat motionless in the bed. Beside her, the device

she was connected to via the drip beeped continuously, sounding for all the world like an asthmatic Darth Vader doing a Road-Runner impersonation. In her ears, the ringing continued. It was fainter, but still there.

She stared at the now closed door, her heart thumping. Her throat filled with a thick lump.

Love.

"Oh boy." Her whisper sounded like a shout in the room.

And then Chris barged into the room, his world-famous grin nowhere to be seen, his normally artfully mussed hair a wild mess.

"Jesus, sis." He hurried to the side of her bed and wrapped his fingers around hers. "Don't you ever fucking do that to me again."

"What? Get blown up?"

He didn't laugh at her lame joke. Nor did the doctor who followed him into her room.

"Ah, there's that wicked sense of humour I remember so well," the doctor who'd tended to Chris in the ER two nights ago deadpanned. "How are you feeling, Ms. Hemsworth?"

Rowan looked up at him, her heart still beating far too fast for its own good.

Love. Christ, Aslin Rhodes loved her.

"Rowie?"

"Do you still hear a ringing in your ears, Ms. Hemsworth?"

She blinked at the steely haired doctor. "A little."

He plucked an instrument from his top pocket, leant forward at the hip and shined a light into her right eye. "I must say, for someone who was knocked backward by an explosion, you are looking remarkably well." He flicked the light to her left eye. "If somewhat shell-shocked."

"I…"

"Aslin said you're feeling better." Chris tightened his

fingers around hers. His stare roamed over her face. "Jesus, sis, you scared the shit out of me."

Rowan smiled at him. "I'm fine, squirt."

"No, you're not." He shook his head. "Someone is trying to hurt you."

Rowan's stomach dropped. "What?"

Chris frowned. "Someone is trying to hurt you. Didn't Aslin tell you?"

"Did he tell *you* that?"

"No. But it's fucking obvious, isn't it?"

The doctor cleared his throat, pocketed his tiny flashlight and pinned Rowan with a steady inspection. "Is this something the officers waiting outside need to hear?"

Rowan shook her head, and then winced a little as a dull pain sliced through it. "No. It's the product of an overactive imagination."

"Rowie," Chris began, but Rowan leveled a hard look at him, and he fell silent.

She returned her attention to the doctor. "How long do I have to be here for, doctor?"

The elderly medical practitioner's lips pursed. "The greatest concern now is traumatic brain injury." He gave Chris a quick look. "That's where the brain gets knocked about in the skull."

"She's got a pretty thick skull, doc."

The doctor chuckled. "Why am I not surprised? Anyway, our scans revealed nothing when you were first admitted, but I want to be sure, which means I'm keeping you in here for twenty-four hours. Minimum."

Rowan frowned. "Twenty-four hours? Really?"

The doctor nodded. "Minimum."

"Can I check myself out?"

Silver eyebrows rose. "Why would you do that?"

*Because I can't be the victim. I won't.*

"Because I'm not good in hospitals."

Chris's warm hand in hers grew firmer. "It's okay, Rowie," he said, his voice low. "You're safe. I won't leave you. Promise."

Rowan's throat constricted. She looked at her brother. At the only person who had mattered in her life since her parents' murder.

And yet now there was another—one who wanted to protect her when the last thing she wanted was to *be* protected. One who could do it—keep her safe—without raising a sweat.

One who loved her.

So why was she so damn confused?

And scared?

# Chapter Twelve

If the cop said another word, Aslin was going to beat the shit out of him.

The officious git stood beside the police tape, hand up, palm out—the same position he'd assumed the second Aslin approached him—and informed anyone who cared to listen that Aslin's trailer was a crime scene and no one was allowed past the tape.

Alsin had no beef with cops. They did a thankless job. They put their life on the line daily. But this cop was in his way. This cop was stopping him from investigating who the fuck was trying to hurt Rowan—no, *kill* Rowan—and being a git about it.

"I'm sure you movie folk think you can do whatever you want," he was saying for the umpteenth time, lip curled in disdain, belly hanging over his belt, "but this *isn't* the movies. It's *real* police work now."

"All I want to do—" Aslin began. For the umpteenth

time.

"Real police work," the cop repeated, enunciating each syllable in an exaggerated volume. "So you will have to—"

"Ever thought of being an actor, sir?"

The cop blanched at the sudden question, his stare snapping to the man striding up to the police tape. "I..."

"Nigel McQueen." Nigel thrust out his hand to the cop, giving the man a wide, beguiling smile. "Director of *Dead Even*. I've been looking for a certain presence for a small but pivotal role in an upcoming scene, and casting hasn't delivered what I'm after. Which is you."

The cop blinked. Looked at Nigel's hand shaking his. Shot Aslin a quick glance. Looked back at Nigel again. "I've never...do you think..."

"I was just watching you deal with my rather intimidating friend here—" Nigel went on, still shaking the cop's hand, "—Nick Blackthorne's personal bodyguard, by the way. Do you listen to Nick's music? Awesome singer. Wrote the theme song for *Dead Even*. Awesome track. He's doing a special concert in Sydney soon, isn't he, Rhodes? Maybe you could get some backstage tickets?"

Aslin regarded the director, keeping his expression set. Nick was doing no such concert. Nick was on his way to New York for who knows how long. But the cop didn't know that, and by the way he was gaping at Aslin, the man was a fan.

"Anyways," Nigel continued. "I'd really like to get some shots of you, just to see if the camera captures your intensity. Is that okay?"

The cop dropped his stare to his hand still engulfed by Nigel's pumping one. Back up to Aslin. To Nigel. "I'm not—"

"Can I get it with the trailer as a backdrop? Like an action shot? If you're what I'm looking for, you'll be shooting with Scarlett Johansson. Have you met Scarlett Johansson, yet? Damn, now that's a fine woman."

Fifteen minutes later, after photographing the cop in various poses around the destroyed trailer on his iPhone, Nigel walked away *with* the police officer in tow, the director describing in great detail the scene the cop would be shooting with Scarlett. A scene, to the best of Aslin's memory, that didn't exist in the script.

Standing at what was once the door to his trailer, but was now a gaping hole of torn metal, Aslin watched the two men disappear around a corner, Nigel dropping him a discreet wink before turning.

Leaving Aslin alone.

Without hesitation, he stepped up into the charred remains of his mobile abode.

He knew what he was looking for—something that would indicate the explosion had been deliberately lit. And something that would tell him who was responsible.

*Ha. You're not wanting for much, are you, boyo?*

The interior was a mess. War-zone destruction. The smell threaded into Aslin's nose, acrid and smoky. It was a smell he remembered all too well. A hideous odor he'd hoped never to breathe in again. It took him back to his last tour of duty, to the shit fire that was Afghanistan. His gut clenched. His muscles coiled. It was a visceral reaction, but he welcomed it. It took his mind from the fact he'd blurted out to Rowan how he felt.

It also took his mind from the fact he actually felt that way to begin with.

Love. Fuck, he was a British bodyguard in love with an American martial arts expert who despised the notion of needing protection.

And someone was trying to kill her.

Cold fury stirred deep in his core, but he ignored it, focusing instead on his surroundings. He cast the destruction a slow inspection without moving, needing to take it all in first. To see if anything immediately caught his attention.

Nothing did.

But then he hadn't spent enough time in the trailer in the first place to know what it really looked like inside, had he? And when he was in it, he'd been losing himself in the rapture of making love to Rowan. The interior could have been a carbon copy of the inside of the Taj Mahal and he wouldn't have noticed.

*Sloppy. Real sloppy. Was a time you didn't miss anything.*

He ground his teeth. Was a time he wasn't in love, as well. Life changed.

*And unless you find out what the fuck is going on, life may change again. For the worse.*

He bit back a low growl at the heinous thought of Rowan being killed and moved deeper into the burnt-out trailer carcass. Shattered glass and debris crunched under his booted feet, the sound a ghost of his former life. How many bomb-destroyed buildings had he searched during his SAS days?

Too many.

But none mattered as much as this one.

This one was going to tell him who was after Rowan.

This one was going to tell him who he was going to break in two with his bare hands.

If only he could find what he was looking for now.

And yet, there *was* nothing. Nothing looked wrong, which was ridiculous given everything in there was now blackened, blistered or charred almost beyond recognition.

The bed—a piece of furniture he'd never even approached— was a sodden lump of blackness, the table and chairs were upended—what was left of them, that was.

He scanned the small kitchenette, noting the blast pattern. The detonation had occurred in that area, but as far as Aslin could determine there was nothing in the kitchen capable of exploding. The stove hot plates—now black warped discs on a charred and buckled silver surface—told him the appliance was electric, not gas, and there was no oven, nor a space in the fire-ravaged cupboards where one might have been pre-blast.

He crossed the rubble on slow, careful feet, running his stare over everything, his mood growing dark.

Nothing.

Not a sodding thing.

*What were you expecting? A sign with the words* "I did this" *pinned to the remains of a lump of C-4?*

He sneered. And then jerked around when a noise came from behind him.

"See anything you like?" A man stood in the gaping mouth of the trailer, white shirt pristine and crisp, black tie perfectly knotted, stare locked on Aslin with drilling intensity. "And while I'm asking questions, who are you?"

Aslin studied him. "Aslin Rhodes."

The man processed the answer before narrowing his light blue eyes. "The owner of the trailer."

Aslin nodded. It wasn't his trailer, per se, but he wasn't ready to divulge anything until he knew who the man was.

"Was there anything of value inside it when it detonated?" the man asked, his inspection on Aslin's face unwavering.

"No."

"But there could have been, correct?"

Aslin didn't answer.

The man cast a quick look over the burnt-out interior surrounding Aslin. "Your girlfriend was about to enter, correct?"

Aslin clenched his teeth. "Yes."

He didn't know if *girlfriend* was the correct word to describe what he had with Rowan, but once again, he wasn't prepared to offer up that information to the stranger yet.

"She's lucky she's alive," the man went on, returning his stare to Aslin's face. "Or maybe, *you're* the lucky one. Given that it was your trailer."

Aslin let his spine straighten. He turned—slowly—to fully face the immaculately dressed man. "And you are?"

Blue eyes flicked over Aslin, from head to toe. "Officer Desmond Russell. Chief arson investigator. Mind telling me why you thought it was okay to cross a police line?"

Aslin held the officer's stare. "Because my girlfriend was almost killed, and I want to know who did it."

Desmond Russell's eyes narrowed a little. "And what makes you think it wasn't an accident?"

"My gut."

"Intelligent gut you've got there."

Aslin snorted. "Some would argue differently."

"What else is your gut telling you?"

"That you're not telling *me* something."

Officer Russell's head inclined. Once. "True. And I'm not going to, I'm afraid. But I can tell you this is a crime scene and you have to exit it. Do you have a problem with that, Mr. Rhodes?"

The urge to tell the arson investigator to sod off welled up in Aslin. He bit it back. Like the cop earlier, the man was only doing his job. Crossing the remains of his trailer, Aslin dropped through the door to the ground, directly in front of Russell. "I don't."

Russell fixed him with another narrowed-eyed stare. "Why's a musician's bodyguard working on a film site?"

Aslin stiffened. "How do you know what I do for a living?"

"I do my job properly, Mr. Rhodes. Before I even look at the scene I know who the parties involved are. Just that little fact can give me a wealth of information of the scene."

"And what does me being Nick Blackthorne's bodyguard tell you about this scene?"

"That an ex-British Special Forces officer would know how to detonate a trailer if he wanted."

Aslin balled his fists. "He would. But he didn't."

Russell didn't break Aslin's stare. "How about I be the judge of that. In the meantime, mind telling me why you had a gas heater installed in the trailer in the middle of summer? I know you Brits constantly complain about the Australian heat so I can't fathom why you'd need a heater in there?"

An icy finger traced up Aslin's spine. The hair on his nape prickled. "Heater?"

Russell studied him for a long second and then, with a dismissive noise, wrapped his fingers around the charred edges of the doorframe and pulled himself up into the trailer. "Don't leave town, Mr. Rhodes," he said over his shoulder before withdrawing a pair of blue latex gloves from his back pocket and stepping out of sight.

Aslin stood motionless, his heartbeat fast, the arson investigator's words ringing in his head.

Heater. He hadn't installed a heater. Hadn't requested one. Why would he? Compared to Britain—and New

York, for that matter—it was bloody hot in Australia, most especially in summer.

So where had the heater come from?

Or more to the point, who had put it in there?

Pulling in a deep, smoke-tainted breath, he turned from his trailer. Nigel McQueen's personal assistant had been responsible for arranging the mobile home. Maybe the young man knew where the heater came from?

Fifteen minutes later, Aslin was more frustrated than ever. Judging by the confusion in the P.A.'s eyes when questioned, followed by the abject terror when Aslin's control began to fray, the young man was clueless. As was Nigel when Aslin questioned him while he was in the middle of placating a very agitated Scarlett Johansson over a stolen kiss from a police officer.

Now, standing on the other side of the clearing from the row of trailers, Aslin stared hard at the destroyed carcass.

Someone knew something. Someone had seen something. There was no way, in a place as crowded with people as the *Dead Even* film site, not one person saw someone carrying something as obvious as a gas heater.

Someone, somewhere, knew something.

He just had to find that person.

His back pocket started to vibrate, his phone's normal ring tone—Queen's "Another One Bites the Dust"—filling the silence.

Biting back a muttered curse, Aslin yanked his cell phone out and rammed it to his ear. "Rhodes."

"You know that fan causing Huntley grief?" Liev Reynold's Australian accent sounded through the connection, his tone on edge. "The one with the red hair security escorted off the site today? She's here at the hospital."

Thick heat knotted like a furious fist in Aslin's gut. "I'm on my way."

He shoved his phone back in his pocket and turned from the trailer, only to find Warren McCreedy directly behind him.

The key grip flinched, stumbling back a step. "Sorry, Mr. Rhodes."

Aslin stopped his hands balling into fists. Just. "That's okay. What can I help you with?"

McCreedy's gaze slid to the destruction behind Aslin for a second before returning to Aslin. "I just wanted to ask how Ms. Hemsworth is?"

The hair on the back of Aslin's neck stirred. "She's well."

McCreedy let out a breath, shooting the trailer another glance. "That's good. It would fuck Chris up big time if anything happened to his sister."

"In what way?"

McCreedy barked out a wry laugh. "She's his world. Without her…well, without her his life wasn't exactly sane."

Aslin cocked his head to the side. A fraction. "Weren't you a part of that life?"

"Yeah, I was. But he's in a better place now. Better mindset and all. Still miss it though."

The cold finger that had traced its way up Aslin's spine earlier returned. Colder. He stared hard at the key grip. "How much?"

The man's eyebrows shot up his head. "Fuck, not enough to hurt Rowan, if that's what you're thinking?"

At Rowan's name, Aslin's anger—already simmering close to deadly rage—grew hotter. He lowered his head, just enough to make McCreedy shuffle back a step. "I'm thinking a number of things at this point in time, lad."

Aslin held him prisoner with his stare, letting the man see the promise in his eyes, letting the key grip sweat for a long moment. And then, without a word, he turned and walked away.

He heard McCreedy's sharp exhalation cut the air behind him. Almost smelt his pungent B.O. as the man no doubt swiped at his face or ran his fingers through his hair. It was the normal response to such an obvious threat.

As soon as Aslin dealt with the fan at the hospital, he'd sit down with Warren McCreedy and have a conversation. A long one. Something about the key grip was…off.

Belinda however, had fled the scene by the time Aslin stormed into the hospital's main entry foyer. Liev met him just inside the door, the Australian dwarfing those around him, his expression set in a lopsided grin. "She took off about ten minutes ago," Liev said, shoving his hands into his back pockets. "Didn't try to come any farther than here. Asked the nurse on the front desk if Chris Huntley was here and okay. The nurse told her she had no clue who Chris Huntley was." Liev chuckled. "I'm not sure the old duck was kidding either."

Aslin forced the tension in his body to abate. He bit back a sigh. The red-headed fan was a persistent one, that was for certain. After the way he'd crash-tackled her to the ground earlier that day, as well as the way she'd been dragged away by the film's security team, he was surprised she'd come this close to Chris again.

The woman was like a shadow. Always…

Aslin's blood began to roar in his ears. His nerve-endings started sparking.

Around. The woman was always around. It didn't matter how many times she'd been chased or thrown off the film site, she always seemed to find a way back on. Perhaps it was time he had a face-to-face with Belinda the crazed fan again?

"Rhodes?"

He turned to the Australian standing beside him, on edge again.

"Are you heading upstairs? To Huntley and his sister?"

Aslin nodded.

"Mind if I call it a night then? I promised my niece I'd take her and her boyfriend to the Justin Bieber concert. I'd hate for her to get crushed in the mosh pit."

"Not at all. Although I'm glad it's you and not me."

Liev laughed. "Teenagers have no clue about music these days. Give me Pearl Jam any day."

Aslin shook his head with a grin. "I'm pretty sure Eddie Vedder lost a leer jet to Nick in a Vegas poker game five years ago."

Liev snorted. "You celebrity bodyguards. I think I'll settle with the political variety. Less insanity."

"And you're not enjoying this job? Tailing Chris Huntley?"

The Australian laughed again. "This, my Pommie friend, is a dream job. One I thank you for. But it's my niece you'll have to answer to if I don't bugger off now, so…" He tapped his fingers to an imaginary hat and walked across the foyer and out the doors.

Aslin stood motionless and watched him go, his pulse a sudden trip hammer in his throat.

*Motionless? Why aren't you heading up to Rowan?*

His pulse throbbed harder. Because he was scared, sod it. The last time he'd seen Rowan, he'd confessed to being in love with her. He had no clue how she was going to react to that bombshell. Nor, for that matter, how she was going to react to his insistence she was the target of an attempted murder.

A chilling ribbon of tension shot up his spine at the thought, followed by a wave of molten fury. He'd find the person responsible and make them regret ever—

His cell phone rang.

The sound of Freddy Mercury singing wailed through the quiet hospital foyer and more than one head turned Aslin's way. He clenched his jaw, yanked his phone free of his pocket and pressed it to his ear. "Rhodes."

"Aslin." Chris's broad American accent shot through the connection. "Where are you, dude? She's checking herself out."

Aslin's eyebrows shot up. "She's what?"

"Rowie is checking herself out. Told everyone here she's fine and dandy, that she doesn't do hospitals and she'll promise to come back if she—"

Aslin didn't wait to hear the rest. He killed the call, shoved his phone back into his pocket and ran for the stairs.

Damn it, why the hell did he have to go and fall in love with a bloody stubborn pain-in-the-arse woman?

# Chapter Thirteen

Rowan didn't need to turn away from the counter to know Aslin stood behind her. She could feel him there—his inescapable stare drilling into the back of her head, the heat radiating from his towering body into hers.

His anger licked against her senses, tangible and potent.

Heart beating fast, she continued to sign her name in the required locations, forcing her focus on the point where pen nib touched paper. She refused to hurry even though a small part of her wanted to throw the pen over her shoulder and run as fast as her bruised—and still-wobbly—legs would go.

Damn it. She'd wanted to be gone by the time he returned.

"You're in trouble now, sis."

She shot Chris a quick sideward glance. "So are you, tattletale."

Her brother laughed, and then did what she was too chicken to do—turn around and look at the Brit behind her. "She's all yours, Rhodes."

Rowan's heart beat faster. She kept her stare on the pen, watching the black ink form the final loop of the last H in her surname on the discharge form.

"Care to tell me what you think you're doing, Hemsworth?"

His deep voice flowed over her like rumbling thunder. Even with the dull pain still at home in her ribs, her body reacted to its sound. Her pussy contracted, her nipples grew tight.

"Checking out," she answered, doing her best to sound nonplussed. She raised her head from the form and smiled at the nurse scowling at her from the other side of the counter. "There you go."

Chris's off-key voice sang softly about being able to check out any time but never leave, his hands tapping on the counter beside Rowan's paperwork.

"And where exactly are you going now you've checked out?" Aslin asked, an edge to his voice.

Rowan's sex constricted again. She was far too aware of the man, of his potent virility and strength. Her brain kept trying to replay his confession of love over and over. Neither helped her now.

Now she just wanted to get out of the hospital and go…

She bit back a curse. Aslin was right. Where *was* she going now?

Still refusing to look at the man behind her, she cast her brother a hopeful look.

"Hell, no." Chris shook his head and took a step back. "I only brought you a new set of clothes 'cause I thought you didn't want to spend all day in a hospital gown. I didn't think you were planning on taking off. As far as I'm concerned, you should be back in the gown and the bed."

"Which is exactly the doctor's opinion," the nurse piped

up, retrieving the pen from Rowan's fingers with a pointed expression.

"I'm fine."

"You're being stupid."

Aslin's calm declaration stoked her anger. She pivoted on her newly booted heel, crossed her arms over her tank-top-covered breasts and glared up at him. "I don't need to be here. The doctor has given me a list of what to look out for. I know not to take aspirin for the next forty-eight hours and—" she cocked an eyebrow, "—I've had worse blows before. Professional martial artist, remember? Being knocked on my ass isn't anything new."

Aslin drew his head closer to hers. "Being knocked on your arse by an explosion is."

"Keep up the attitude, soldier boy, and I'll put you on your *arse* to show you just how fine I am."

Something dangerous flared in Aslin's eyes. "Right," he murmured. "That's it."

He straightened, shoved a hand in his hip pocket, withdrew it and turned to Chris. "Here you go." He tossed something to her brother, the distinct sound of metal clinking telling Rowan it was a set of keys. "Where's Jeff and the SUV?"

Chris snatched the keys from the air, surprise pulling at his eyebrows. "Jeff is in the cafeteria, no doubt trying to hit on someone. The SUV is on parking level four."

As Rowan gaped at them both, Aslin nodded. "The Ducati is yours for the rest of the day. Get Jeff to the car in five minutes." He turned to face her. "You want out of here. Fine. I'll take you out of here. Back to my hotel room. At least there I can keep an eye on you."

"What?" she burst out.

"Oh, good idea, Rhodes." Chris grinned.

"Very good," the nurse agreed.

Rowan's pulse pounded. "*Not* a good idea."

"Why?" Dark emotion flared in Aslin's eyes, but what that emotion was Rowan couldn't tell. "Are you scared of me?"

Scared? Oh God, scared couldn't be further from the truth. And yet that's exactly how her body was reacting. Her heart raced, her palms were sweaty, the hair on her nape was on end and her mouth was dry. If it wasn't for the fact her damn pussy was contracting and constricting and fluttering like mad she'd say scared was *exactly* how she felt.

But all those very feminine, very sexual things *were* happening to her. At the thought of being in Aslin's hotel room. Alone. With him. With the man who'd told her he loved her.

The man she was more than half in love with in return.

*Half? Huh. You're freaking head over heels, fully, totally and utterly in love with him. Admit it.*

She clenched her jaw and tilted her chin. "No. I'm not scared."

And to prove it, she stormed toward the exit, hitching the shorts Chris had snagged from the wardrobe department higher up on her butt to hide the fact her head was still wobbly and her balance was still…unbalanced.

Behind her, Chris laughed, and then she heard him say, "Get your ass into gear, Jeff. You're taking Aslin and Rowie wherever they need to go. You can hit on the natives later."

She stopped at the closed elevator door and stabbed the down button.

"Well?" she snapped, turning to glare at Aslin at the counter.

But he wasn't at the counter. He was right behind her. So close she could feel his heat on her body. So silent she hadn't heard him move.

Damn him.

And damn her nipples for puckering so hard at his proximity. And his...his...fuck, damn his everything.

His gaze melded with hers and the corner of his lips curled. "Ready for me to take care of you, Ms. Black Belt?"

She narrowed her eyes, tilted her chin and ignored the way her sex throbbed with increasing want. "Ready for me to—"

The elevator binged and opened before whatever pathetic comeback was going to fall from her lips could. She started, her cheeks filling with heat at the very sudden and very raw look of desire that crossed Aslin's face a second before he cupped his hand around her elbow and guided her inside the empty elevator.

"I'm looking forward to this," he said

He pressed the button for parking level four without looking at her. Nor did he say a word or cast her a look for the duration of the descent. By the time the doors opened with another soft chime, Rowan's heart was slamming so fast and hard in her chest she wondered if—given the fact she'd survived an explosion only that day—she should call a doctor? By the time she stepped out into the parking level, she was almost gasping.

"Over here, Mr. Rhodes."

The familiar voice jerked her attention to her left, and she found Jeff Coulten, the most affable member of Chris's formal entourage, standing beside a blue Audi SUV, his hand on the rear passenger door's handle.

"Let's go. Or do you need me to carry you?"

Rowan snarled at Aslin's question, shucked her elbow from his grip and stormed over to the SUV.

It would have been all so impressive if she could have

made the journey without stumbling mid-distance.

Aslin slipped his arm around her waist before she could fall too far to the side. It was all Rowan could do to keep walking forward. Her head ached, her ears still sung and her body was telling her under no uncertain circumstances had she been beat up. But at the firm contact of Aslin's hand on her hip, all worry about remaining on her feet vanished.

For the first time in her life since her parents' murder, she allowed herself to lean on someone.

"It's going to be okay, love."

Aslin's low murmur drew her gaze up to his face and she swallowed at the undeniable tenderness in his eyes.

"Is it?" she whispered.

"I won't let it be any other way."

And then they were at the Audi. Jeff asked how she was in his usual amiable way, Aslin helped her into the backseat and her body told her she needed to rest.

But she didn't want to rest. All she wanted to do was wrap her aching, bruised body around Aslin and make love to him until she couldn't move at all.

"You okay?"

She lifted her gaze, finding Aslin sitting beside her in the back. His eyebrows were knitted, worry on his face. A distant part of her mind told her he was wearing his emotions much more openly then when she'd first met him. The British super soldier slash muscle for hire she'd encountered on that first day, a lifetime ago, wouldn't have let anyone see what he was feeling.

He paused clipping his seatbelt, studying her face. "You do realize you're being a stubborn pain the arse, right? Not staying here?"

She let him see her smile. "I do."

His answering smile was crooked. "As long as you know."

Thirty minutes later, they were pulling to a stop outside the Sydney Hilton, Jeff filling in the silence the whole way there as only Jeff could—with a constant chuckled narrative about the world around him.

Rowan was glad for it. There were words in her head that wanted to come out, words like I and love and you. Every time she looked at Aslin sitting beside her, his focus fixed on the road ahead, his sublimely muscled body held tense and alert, she wanted to press her cheek to his chest. She wanted to smooth her arms around his torso, let herself surrender to the strength and protection he wanted to give her, and tell him she loved him too.

Oh God, she wanted that.

But that want, that need was beyond any she could bear. So instead, she welcomed Jeff's constant chatter, ignored his rather questionable driving skills and sat silent.

Knowing she would soon be alone with Aslin in his room.

A room in one of Sydney's more prestigious establishments. "I still say this is swank accommodation for a bodyguard," she commented, looking at the very luxurious exterior as the valet opened her door.

"Where did you think I would stay?" Aslin's deep rumble behind her made her tummy flutter. "A Best Western?"

She shot him a quick glance over her shoulder. "So Blackthorne pays you well then?"

"Blackthorne pays me very well. Look it up on the Forbes Top 100 Highest-Paid Bodyguard List. I'm Number Two."

Rowan couldn't stop her eyebrows shooting up. "There's a Forbes Top 100 Highest Paid Bodyguard list?"

Aslin grinned. "No. Now get out of the car, Hemsworth, before I come around there and lift you out."

If she were feeling more capable, she would have hit him. But she wasn't. She hurt. She really did. Shutting out the pain wasn't easy when she was spending so much effort suppressing the need to blurt out how much she wanted him.

Climbing from the backseat, she bit back a wince as her heels hit the ground.

Aslin was there before her in a heartbeat, worry etching his face, scooping his hand up to hers to help her out. A small part of her wanted to tell him to piss off. The rest of her—not only the broken, sore bits, but the bits governed by her heart—surrendered to his attentive concern.

When was the last time she'd let anyone take care of her?

There was no immediate answer for that, and when she went searching for it, a cold emptiness stroked her soul.

Her life had been all about Chris for so long she'd forgotten what it felt like to be someone else's *anything*. For the first few years of Chris's career, she'd stayed in the background, focusing on her tournaments and martial arts school for kids, determined to let him find his own feet. He was a young man in his early twenties, after all. She knew she'd come close to coddling him since their parents' death. But then the entourage had formed around him, the wild parties had begun, the excessive indulgences, the reliance on Tilly to do things for him above and beyond that of a personal assistant, and Rowan hadn't been able to stand idly by any longer. From the minute she'd stepped back into the role of big sister, her life had been about her brother and being the most invulnerable fighter she could be.

Letting anyone care for her...

Rowan's heart tripped a beat and her mouth went dry. It wasn't just that she was in love with Aslin Rhodes. She *trusted* him.

Trusted.

Which was impossible. She trusted no one. Apart from Chris.

She swallowed, staring at him as he stepped back from the car, her hand in his.

His forehead creased. "What?"

"I—"

"Want me to stay, Mr. Rhodes?"

Rowan turned to look at Jeff, who grinned at them both through the driver's side window.

"No." Aslin drew closer to her as he closed the door behind her. "Go back to Chris. And tell him if he damages my bike, I'll damage him."

Jeff laughed. "Will do."

With a quick nod to Rowan, Jeff gunned the Audi's engine and tore away, leaving the valet parking attendant coughing on his fumes.

"Sorry about that," Rowan said to the young man. She dipped into her shorts' pocket to look for a tip before remembering they were from Wardrobe and empty of money.

"C'mon." Aslin smoothed his hand down her back and around her waist. "Let's get you off your feet and into my bed."

Rowan couldn't help but chuckle. "Is it always going to be this way with you, Rhodes? Bossy, arrogant and presumptuous?"

He flicked her a quick sideward glance. "Yes. It is."

The corners of his mouth twitched, destroying his attempt at brooding menace.

Rowan loved it.

Loved it. Loved him.

By the time they arrived at his suite on the fourteenth

floor, she knew she couldn't keep it in any longer. Knew she had to tell him, show him, before she exploded like his trailer.

The sound of the door closing behind her was all she needed. She may have only been two steps into his suite, she may only have left hospital half an hour ago, hell, she may have only just survived some messed-up attempt on her life six hours ago, but she couldn't wait any longer.

She turned to Aslin, hooked her fingers over the waistband of his jeans directly above his fly and tugged. She pulled him along as she walked backward toward the suite's massive king-size bed.

"What do you think you're doing, Hemsworth?" His deep voice played with Rowan's sanity. Stroked over her senses. Teased her control.

"I'm seducing you, soldier boy. What's it look like I'm doing?"

He shook his head, curling his fingers around her wrist to remove her grip on his waistband. "No you're not. I didn't bring you here to—"

Rowan took a step back, slipped her hands under her shirt's hemline and pulled the item of clothing up over her head.

Aslin's argument was abruptly silenced. His nostrils flared. His gaze fell to what she'd revealed—her unrestrained breasts, her puckered nipples.

The muscles in his jaw bunched, his throat working as he studied her offering to him.

"I want you inside me so bad it hurts," she stated, never so sure of anything in her life. "Make love to me. Now."

He lifted his stare to her face. "No, love, you hurt because someone tried to kill you this morning. And as much as I want to, if I make love to you now, I'll only hurt you some more."

Rowan shook her head, her fingers moving to the fly of her shorts. "No you won't. I trust you."

And before he could utter another word, she released the opening of her shorts and let them fall from her body.

Chris had not delivered underwear with him when he'd brought the shirt and shorts. He never wore underwear himself, so why would he think to bring some for his sister? Rowan had never been so thankful for that shortcoming.

The second the soft denim of her shorts pooled around her ankles, she knew she was exactly where she wanted to be.

The second she stepped out of the bunched item of clothing and destroyed the space between her and Aslin, she knew she was doing exactly what she wanted to do.

The second—the very *second*—she took Aslin's large, strong hands and placed them gently on the curve of her hips, gazing up into his dark, desire-filled eyes, she knew she was exactly with the only person she ever wanted to be with again.

And when he groaned, a barely audible sound of raw need and tenuous control that she felt it in the pit of her belly, she knew he was the person she was meant for.

He was the strength she never allowed herself to believe she needed.

The protection she'd never sought.

The man she didn't know she longed for.

"Aslin," she murmured, smoothing her hands up his chest, reveling in the coiled steel of his pecs, "you'll only hurt me if you say stop."

"Oh, fuck me." The words were a hoarse moan. His stare was locked on her, his jaw tight. "I should say stop. You're in no condition to make love, Rowan. I'd be a sodding, selfish bastard if I — "

She turned and walked away from him, three steps, four, until she reached the bed, the massive bed beside the floor-to-ceiling window with its views of Sydney beyond. She stopped and climbed onto the soft mattress, one knee and then the other, presenting him the sight of her naked ass, her moisture-slick pussy, before lowering completely to the bed on her side and gazing back at him.

"I trust you, Rhodes," she said, watching him watching her. "I trust you, I'm in love with you and I know you won't hurt me."

He didn't move. "Say that again."

"I trust you. I love you."

His Adam's apple worked up and down his throat. He walked to the bed, his stride long and steady.

"Say that again."

She smiled at the tenuous control in his deep voice. "I trust you, I love you and I know you won't hurt me. Now shut the fuck up and make love to me. Before I risk reinjuring myself by handing you your ass. Again."

His nostrils flared. "One of these days I'm really going to regret being bested by you."

"You are?"

Aslin shook his head. "No."

Rowan laughed, and then the sound faded away as Aslin's hand circled her ankle.

She held her breath, unable to tear her stare from his face as he lowered his gaze to where his fingers wrapped her flesh.

He smoothed his palm up her calf, not a lot, but enough to send a shiver through Rowan's entire body. She moaned, her nipples pinching tight at the caress.

His chest rose with a long, deep breath, his fingers

splaying a little as he pressed his knee onto the bed beside her leg. She slowly rolled onto her back, parting her thighs to grant him more room on the bed.

He drew in another breath and lifted his gaze to her pussy. His throat worked again, the muscles of his jaw knotting, his battle with control turning his muscles to coiled steel. His undeniable, restrained power flooded Rowan's sex with moisture. She was right to fall in love with this man. As unexpected as it was, it was so right.

Perfect.

She shifted a little, biting back a soft wince as her bruised rib did its best to remind her she'd recently been in an accident.

Aslin's stare flicked to her face at the low sound, the tension in his body claiming his face.

"Rowan..." he murmured, straightening away from her, his fingers sliding off her calf.

She stopped his retreat with a quick hand, shaking her head as she maneuvered onto her knees before him. "I'm fine, Aslin. I hurt more when you aren't touching me."

And to prove her point, she lifted his hand and placed it on her breast.

# Chapter Fourteen

A ragged groan tore from Aslin's chest. He gazed into her eyes, so close her warmth folded around him, and yet still so far away. Too far away. Just one hand on her body. One.

It wasn't enough.

It made his head swim and his body burn.

But as much as he wanted to shove Rowan backward, cover her body with his and bury himself to the hilt in her tight, wet sex, he couldn't. He shouldn't even be touching her now.

As if aware of his torment, Rowan took charge.

Without a word, she captured his other hand in a gentle grip, lifted it to her mouth and pressed her lips to the centre of his palm.

The cut on her bottom lip from the explosion scratched against his skin, and with the sensation came guilt.

"Rowan." He tried to pull his hand away, but her fingers on his wrist grew firm.

"I've spent my entire adult life conditioning my body to

switch off pain, Rhodes," she said, her breath warm on his palm, her gaze holding him prisoner. "Training my brain to deny its presence. What I haven't done is teach my body and mind and soul to ignore the pleasure you awaken in me."

The words sent exquisite pressure into Aslin's groin. He pulled in a deep breath, knowing he should insist what Rowan wanted—fuck, what he wanted—couldn't happen now. Later. When she had recovered more from the explosion.

But he couldn't. Not with the heat from her naked body kissing his. Not when she pressed his right hand to her breast. Not when desire burned so openly in her eyes.

"The pleasure you awake in me now, Aslin," she whispered, rasping her lips against his palm, "just by being here, loving me, is far more potent and consuming than *any* discomfort my injuries may cause. I love you, soldier boy. Love you."

It was those words that destroyed his control. Those words that shattered his resolve.

Love.

She loved him.

The only woman he'd ever felt love for loved him back. And wanted him to make love to her now. There was no coming back from that.

He smoothed his hand from her breast, down over her broken ribs, lingering there for a still moment. "I will do everything I can not to hurt you," he whispered. "But I need you to tell me if this does."

She nodded, her eyes shining. "I promise."

His gut clenched, her trust in him almost undoing him completely. He was used to people trusting him. His unit had trusted him when he was a soldier, Nick had trusted him to keep him safe for fifteen years, but this was different. This was…

*Precious.*

Smoothing his hand from her injured ribs, he allowed his palm to skim over the curve of her hip before journeying the perfection of her butt cheek. Its toned shape felt sublime beneath his hand. Rowan's low groan told him she craved his touch as much as he craved her body.

Not just her body. All of her. Her stubbornness. Her inner strength. Her determination.

All of her.

With gentle pressure on her arse, he drew her closer to his body and lowered his head until his lips brushed hers.

The kiss was more tender than any he'd given. Barely a contact of skin to skin. As much as he wanted to plunder her mouth, he knew the split on her bottom lip wouldn't allow him.

So instead, he feathered her parted lips with the softest of kisses before moving to her throat. She curved her neck, allowing his mouth to travel her throat. He tasted every inch of her flesh, desperate for her. He nipped at her skin with his teeth and sucked at the spot until she whimpered. Her hands found his hair, tangling in strands.

"Oh…"

Her shaky sigh ignited fresh need in Aslin. He groaned in response and dragged his lips up to her ear. She rolled her head and he sought out the tiny dip near her pulse and flicked his tongue over it before nipping again.

"Aslin…"

Rowan's moan vibrated through him. He lowered his mouth, exploring her collarbone, kissing the faint bruise there. A shard of anger surged through him, the cold memory of what caused the bruise assaulting his rapture.

Someone was trying to—

The torturous thought was lost to him when Rowan's hands directed his lips to her breast.

He suckled on one puckered nipple, rolling it between his teeth and laving it with his tongue.

She moaned and panted words fell from her. Words like yes, more and harder.

He refused to allow himself. One of them needed to remain in control. It would be too easy to succumb to the desire engulfing them both. To live in the moment and forget her injuries. He had no doubt Rowan could deny the pain in her body, but he would not allow himself to cause any.

Not physical pain.

Sexual pain…pain from the pleasure he gave her? That was a different matter.

And so he continued his tender worship of her nipple, her frustrated cries for more feeding the fire in his groin.

He slid his mouth to her other breast, cupping its weight with a gentle hand as he licked at her nipple. One swipe of his tongue. Two. Three.

"Please, Aslin." Rowan's voice was a husky whisper. "Harder, please?"

He closed his lips around her taut nipple and sucked once.

"Yes." She arched into him, bunching her fists tighter in his hair.

He sucked again, a little harder this time, and then dragged his mouth up to her jaw.

"I don't want you gentle," she protested, shifting on her knees until she was closer to him. "I can take it. I—"

He brushed his lips over hers, silencing her protests. "Shush." He chuckled. "I'm in charge."

Her own laugh bubbled up her throat. "Fine. But I'm not going to be injured forever, ya know."

Aslin lifted his head and grinned down at her. "Oh, I know. But for the moment, you are, which means I'm in charge. Got it?"

She arched an eyebrow. "Yes, sir."

He squeezed her butt. A little. "You'll pay for that later. But for now, I'm going to carefully lay you on your back. You're not allowed to touch me. You're not allowed to move. Do you understand?"

"What if—"

He gave her a stern look. "You are not allowed to move. I may be dangerously close to losing control, but I still *am* in control. And that means I can walk away if you don't do as I say. Wrap your arms around my neck."

Rowan did as he ordered. The second her breasts and belly pressed to his torso, his cock throbbed with exquisite agony. Hot blood flooded its length, turning it to a rod of excruciating need. He denied its demands, finding Rowan's gaze with his stare as he smoothed his arm around her uninjured side and back. Leaning slightly forward, he planted his free hand on the bed, supporting as much of their combined weight as possible. "Ready?"

She nodded.

He lowered her slowly, slowly, onto the bed, watching her face for any sign of pain. There wasn't any. None at all.

Just an undeniable desire and hunger.

The moment he felt the mattress take her weight, he straightened, sliding his hand from behind her back.

She adjusted her legs, keeping her knees bent on either side of his thighs, her stare never leaving his face.

"Put your arms where they won't hurt."

Without a word, she slid the backs of her hands over the duvet until her arms were resting slightly from her body. Aslin's stomach clenched at the bruise staining her flesh over her ribcage. He bent, placed his hands on the bed and brushed his lips against the injury.

"Oh God." Rowan's breathless whisper stroked his senses.

He kissed her flesh again, just as softly, barely making contact.

A delicate shiver rippled through her. "I've…I've never had anyone kiss me better before."

He lifted his head and gazed down at her. "I've never been in love before." The confession left Aslin before he could stop it.

Rowan's lips parted. "Jesus Christ, Rhodes, I want you inside me. Please?"

In response, he repositioned himself between her legs, skimmed his palms down the length of her thighs to her knees and oh so gently lowered his mouth to her pussy.

She gasped at the first swipe of his tongue over her folds.

He stopped. Lifted his head. Studied her. "If you feel any p—"

"Again, Rhodes."

"Now who's being the bossy one?"

Chuckling, he lowered his head back to her sex and ran his tongue over her clit.

"Oh, yes." Rowan's sigh fueled his pleasure. He lapped at her pussy, keeping each stroke measured and tender. With every pass of his tongue on her clit, her moans grew louder. He feasted on her juices, reveling in her flavour as he lapped at her sex. Beside his head, her legs trembled. He paused, knowing she was close to release. Her ragged pants and whimpers told him so. But he didn't want her coming yet. There was so much more he wanted to give her. He wanted to take her so much higher.

Raining a slew of soft kisses along the inside of her

thighs, he replaced his mouth on her sex with his fingers. He parted her folds, rolling her clit under the pad of his thumb.

Rowan's breath hitched and a soft gasp escaped her. Followed by a low moan as he slipped his index finger into her moist slit.

"Oh God, Aslin."

Her legs trembled again. He continued to explore her inner thighs with his lips as he gently wriggled his finger deeper inside her, seeking out the inner sweet spot of her sex.

She whimpered, her pussy sucking at his finger with constricting pressure.

Aslin's head swam again. His cock ached, engorged with need. He refused to acknowledge its torment. Rowan's pleasure was his only purpose.

Withdrawing his finger from her sheath, he stroked her clit again. Little circles of increasing pressure and speed. She called his name, a husky plea he wanted to surrender to.

Instead, he dipped into her pussy, two fingers this time, scissoring them within her feminine walls as he moved his lips to her belly. He painted the flesh around her navel in a string of soft kisses, journeyed the subtle line up her abdomen with his tongue. She moaned, her eyes closed, her breath rapid and shallow.

When he reached her breasts, when he claimed one distended nipple with his mouth, her pussy squeezed his fingers.

"I'm…I'm going to come soon."

Her panted words flayed Aslin's control. Fed his desire.

He suckled on her nipple with growing need. If he didn't stop soon, he would be unable to.

Forcing himself to release her nipple, he worked his way back down her body with feathery kisses on her skin, tender swipes of his tongue, his fingers stroking her inside the whole time.

Making love to her in the most gentle way he could. Giving her the pleasure she so desperately sought.

Returning his mouth to her spread folds, he stroked his tongue over her clit, bathed her clean of her cream before sucking on the tiny knot of sensitive nerve-endings again.

Rowan cried out, thrusting her hips upward.

Aslin suckled again, nipped her clit with his teeth, and then, as her hips bucked once more, penetrated her sex with his tongue.

As deep as he possibly could.

Rowan's orgasm gushed over his tongue, his lips. He drank in her flow, even as his other senses feasted on her release—her raw moans, her musky perfume, her quivering thighs framing his head…

She came and he continued to make love to her with his tongue, addicted to her pleasure. Greedy for it.

And when the pulsing pressure of her inner walls began to fade, he laved his tongue over her clit again and dipped his finger inside until another orgasm claimed her.

And one more.

It wasn't until his cock screamed at him for its own release that he pulled away from her body.

He straightened to his feet, on fire. In pain. Fuck, so much pain.

"Aslin?"

He sucked in breath after breath, refusing to open his eyes. If he looked at her now…

The rustling sound of material told him Rowan was moving. Reaching for him.

He jerked open his eyes. Took a step back.

"Aslin," she whispered. "Let me—"

He shook his head. "If I let you touch me, love, my control is fucked. I promised I wouldn't hurt you, but if you touch me…"

The rest of his statement hung on the air between them, as taunting as the flush in her cheeks, as tormenting as the scent of her release in his breath.

His cock throbbed, pushing against the zipper of his jeans, engorged.

"Then I won't touch you." Rowan shifted on the bed, facing him on her knees. "But let me watch. Please? Let me see how much you want to fuck me. Look at me as you fuck your own hand and imagine it's my—"

Aslin tore open his fly before she could finish.

His cock sprang free, jutting upright, no longer imprisoned by his jeans. He wrapped his hand around its swollen length, grounding out a harsh breath as even that contact sent shards of concentrated pleasure into his core.

"Look at me," Rowan murmured

He snapped his stare to her face, his hand choking his leaking dick.

"Imagine that's my cunt engulfing your cock, not your hand."

Her words pushed him over the edge. He punished his erection, pumping its length with savage force. Up and down, slamming the side of his clenched fist to the root of his shaft every time, staring at Rowan as he did so.

Unable to look away from her.

He ground his teeth, refusing the groan in his chest. Trapping it there as he fucked his hand and stared into Rowan's eyes.

It was the most raw, truthful connection he'd ever made with a living soul.

*I love her. I love her. I love her.*

The feverish, heady thought roared through his head. His release erupted from him, detonating in the deepest part of his groin before radiating out to his balls, the base of his spine, his anus. It shot up his spine like a current of white-hot fire. It sank into the pit of his gut. He sucked in breath after breath through clenched teeth, watching Rowan witness his climax, wanting her to see exactly what she did to him.

His seed spurt from him. Arcs of white, ropey fluid that shot up into the air.

"Oh God," Rowan moaned, "I can't…"

Before Aslin could move, before he could register what she was doing, she moved off the bed and sank to her knees before him. Her hand covered his come-slicked one on his dick and she slid her lips over the bulbous head of his cock.

His seed flowed into her sucking mouth, over her tongue. She pressed her teeth at his flesh.

Searing pleasure consumed him. He threw back his head and finally allowed his suppressed roar to tear from his throat as his hand still pumped his spurting erection with Rowan's hand covering his.

And then it was over.

Strength deserted him.

He crumpled to the floor, the sounds of his panted gasps joined by Rowan's laughing joy as she stretched out between his legs on the floor, resting her cheek on his inner thigh, combing her fingers through the pubic hair on his scrotum.

"You weren't meant to move, Hemsworth," he rasped, his gaze jumping blankly around the ceiling as he fought for breath in his lungs.

At his groin, Rowan chuckled. "I may regret it later." She stroked her fingers over the flat plane of flesh next to his hip. "But I don't give a fuck right now."

"Remind me to tan your backside when you're better."

She lifted her head and grinned at him down the length of his body. "You can do other things to my backside when I'm better if you like."

Aslin's gut tightened at the thought. He groaned, returning his gaze to the ceiling. "Rowan, I've already exerted all the control I possess. If you keep talking like that…" He let the promise remain unspoken.

She laughed.

Five minutes later, Aslin realized he was slipping into sleep. And still on the floor.

Lifting his head, he peered down at Rowan, a smile on his lips.

She was sound asleep, her cheek resting just above the root of his cock, the fingers of her hand loosely cupping his balls.

The overwhelming desire to not disturb her, to stay exactly where they were welled through him. For a heartbeat. Commonsense told him the floor was *not* the place for a person who'd survived an explosion to be.

No matter how sated and peaceful her sleeping expression.

He shifted beneath her, an inch at a time, determined to not wake her. It took patience, stealth and muscle control, but Aslin didn't care. He not only didn't want to wake her, he wanted to be certain he didn't hurt her.

Finally on his feet, he allowed himself a moment to study the bruises on her body. Her ribcage was going to be sore for many days, and the cut on her lip would make kissing out of the question. She wouldn't like that. Hell, he didn't like it either, but that was the way it was.

*So sodding well control that dick of yours, boyo.*

Aslin let out a slow breath. What they'd done just now…

Guilt wormed its way through his happiness, cold and

tainted.

He let out a slow breath and lowered himself into a crouch. With as little movement as possible, careful not to press any part of his body against her ribcage, he slid his arms under back and knees and lifted her from the floor.

She moaned, her eyebrows pulling into a small frown before she curled into his chest. Sounds slipped past her lips, words he couldn't make out. He held her motionless for a long second, her cheek on his shoulder, her lips on the side of his neck, her body snugged against his chest, and he knew without doubt he would kill anyone who tried to hurt her again.

Which meant the person responsible for her being injured today better hope it wasn't Aslin that tracked them down.

Because if Aslin *was* the one that found them before the cops, they wouldn't live another minute.

And he would end their life with an extraordinary amount of pain.

# Chapter Fifteen

Filming was shut down until further notice.

Nigel McQueen, having recovered from his meltdown the day before, was now—according to Tilly—spending his time co-operating with the police investigating the trailer explosion or arguing with the studio suits. Apparently the suits were threatening to pull funding if filming didn't recommence within twenty-four hours.

Nigel was calling for blood. Everyone was being interrogated. The director's famed intensity and relentless focus was now being turned on cast and crew. No one was spared his suspicions.

"He's even questioned Chris and Mr. Rhodes," Tilly said, shaking her head. "Which is ridiculous. Why would your brother and your lover try and hurt you?"

Rowan dragged her hands through her hair, bit back a sigh and stared at the young woman sitting opposite her. "What are the police saying? Do they have any leads?"

"If they do, they're not sharing." Tilly popped a

strawberry into her mouth from the breakfast platter she'd ordered after arriving in Aslin's suite thirty minutes ago. "But the feeling on set is they think it was an accident. Apparently there was something wrong with Mr. Rhodes's trailer that was meant to be fixed before being delivered."

Rowan's stomach rolled. An accident? Was it possible? She thought of Aslin's insistence someone was out to harm her. She thought of the bruise covering her broken ribs.

Just an accident?

"I told Chris to go." Tilly's chipper voice tickled Rowan's frustration. "He didn't want to, but I said you'd be fine. And Mr. Rhodes was going to be there, so I knew you wouldn't worry about him being attacked."

Rowan blinked, forcing her focus back on her brother's personal assistant. "Sorry? What didn't Chris want to do? Where is he now?"

Tilly smiled, her eyes wide and excited. "He didn't want to go surfing. But when I called Mr. Rhodes this morning and asked him to guard Chris, Chris was more than happy to head to the beach. He's been working so hard he needed a time out, don't you think? Jeff and Ross are with him. I procured boards and wetsuits from a local supplier and promised they could use Chris's image in their advertising in exchange."

The pit of Rowan's stomach clenched. Tilly was organizing Chris's days. Two members of his former entourage, the jovial clown and the surly sponge, were with him. It was just like Rowan didn't exist.

"Don't worry," the young woman went on, topping off Rowan's cup with hot, black coffee, "I covered his face with sun block and told Mr. Rhodes not to let anyone near him when he comes out of the surf."

"Thank you." Rowan was surprised by how calm her

voice sounded considering how unsettled she was at Tilly's words.

That Rowan had woken this morning to find Aslin missing may have something to do with her unease. That she'd felt lost when he wasn't there flustered her as well. At least she knew where he was now.

"He's very scary when he wants to be, isn't he?"

She blinked, Tilly's statement jarring her. "Who?"

"Mr. Rhodes," Tilly answered. "He wasn't very happy to leave you alone, but when I told him Chris would be an open target on the beach for any crazed fans, particularly that red-headed woman who keeps stalking him, he agreed to go." She reached forward and patted Rowan's hand. "And no need to thank me. I'm just doing my job, Ms. Hemsworth. I've been doing it now for over five years. I'm very good at it."

Shifting on her chair, Rowan bit back a soft hiss. Her ribs still hurt more than she wanted them to. "Is there anything else?"

"No. Chris told me to tell you to take it easy and get better as soon as you can. Oh, he's attending a party tonight thrown in his honour by a local night club. Ross said he'll go with him so Mr. Rhodes can come back here to you."

Rowan frowned. "A party? Where?"

"Somewhere near the water. He's quite excited about it. Said he hasn't been to a good party for a long while. I know Warren is keen to spend some time with him like they used to. I told Warren to call me when they are done and I'll arrange for Jeff to collect them and bring them back to Chris's suite. I'll make sure I'm there to get him into bed *alone*. I know how you don't like him bringing his sexual partners back to his room when he's on location." She wrinkled her nose. "I don't either. So much hassle to deal with the next morning."

She rose to her feet, scooping up a croissant from the platter of food on the coffee table. "I better go. Chris asked me to organize lunch for him and the boys. He wants to book out the revolving restaurant at the top of the Sydney Tower so they can relax before climbing the Sydney Harbour Bridge. I reserved all the allocated times for today so they can do it without being mauled by fans." Taking a bite of the pastry, she gave Rowan a flakey smile. "Oh, I almost forgot. He told me to tell you not to worry about him at all. He's being well cared for."

And with that, Tilly vacated Aslin's hotel room. Leaving Rowan alone and unsettled.

Parties, booking out restaurants, throwing his money around. It was like the second she was out of the way, Chris had leapt back into the extravagant, excessive lifestyle she'd worked so hard to educate him away from. What did that mean?

*That he never wanted you taking charge in the first place? That he preferred his personal assistant's care? Christ, the woman was positively glowing with joyful pride.*

She pushed herself from the chair, grinding her teeth against the dull pain pulling at her ribs. The ringing in her ears had been gone this morning when she woke, as was the ache in her head and extremities, but her ribs still felt like shit.

It had something to do with the chunk of Aslin's trailer that had slammed into her as she'd been flung backward. The doctor had informed her she was lucky to not have her lung pierced by splintered rib bones.

Rowan didn't feel lucky. She felt pissed. How many side kicks, back kicks, spinning kicks and fists had she taken to the ribs in her life without this kind of residual pain? And yet here she was, hissing like a freaking kettle whenever she moved?

Thank God Rhodes wasn't here to witness it. He'd call her a *big girl's blouse* again, whatever the hell that meant. Something about the glint in his eyes told her she'd want to thump him if she knew.

Refusing to limp, she walked to the window and glared out at the city beyond the glass. She was edgy.

Maybe because she'd woken up alone when she'd expected to wake up beside Aslin. Maybe because she was feeling displaced from her brother.

Maybe because she felt…defeated.

Biting back a growl, she crossed the room to her backpack, withdrew a clean set of underwear and then walked—*without* limping, dammit—to the bathroom. Perhaps a shower would clear her head? Wash away the self-doubt trying to eat her up?

Forty minutes later, she killed the water, stepped out onto the plush white mat, wiped her hand over the steam-fogged mirror and stared at her reflection in the streaky glass.

She let out a long breath.

The shower hadn't washed away anything it seemed, except the slight crust of dry blood above her eyebrow.

She ran her gaze over her body, for the first time since leaving the hospital truly aware of the damage the explosion had caused her. Small bruises and grazes marred her flesh, most on the side she'd landed on after being propelled backward by the blast. There was a nasty bruise on her hip, about the size of a golf ball, and another on her arm that ran from elbow to shoulder. All spoke of a serious blow, none more so than the one that covered her ribcage.

Frowning, Rowan narrowed her focus on the injury. It was discolouring, a faint tinge of green starting to bloom in the mottled purple stain. She touched her fingertips to it, prodding a little to see how much pressure it could take before hurting.

Cold shards of pain sank into her side after a second and she removed her fingers, happy with the result.

Yesterday, just the slightest pressure had made her wince. Today, her body was on its way to healing. That was a good thing. As was the way the split on her lip looked this morning, just a tiny line of red curving from inside her mouth. In fact, apart from the bruises, she appeared okay. Physically. Not at all like a woman someone had tried to blow up.

Her eyes however…

Rowan stared hard into her reflection, her stomach churning. She recognised the shadow there. It was the same haunted darkness that had lingered there for many months after her parents' murder. It told her she *wasn't* okay, wasn't just nursing the injuries of a brutal full-contact sparring session or competition.

It told her she was dealing with shit beyond the norm.

It made her want to scream. And hurt somebody.

A choking sob welled up in her chest, thick and heavy. She swallowed it down and turned from the mirror, snatching up her clean thong.

She'd sworn never to feel like this again. She'd promised herself. Feeling like this made her weak. She wasn't weak. She wasn't.

Shoving her legs into her thong, she yanked the black cotton up over her ass, ignoring the biting ache in her side at her abrupt movement. Pain could be turned off.

Pain could be denied.

She was denying it now.

She'd get dressed, call a cab and go find Aslin at Bondi

Beach. Talk to Chris. Ask him if she was being too much of a PITA big sister.

Walk in the sun and find her centre again.

Pulling her shirt on was a problem, one she hissed and winced through. It didn't help she was down to just a snug black racer-back tank top now that the shirt she'd worn yesterday had been cut from her body in the hospital, and the shirt she'd worn on the flight to Australia was crumpled in the bottom of her bag. She'd buy a tank or tee today at the beach. There would no doubt be plenty of places she could purchase a touristy shirt that would do the job. As for her legs…

Rowan pulled out the only option left in her bag, a pair of lime green satin hotpants she'd packed in case Chris had wanted to hit the dance clubs one night.

The last thing she withdrew from her depleted clothing supply was a pair of knee-high lace-up Chucks. Not exactly beach-combing footwear but better than her cowboy boots, which hadn't survived the blast unscathed.

She fastened her hair in a ponytail, wiped away the small beads of perspiration the exertion of getting dressed had created from her forehead, scooped up her handbag and walked toward the suite's door.

And stopped when her fingers wrapped the doorknob.

Stopped.

Stood frozen.

She stared at the polished brass knob, its chilly surface like a branding heat on her palm. Her heart slammed into her throat. Her blood roared in her ears. A million pin-pricks of fire danced over the back of her neck. Her breath grew trapped in her constricting chest.

She stared at the doorknob.

At her fingers squeezing its form.

Stared at it. Willed her hand to turn it. To open it.

And let out a strangled sob as she stumbled back a step.

"Oh, fuck," she burst out, tears stinging her eyes. "Fuck. What the fuck is—"

Refusing to finish the sentence, she grabbed the doorknob again.

This time she felt the explosion's force lash at her face, her body. She sucked in a breath, her stare locked on the doorknob, as immobile as she was.

*Open the door, woman. Open the door.*

She ground her teeth, her knuckles white, her fingertips aching as she drew on every fibre in her body to turn the doorknob.

And her hand refused to move.

"Oh God." She fell back from the door, her gut a ball of knotting fear, her chest so tight breath refused to come. "Oh God, no."

She stumbled backward, her feet moving her from the door even as she stared at it through the blurring heat of her tears.

The backs of her knees collided with the edge of the bed and she collapsed onto it, unable to stay on her feet.

Unable to tear her stare from the door. The fucking door and its fucking doorknob.

Oh God, what was wrong with her? What was—

The door opened.

"Rowan?"

Aslin stood in its frame, filling it with his muscled strength, his undeniable power.

She swiped at her eyes, forcing a smile to her lips. "Hey, I was just coming to you guys."

He stepped into the room, pocketing his keycard as he let the door swing shut behind him. "What's wrong?"

Rowan shook her head. "Nothing. Just hurt myself doing up my shoes."

He walked over to her, his gaze locked on her face. "I don't believe you. Tell me what's wrong."

The laugh she gave him was brittle. She knew it, and by the way Aslin's eyes narrowed, he knew it as well. "Seriously. I'm okay. I wished I'd packed a pair of flip-flops though. Lacing these up—" she lifted a foot off the ground and pointed her Chuck-encased foot to show him what she was talking about, "—was a bitch."

He crouched before her, his hands smoothing up her legs to come to rest on her thighs, a slight pressure on her elevated leg returning her foot to the floor. "I don't believe you."

"Of course you don't." She grinned at him, wishing to hell her heart would slow the fuck down. "It's your nature to be suspicious. Now shut up and kiss me. My lip is almost better and you owe me one for taking off this morning while I was still asleep. How is Chris by the way? I thought you were guarding him while he surfed. Is he finished?"

Aslin didn't reply, his inspection inscrutable as he studied her face, his palms warm on her bare thighs.

She resisted the urge to fidget. "What about lunch?" she asked, trying to distract him. The last thing she wanted was him knowing she was too freaking pathetic and scared to open the door. "Aren't you going to follow him to the restaurant?"

"What restaurant?"

"The revolving one on top of some tower."

Aslin's inescapable scrutiny turned into a frown. "Chris is not having lunch at 360 Bar and Dining. Jeff just dropped him back at his suite. He's planning on spending the rest of the day preparing for the scene being shot when filming recommences."

A tingling pressure slid up Rowan's spine. "Tilly said he'd booked out the entire restaurant. He and the guys were eating then climbing the Harbour Bridge after. And then there was a party tonight at some club."

"Guys?"

"McCreedy and Jeff."

Aslin shook his head. "No. No lunch. No bridge climb. Just a quick surf this morning before the normal Bondi crowd arrived. And your brother is too worried about you to go to a party. Warren mentioned one, but Chris said he wasn't interested."

Rowan chewed on her bottom lip and then flinched when her teeth pressed on the tiny split there.

"That hurt?"

Aslin's voice—deep and laced with gentle humour—played with Rowan's senses. She met his gaze, her belly twisting at the love she saw in his eyes. Everything else may be a confused mess at the moment, but she could not doubt what he felt for her. What she felt for him.

"Tilly had it right," he suddenly said, his hands skimming over her hips in a caress that made Rowan's heart quicken. "I think lunch somewhere special is a perfect idea. Especially when you are wearing the sexiest bloody outfit I've ever seen. There's this quirky little café in Paddington I'd love to take you to. The locals guard it like a national secret from the tourists and, unless they've changed the chef since Nick ate there last, they make the best macadamia-crusted swordfish. How's that sound? Do you think your beat-up, broken body can take it?"

She nodded, willing the butterflies in the pit of her belly away. "That would be lovely." She'd call Tilly later. Ask why the young woman had implied Chris was falling back into his old ways. There had to be a reason. Whatever it was, it better be a goddamn good one or Rowan would give her a piece of her mind.

For a moment, Aslin didn't move, studying her from his crouch between her thighs with an unwavering inspection. To Rowan, it felt like he was seeking something deep within her soul. And then, before she could confess everything—how angry she was at feeling so weak, how confused she was by Tilly's words—he dipped his head and brushed his lips over hers in a kiss so light she barely experienced its physical touch.

But her heart, already beating too fast, leapt into a rapid pace and her breath caught in her throat.

She watched him rise to his feet and hold out his hand to her. Just one. "C'mon," he murmured. "Let's go pretend we're normal people for a while."

"As opposed to what?"

He grinned. "As opposed to the number-two trending topic on Perez Hilton's blog. Have you *seen* the images of us making out on my bike posted there?"

She laughed and allowed him to help her to her feet. She even let him see the slight wince that escaped her when her ribs protested at her shift in position. With another kiss even more tender than the first, he crossed to the door, his fingers threaded through hers.

He stopped when she stiffened the second his hand closed over the doorknob.

*Not again. Not again.*

Aslin turned to her, slowly, his fingers never releasing hers. "What's wrong?"

She drew a deep breath, fighting to keep her heart under control. "I…" She couldn't say it. She couldn't say she was apprehensive.

Scared.

Studying her for a silent minute, his body as still as hers, he finally released his grip on the doorknob and turned to face her fully. "Perhaps room service is a better idea."

Prickling anger sliced through her. Anger at her woeful state. Anger at the unknown person who'd made her this way. Anger at her inability to deal with it. She drove her nails into her palms and ground her teeth. "You think I'm scared? That I can't walk through the door?"

Aslin shook his head, closing the small distance between them with a single step before framing her jaw with his hands. "I think you've forgotten what I once was. A soldier. I've been in more than one explosion, Hemsworth. I was in a Pinzgauer in Afghanistan that hit a mine and flipped three times, almost killing us all in the process. I know about PTS. It took me for sodding ever to climb back into a truck after that without breaking out in a sweat and having heart palpitations. But I did. And I know you will open a door. You're too strong, too stubborn not to." He stroked his thumb over her bottom lip, his gaze holding hers. "But until you're ready, I'm not remotely interested in what's on the other side of that door."

A choking lump filled Rowan's throat and she sucked in a soft breath, her chest aching. "I feel so…so…"

"Shhh," he whispered, a gentle smile playing with the corner of his mouth. "It's not important right now."

Rowan frowned, wishing to fuck she could stop shaking. Oh God, where did this wonderful man come from? And how was she so lucky he fell in love with her? "What is important?"

His smile grew into a slow grin and he lowered his head closer to hers. "Making love to you. Stripping you out of these sexy-arse shorts and boots and making love to you.

Not doors and whether they are opened or not. Doors and what's on the other side have no bearing on what really matters—us. Understand?"

He kissed her before she could respond. A little harder this time, but not much.

Not enough for Rowan. She slid her palms up his chest, tangled her fingers in his hair and parted her lips to his mouth, deepening the kiss.

A low growl rumbled in Aslin's chest. He stole his hands around her waist, bunching the material of her shirt at the small of her back. He swiped his tongue over hers, once, twice, and then he pulled away and stared down into her upturned face, his breath shaky. "Gentle, love. You'll hurt your—"

"Fuck gentle." She fisted her hands tighter in his hair and pressed her hips to his. "I'm done with gentle. I want you inside me. And I don't want you to hold back. Understand, soldier boy?"

Aslin claimed her lips again, and this time there was nothing tender about the kiss. He feasted on her mouth, his tongue wild as it mated with hers. She groaned, the pleasure of his touch already a salve to the minute pain in her lip. She dragged her hands down over his shoulders, across the broad expanse of his chest. His pec muscles coiled beneath her palms, a reflex action that flooded her pussy with eager moisture. She dragged her thumbs over his nipples, loving the way he groaned in response. He swirled his tongue over hers, smoothed his hands down to her butt. With steady pressure, he began walking, guiding her backward as he continued to worship her lips with his kiss.

Four steps later, Rowan's calves bumped the edge of bed.

She knew what Aslin was going to do without needing

to ask. His lips moved from hers, trailing a path of wicked kisses down her throat as he slowly lowered her back to the mattress. A small part of her wanted to demand he throw her on the bed, the way he would if she wasn't still recovering, another more rational part loved that he didn't. He was giving her what she wanted and still caring for her. There was nothing better, more perfect than that.

As soon as her back rested on the bed, he captured her breasts with his mouth and hands. He suckled on one erect nipple through the cotton of her shirt as his fingers pinched and rolled the other. She moaned, her eyes fluttering closed at the pleasure radiating through her.

Overwhelming her.

"More, Aslin," she murmured. "I need more."

He complied. Before the plea finished falling from her lips, he'd nudged the hemline of her shirt high with a firm hand, his kiss exploring the flat plane of her belly he'd revealed. She hitched in a breath and pushed her hips upward.

A slight tug on her fly told her he'd done what she ached for him to do. As did the cool air flowing over her newly exposed pussy mound. He covered the curve of her mons with a rain of tiny kisses, working her hotpants over her hips with his hands.

"M-my boots," she whispered, shifting enough on the mattress to aid his removal of her shorts and thong.

"Can stay on," he rumbled back, flicking his tongue over the sensitive area of flesh where her thigh became her groin. "They're too fucking sexy to take off."

She laughed at his growled statement. And then whimpered when his tongue dipped into her folds to lap at her clit.

He made love to her sex with his mouth, licking and

nipping at her clit, delving into her slit over and over again. Three times, the surging heat of an orgasm approached her. Every time, Aslin pulled away, returning to her swollen breasts and straining nipples until she was begging him to make her come.

Three times.

Three times, he explored her sex with such fierce, thorough purpose until she was on the brink of a detonation and yet each time he denied her that release.

When he rose to his feet, she glared up at him, her heart an insane hammer in her chest, her pussy a constricting world of need. "What are you—"

Her protest died as he stripped his clothes from his body without a word.

Oh boy.

She'd never seen him so erect, so engorged. His cock jutted upright from his dark pubic hair, its thick venous length a sublime arc crowned with a bulbous head of the deepest blood-red purple. Tiny beads of moisture anointed the tip. Rowan's mouth grew wet with saliva at the sight even as her pussy flooded with liquid warmth.

"I know you don't want me to be careful, love." Aslin's husky rumble drew her gaze to his face and she swallowed at the raw desire in his eyes. "And I know you're tough, the toughest person I've ever known, but I won't be able to live with myself if I hurt you." He snared his jeans from the ground, removed his wallet from a pocket and withdrew a condom. "So I'm going to do this *my* way."

"Aslin…" she began, her pulse pounding.

"My way," he repeated, sliding the latex sheath over his erection before slipping a hand beneath her right leg as he stepped back between her thighs.

He bent over her, drawing her right leg up to hook her

knee over the crook of his elbow, his forearm protecting her ribs from her thigh. He placed his other elbow on the bed beside her, the action allowing his cock to nudge her parted folds. She drew in a swift breath, the pressure on her clit almost too much to survive. Her body was on fire. So attuned to his. So aware of the moment about to—

With one slow, fluid thrust, Aslin sank into her.

She cried out, arching into his deep penetration, scraping her nails at the muscled perfection of his shoulders.

"Fuck, I can't..." His breath was ragged. "You feel so fucking good, love. So fucking..."

He slowly withdrew, to the distended rim of his cock's head, and then filled her once more, stretching her pussy lips to their limit, protecting her rib with his position and strength.

She cried out again. Louder this time, the orgasm he'd denied her three times rushing at her. Mounting pressure sent shards of exquisite tension up her spine, into the pit of her belly. Building heat that squeezed her anus tight and filled her aching breasts with swollen want.

And all the time, Aslin took her body. Thrust in and out, his pace slowly increasing, his strokes sinking deeper and deeper, his stare melding with hers.

She felt no pain in her wounded body. Only pleasure. Absolute pleasure.

Elemental and consuming and unspoiled by pain.

She raked her nails over his flesh and whispered his name and gazed into his eyes, reveling in the fire in their dark depths. Fire for her. Love for her.

Fathomless desire and need and love.

He was hers and she was his, and nothing in the world would change that.

When her orgasm finally smashed into her, when her

body was undone by sheer paroxysms of pleasure, Aslin came as well. Silent. Powerful.

His seed erupted from his cock in wild spasms, filling the condom. She could feel it surging through his length as it left him. The sensation was sublime, amazing, and she came again. And again. Three times.

Three times.

And then there was a fourth, so powerful that swirls of coloured lights filled her vision, and all she could do was cling to the man she loved and call his name forever.

# Chapter Sixteen

"The power of the almighty dollar," Nigel McQueen said, taking his megaphone from his assistant. "Not even the cops can compete against it."

Turning away from Aslin, the director strode across the old Hyde Park Barracks' ground floor—now turned into a gunfire-devastated scene of destruction by the set-design department—and called for silence.

After four days of not a single frame being shot, silence fell over the set in an instant. Aslin suspected every crew and cast member present knew now was not the time to test the director.

Four days of no filming made for one very agitated, stressed and intense Nigel McQueen.

Four days of no filming for Aslin however, meant four days of quietly investigating every possibility presented to him regarding Rowan's attacker.

Of repeated frustration when every possibility lead

nowhere.

Even the police seemed to believe the detonation of his trailer was an accident. When they'd finished with that, they'd begun to ask about the accident in the dormitory, questioning how a beam installed by the crew could splinter and fall to the ground. Aslin had done his best to glean anything from their behaviour and body language, but there was only so much a fight consultant was allowed to hear.

He'd suggested it wasn't an accident when they'd spoken to him about it. Or should that be interrogated? It didn't take more than two questions for Aslin to realize the investigating officer was suspicious about him.

To give the cop his due, Aslin would be suspicious as well. The accidents hadn't started until he arrived, and he always seemed to be connected or involved in some way. He was in Chris's trailer when the steps were tampered with, he was on set when the beam splintered and fell, and it was his trailer that had exploded.

That didn't assuage his simmering rage in any way. Nor did it help him find out who was targeting Rowan.

And despite all the possibilities that lead nowhere he still couldn't shake the belief Rowan was in danger. He'd investigated crew members that had shared angry words with Rowan during the first U.S. section of shooting, only to discover they were not a part of the Australian team. He'd spoken to Chris's agent about any fan mail that may have mentioned Rowan, learning there was none. Hell, he'd even tracked down the owner of the empty gas-heater box found in one of the film set's dumpsters, his hopes shattered when it belonged to a member of the makeup team who'd come down with the flu.

Four days of coming up empty and stalking shadows.

And four days of falling deeper and deeper in love with Rowan.

When he wasn't on set trying to find a lead, Aslin was with Rowan. Often they were both with Chris. The actor had settled into a relaxed routine since filming shut down. He'd collect Aslin from the Hilton in the morning, go for a surf with Jeff and Warren while Aslin watched from the sand, drop Warren back on set and spend the day hanging out with Aslin and Rowan. He never questioned his sister why she hadn't left Aslin's room. He spent most of the time with his feet up, flicking through his dog-eared script, discussing certain aspects with Aslin, talking over future film offers with Rowan.

Occasionally, Tilly would call or arrive to deliver something—script changes Nigel had decided on, gifts from Australian fans, requests from local media for appearances, but for the most part, he was just a young man hanging out, making his sister laugh.

For that, Aslin would protect the actor with his life.

Because every time Rowan laughed, Aslin's life gained greater meaning. Deeper purpose.

Every time she smiled, he knew what his future held. Not the life of a rock-star's bodyguard. Not the possibility of returning to the UK for active duty again. Not even the uncertainty of a future career.

Her. Forever. No matter where she was, where she went.

Nick had paid him well during his time, very well. He didn't need to earn a cent for many years if he didn't want to. And he didn't. He just wanted to be with Rowan.

Four days had shown him that.

Four days of relaxed company, eating room service, watching television, enjoying Chris's company as Aslin allowed Rowan to heal.

Four nights of making love to her until they were both weak and breathless and dripping in sweat.

If anyone had told him sex was a better workout than an hour or two at a punching bag, he would have laughed at them. But it was. And the more Rowan's physical injuries healed, the more fierce their lovemaking became.

A warm tension curled deep in the pit of Aslin's stomach at the thought. More than fierce. Profound.

Last night, after Rowan had promised to tie him up and spank him if he didn't make her come three times in a row, he'd chased her around his suite, both laughing themselves silly. He'd chased her and she'd run, only to be finally cornered at the door.

He'd pinned her there with his hips, his erection grinding to her belly, tormenting her with his lips as he told her *she* was the one going to be spanked, thank you very much. *She* was going to be spanked and he was going to be the spanker.

She'd wriggled against him, laughed her denials and reached for the doorknob at her hip. She'd twisted it and yanked the door open before he knew what she was doing, squealing in delight as she tumbled over the threshold.

They'd both stood frozen for a split second—Rowan in the hallway, naked as the day she was born, Aslin staring at her from inside, equally as naked.

"Holy shit," she'd burst out, her eyes sparkling with sheer happiness, her fingers pressed to her smiling lips. "I opened the door, Rhodes. I opened the fucking door!"

He didn't get the chance to respond. Laughing, she launched herself back into his suite. She wrapped her legs around his hips, her arms around his shoulders, and then they were both on the floor. Rowan kissed him, laughing and crying over and over that she'd opened the door, she'd opened the fucking door, as the door closed behind her.

They'd made love. He'd given her her demanded three-orgasm climax, and then they'd showered and gone *out* to the movies, catching a late showing of the newest superhero film playing.

Life couldn't be more wonderful.

Except for the nagging belief she was still in danger.

"Are you ready, Chris? Vin?"

Nigel's amplified voice sounded through the silence, jerking Aslin back to the here and now. He looked over at the scene about to be shot—an intense moment when the film's antagonist declares his intentions to Chris's hero before supposedly shooting himself in the head.

Aslin wasn't needed for this scene. In fact, he wasn't required at all for the rest of scheduled shooting. His job as a consultant during the Australian component of filming was essentially finished.

But Nigel had asked him this morning to remain in the role until wrap, which meant Berlin, followed by London and finally Hollywood.

Aslin hadn't told Rowan. He had to tell Nick first.

"Just going outside for a sec," he whispered in her ear, unable to wait any longer to do so. "Need to talk to my old boss."

She'd studied him for a long beat. "Old?"

He dropped a kiss on her lips and walked away before she could whisper the question he wasn't ready to answer yet.

"Aslin?" Chris's voice drew him to a halt and he turned back to the set. "Any chance you can grab my script from my trailer while you're out? Fucking left it there. Tilly, can you give Mr. Rhodes the key?"

"I can get it, Mr. Huntley," Tilly called from beside a tungsten light.

"It's okay, Tilly." Aslin calmed her eager-puppy expression with a wave of his hand. "I can do it."

He waited for the young woman to hurry over to him, giving her a smile as she handed him the key. "Thanks."

"Okay, *now* are we ready?" Nigel called into his megaphone as Aslin turned and exited the building.

Chuckling, Aislin pulled his phone from his back pocket and dialed Nick's Upper West Side apartment as he walked across the old Hyde Park Barracks' large courtyard.

Nick didn't answer. Aslin didn't expect him to. It was early evening in New York after all. The Blackthornes would no doubt be out having dinner. "Heya, boss," he said when the singer's answering service activated. "I'm pretty certain you know what I'm going to say. Give me a call when you're ready."

Disconnecting, he shoved the slim phone back into his pocket. A sense of disconnected grief stirred within him. He'd been Nick Blackthorne's bodyguard for close to sixteen years. He'd watched a lost, brash, egotistical young man grow into a mature, centred, loving father and husband. He'd shared a life with the singer. And yet, while he could hardly believe he was bringing that life to an end, another one waited for him.

One that he could no more deny than drawing breath.

Two steps later, his phone rang. "Rhodes," he said, pressing it to his ear.

"Heads up, mate," Leiv Reynolds's broad accent came through the connection. "Inside word says the arson investigator has declared the explosion deliberate. His report states the ignition was caused by gas leaking into your trailer from the gas heater found inside it. He also detected nylon residue across the floor from the door to the stove. It's likely it was triggered to ignite when the door was opened."

Aslin's gut rolled. He stared at nothing, his pulse a deafening hammer in his ear. "How do you know this?"

Reynolds snorted. "I'm a firefighter when I'm not a bodyguard, Rhodes. Remember? I've got connections."

The hair on the back of Aslin's neck stood on end. He gripped the phone harder. "Do you know if the cops have a suspect?"

"That I don't know, mate. But it looks to me like someone's out to cause some fucked-up shit over there."

Aslin bit back a curse. Fucked-up shit was right.

"I've got an incoming call, mate," Reynolds said. "I'll call you back when I know more."

Shoving his phone into his pocket, Aslin ground his teeth. All his suspicions had been confirmed. The explosion had been a deliberate attack. Nylon on the floor, like that left behind by incinerated fishing line…

He clenched his fists, rage simmering below his calm. Hurrying to Chris's trailer, he unlocked the door and leapt inside the dim interior, his mind playing over everything Reynolds had told him.

"Shit." A soft hiss came from his left.

Aslin snapped around, seeing a shape in the shadows of the trailer's eating area. He saw Warren McCreedy's eyes widen with recognition.

Something small and dark was flung at him. A wallet? He couldn't tell. Didn't have time. The wild punch came at him before he could dodge it. He took the blow, rolling with the force before slamming his right palm upward into

McCreedy's elbow and his left fist down onto the man's biceps.

The man screamed, the wail barely drowning out the splintering sound of his elbow joint shattering.

Aslin pulled back enough to allow McCreedy to stagger his own step backward. Enough to let the man make the next move.

Which he did. A wild lunge at Aslin, his uninjured arm lashing out in a quick punch Aslin ducked effortlessly.

The man fell forward and then stumbled backward as Aslin's fist slammed up into his gut.

And still McCreedy fought on, driving his knee upward, aiming for Aslin's groin. "Fucker!" the man snarled. "You fucking broke my—"

He lunged again, aiming for Aslin's jaw with his still-working fist.

It bounced off Aslin's deflecting forearm, the block sending McCreedy staggering sideward. His hip smashed into the trailer's kitchen counter and he threw back his head and wailed, a second before grabbing the glass blender jug Chris used every break between shoots.

"Fucker." McCreedy swiped the jug at Aslin, his eyes feverish, his broken elbow a jarring angle at his side. "You fucking fucked everything up."

Adrenaline flowed through Aslin's veins like liquid electricity. "Fucked what up, Warren?" he asked, keeping his voice curious and his stare locked on McCreedy's face. "Stopping you from stealing from Chris? Is that what you're doing here?"

"You fucking know what." Spittle splattered from the man's lips. "Me, Chris, Rowan…everything."

Icy calm descended over Aslin. Resolute and infinite.

He curled his fists, his muscles coiling, his blood on fire. "Rowan? You're the one trying to hurt her? So you can be part of Chris's world again? A world she took away from you when she disbanded his entourage?"

"Hurt her?" McCreedy's shout reverberated around the closed space. Eyes bulging, he shook his head, his hand shaking as he brandished the blender jug like a blade. "Why the fuck would I want to hurt her? I fucking love her. I want to fucking be with her. And you fucking came along and—"

He threw himself at Aslin, the jug swinging for Aslin's head.

Aslin blocked the feral attack, snatching McCreedy's wrist before the jug could strike, and slamming an uppercut into the man's pudgy gut. Once. Twice. Three times.

McCreedy crumpled to the floor, the jug spilling from his fingers, his moans filling the trailer.

Aslin pinned the man's wrist to the ground under the ball of his boot and hooked a fist into his loose, sweat-soaked shirt. "Tell me again and I promise I will let you live. Are you trying to hurt Rowan?"

McCreedy shook his head, tears streaming down his cheeks, snot bubbling from his nostrils. "I love her," he blubbered, eyes squeezed shut, face a distorted mask of terrorized misery. "I wouldn't hurt her. I love her. I love—"

"So you've been trying to get rid of me?"

"No, no, no." Fresh snot oozed from McCreedy's nose. "I haven't done anything. Honest. I wouldn't. Shit man, you scare the shit out of me. I just want to be with Rowan, that's all. I love her."

"Why did you attack me when I came in?"

McCreedy whimpered. "I—I dunno. I saw you and panicked. I don't want Chris to know I've been stealing from him. I don't. I—"

Aslin rose to his feet, kicked the jug away and stared down at the sobbing man. His gut churned. His fury dissolved into disgusted pity. "I'd suggest you leave. Now. Say goodbye to Tilly. Tell her you've been lying to her all this time and she needs to find someone else who deserves her. Write Chris a note telling him you quit. Tell him you're not cut out to be a key grip. Tell him you're going back to the U.S."

He leant forward again, letting McCreedy feel the heat of his breath on his face. "And if I find out you're lying, if I discover it *was* you…the world is not big enough to hide from me. Do you understand?"

McCreedy sobbed, snot and spittle glistening on his lips. "I understand. I promise, I understand."

Aslin straightened, ran his stare over the gibbering, cowering man at his feet and then turned to the door. "Go."

McCreedy scurried to his feet and ran for the exit, stumbling down the steps in two clumsy strides.

At the sight of a dark stain spreading over the arse of McCreedy's jeans, Aslin shook his head. "Pissed himself," he muttered. "Proof enough he's not the one, boyo."

He scooped up Chris's script and the glass blender jug, returned the jug to its cradle and exited the trailer. Locking the door behind him, he pocketed the key and tucked the script under his arm. Apart from a slightly aching jaw, there was nothing about him that spoke of a physical altercation. Which was good. The last thing he wanted was Rowan on edge. If Warren McCreedy was smart, he'd book the first flight back to the U.S. and leave Rowan and Chris alone.

Walking back to the set, a ruckus to his left drew his attention. The last day of filming at the old Hyde Park Barracks meant the external location just outside the building's front door was close to the street. Close enough the public could line the perimeter in the hope of catching some of the Hollywood action taking place in their world, or spy one of their favourite actors. Since the trailer explosion, that fence perimeter had been kept clear. But by the look of the people pressed against it now, security had reopened access.

Men and women—predominately women, Aslin noticed—swelled against the waist-high barricade, most holding cameras, smartphones and printed images of the film's main stars. They pushed against each other like a wave, jostling for the best position for the ultimate view beyond the fence.

He flicked the crowd a quick look, surprised when more than one person called out his name. Apparently his appearance on the gossip blogs and websites had elevated him beyond Nick Blackthorne's nameless bodyguard.

Biting back a growl, he continued to stride to the barracks. But he snapped back to the crowd when his distracted brain finally registered who was standing front and center at the fence.

Belinda.

The red-headed fan stared at him, trepidation etched on her face.

Aslin frowned. She didn't look like the same defiant, determined woman he'd first met at the harbour-side café a week ago. Her hands gripped the steel barricade like it was a lifeline, the *Twice Too Many* shirt she'd been wearing on two of their interactions absent today.

Aslin's gut clenched. He studied her, every fibre in his being telling him…

*What? That it's her? That she's the one trying to hurt*

*Rowan? No. That's not what your gut is telling you. So what is it?*

Acting purely on instinct, he crossed the distance to the fence, lifting his hand to the security guard who began jogging toward him from his post. "It's okay," he said, raising his voice enough for the guard *and* Belinda to hear. "I'm just going to have a chat with someone I know."

The guard nodded, falling back to where he'd been standing. Belinda stiffened, her knuckles growing white as Aslin approached her.

But she didn't run away. For Aslin, that spoke a thousand words.

"You're not here to cause trouble, are you, Belinda? I'm not in the mood to deal with you again."

She flinched at his menacing tone, but shook her head. "No. I've been warned by the police if I cause another incident I'll be arrested."

Aslin narrowed his eyes, ignoring the onlookers crushing around her. Something itched at the back of his mind, something about the woman before him. Something from a few days ago. But what? "You're taking a risk being here. Surely you know now you can't gain access to Mr. Huntley?"

A woeful grimace pulled at Belinda's mouth. "All I wanted was an autograph. Freddy Hill dared me a hundred dollars."

"Freddy Hill?"

"A guy I work with. He dared me to get Chris to sign my chest for a hundred bucks." The grimace turned to a snort, disgust twisting Belinda's face. "It's pathetic, I know, but with a hundred bucks I could buy my daughter the dress she wants for her year-twelve formal." She laughed, a wholly miserable sound. "Plus Chris Huntley would have been touching my boobs. A man hasn't touched my boobs for years. I couldn't *not* try."

Someone behind her laughed. "I'll touch your boobs, honey."

Aslin turned his stare on the guffawing man, a disconnected sense of satisfaction stirring in him when the idiot with apparently no social skills cringed backward and was swallowed by the crowd.

"That was it?" Aslin asked, returning his attention to a red-faced Belinda. "Just an autograph?"

She nodded. "I came so close. I made it onto the set so often, more than you or the security guys were aware of. So many times I could see Chris but couldn't get to him." She snorted again, giving Aslin a sardonic grin. "*You* were everywhere, pain-in-the-arse Pom. And if it wasn't you, it was his assistant. Everywhere I went to approach Chris, *she* was there. Shit, she almost busted me near your trailer on the day you caught me pretending to be an extra."

Prickling heat razed over Aslin's flesh. "Say that again."

Belinda frowned. "I was walking past your trailer—I knew it was yours 'cause I'd watched you and Chris's sister go inside." She paused, a smirk twisting her lips for a second. "Saw you both fall out of it too."

Aslin didn't react to her goad, keeping his stare fixed on her face.

"I was walking past your trailer trying to find where the other soldier extras were and she almost ran into me as she was coming out of it. I'm just glad she was…"

Whatever Belinda said next, Aslin didn't hear.

His whole body tingled. Every nerve ending and cell thrummed with dawning realization.

He spun on his heel and ran for the barracks, his blood

on fire, cold rage roping through colder fear.

Tilly was with Rowan. Who the fuck knew what she was going to do next.

"Hey!" He heard Belinda shout behind him. "Hey, you rude Pommie prick! Can you get—"

Without slowing his pace, Aslin tossed a look at the security guard gaping at him from the barricade. "See that woman there?" He jabbed a finger at Belinda. "She gets an all-access pass onto the set today. On my say so. Tell Mr. Huntley he owes her an autograph on her chest."

And with that, he broke into a sprint, the ecstatic squeals from Belinda behind him fading to nothing as the roar of his murderous rage consumed him.

He didn't answer his phone when Liev Reynolds rang. He didn't need to. He knew exactly who the person was trying to kill Rowan.

And exactly where to find her.

# Chapter Seventeen

"I need to collect the board Mr. Huntley has been surfing on," Tilly whispered in Rowan's ear. "I promised him I'd pick it up from the surf shop this morning and I forgot." She slid her gaze to where Chris was discussing his delivery with Nigel, before giving Rowan an apologetic smile. "Can you help, please? I think the owner of the shop is going to ask if Mr. Huntley will let him keep it, maybe autograph it so it can be a tourist attraction in the store, and I know you're better at making people feel okay when told no."

A frown pulled at Rowan's eyebrows. "Does he really want to take it back to the U.S.? He's got more than one board at home."

Tilly nodded, her blonde ponytail dancing about her head. "That's what he told me last night. Apparently, after he and Mr. McQueen finished dinner, he went to see you and Mr. Rhodes at your hotel, but neither of you were there so he called me. I also need to organize a case of the board wax he's been using here. He likes it more than the wax he uses at home."

"A case?"

Tilly shrugged. "You know what he's like. How fickle he can be with stuff like that. Sometimes I don't think he knows what's good for him. It's my role to look after him however, so I will do what's needed."

Rowan suppressed a sigh, pulling a face instead as she studied her brother. It *was* Tilly's job, she guessed, but damn, Rowan had hoped Chris had moved on from the selfish, extravagant whims of his fame.

"Do you mind coming with me, Ms. Hemsworth? It will make it so much easier."

Turning back to the young woman waiting with such a beguiling expression on her pretty face, Rowan nodded. "Sure. I'll help. It's kinda embarrassing I've been in Australia for a week and haven't visited its most famous beach, I guess." She chuckled. "In fact, only a few days ago I'd planned to buy a T-shirt from there. Something to remember Sydney by."

The sentiment made Rowan laugh again. As if she needed a shirt to remember her time in Australia. Her life had been turned upside down in Australia. She'd come to the country planning on helping her brother during his break-out movie role, help him stay grounded and focused, and instead she'd been blown up, fallen in love and now faced the daunting task of asking Aslin to quit being Nick Blackthorne's bodyguard and come with her for the rest of the shoot. And hopefully, for the rest of forever.

As soon as he returned from wherever he'd gone, she was plucking up the courage to, effectively, propose to him. After ten years of being afraid to give her heart, her time, her vulnerability to anyone but Chris, she'd finally realized she was stronger, so much stronger when she wasn't alone.

It had nothing to do with Aslin's size and strength, and everything to do with the person she was when with him—a person not afraid.

Who would have thought her life could change so much?

"Achieving what you plan is always a good thing," Tilly said, bringing Rowan's attention back to the young woman. "My dad says you never quit on your plans, no matter what you have to do."

Rowan smiled. "Sound advice."

Tilly's own smile grew wide as she hitched her tote up higher on her shoulder. "I think so. Ready?"

With another quick look at Chris, a look met with a cheesy, cross-eyed grin from her brother, Rowan followed Tilly from the set.

"My dad taught me a lot of things I've needed in life," the assistant piped up the moment they'd exited the old building. She turned right, heading in the direction of the crew parking area behind the mobile storage sheds. "Of course, you didn't get that chance with your dad being—"

She stopped, slapping a hand to her mouth, her cheeks turning red. "God, I'm sorry, Ms. Hemsworth."

Rowan shook her head. "It's okay, Tilly."

It wasn't, of course. Rowan's heart ached. She rarely let herself think about her parents since their murder. It was less painful that way.

"I know you don't talk about your mom and dad. Chris says it's because it makes you feel weak."

Itchy heat razed over the back of Rowan's neck. "He what?"

"He talks about them all the time," Tilly went on, starting to walk again, her strides long and confident. "I gave him a framed painting of them I had commissioned for his birthday last year. He loved it. I've never seen him so happy.

Ever."

Cold disbelief curdled in Rowan's stomach.

Tilly stopped again, turning back to Rowan. "I did it again, didn't I? I need to shut my mouth. I'm sorry. That was silly of me. Warren and I had a fight last night and my head is all over the place. I'm sorry. I really didn't mean to offend."

Rowan stood motionless, staring hard at the young woman before her. Tilly had always been a bit ditzy, but Chris had insisted that was part of her charm. She'd been his assistant for five years now and, as far as Rowan could tell, this was the first time she'd been anything apart from the perfect P.A.

Perhaps heartbreak was undoing her a little?

*No. There's something more. Something important you're missing…*

"I understand if you'd rather not help me." Tilly let out a sigh, eyes downcast. "I'm sorry."

"It's okay, Tilly." Rowan closed the distance between them and smoothed her palm up Tilly's arm. "Honest. Let's pretend it never happened."

Bright blue eyes glinted with tears as Tilly smiled up at her. "Thank you, Ms. Hemsworth. You won't regret it."

They continued walking, Tilly prattling on about what she'd seen in Australia and what she planned to do when back in the States. It was all very elaborate and seemed to involve moving into a house beyond her means.

"But it will be okay, because I've planned everything toward this end," Tilly whispered, as if confiding a great secret. "And as my dad always said, you never quit on your plans, no matter what you have to do."

Rowan's tummy fluttered, an uncomfortable sensation only intensified when Tilly slipped her hands around Rowan's elbow and squeezed tight.

Something about what Tilly had said sounded wrong.

"He sounds smart, your dad." Rowan looked at the younger woman. "What does he do?"

The young woman's smile turned dreamy. "He was Paramount Studio's chief pyrotechnics operator for a long time. Taught me all sorts of useful things."

"Was? Doesn't he work anymore?"

Tilly shook her head, her eyes growing wide. Surprised. "Oh, no, he's dead now."

"Dead? But you said earlier—"

"He died when our house blew up six years ago," Tilly went on, as if Rowan hadn't utter a word. "Terrible thing. The gas pilot light somehow ignited. The cops never figured out why."

Rowan blinked. The flutters in her belly turned to heavy knots. "But you said—"

"Of course, *I* know how it happened." Tilly smirked. "Here we are." Her fingernails dug into Rowan's arm for a painful moment. "Now, where are the keys?" She frowned, releasing Rowan's elbow to rummage around in her bag. "Can you see if I left them in the van, please, Ms. Hemsworth? I can't do what's needed for Chris if I don't have the keys, can I?"

Rowan stepped away from her brother's assistant. She frowned at the young woman, a churning unease rolling through her before she slid her attention to the white van parked beside a wall of storage crates before them.

A tingling tension razing her flesh, she walked to the driver's door and peered through the window. Something told her there wasn't any chance of spying the keys in the ignition.

Something was going on. Something…

*Chris. She called him Chris. She never calls him Chris. It's always—*

She saw movement in the window's reflection before she heard the click of the Glock's slide.

Spinning, Rowan dropped to the ground, her broken ribs screaming in pain as her knee slammed into her side.

"It's a prop!" Tilly shouted, waving the gun above her head. "It's a prop. I forgot I had it in my bag."

Rowan crouched on the ground, staring up at the young woman, every fibre and molecule in her being telling her the situation was wrong. Wrong. Her side throbbed with a hot tearing pain that radiated out from her bruised ribs.

She watched Tilly, her hands splayed on the ground, her breath rapid, her heart slamming fast.

"Sorry," Tilly held out her empty hand, palm outward, her smile sheepish. "Didn't mean to scare you, Ms. Hemsworth. Why would I want to shoot you?"

Heart racing, Rowan began to stand.

"When I can burn you alive in the van instead?" Tilly snarled, lunging forward to smash her foot, heel first, into Rowan's face.

Excruciating agony detonated in Rowan's nose, her lips. She reeled backward, her head smacking into the side of the very van Tilly planned to incinerate her in.

"The beam didn't work—" the young woman slammed her foot into Rowan's side, "—the trailer didn't work." She kicked her again. "But *this* will."

Rowan blocked the kick before it could land, but the force of Tilly's leg drove her elbow into her broken ribs. Fresh pain ripped through her, stealing her breath. She staggered sideways, refusing to fall completely. Or to cower.

"Don't you realized that *I'm* what Chris needs?" Tilly went on, slamming another foot into her side. "Not you."

Rowan rolled with the kick, agony tearing through

her side. Something wet and warm slicked her top lip. She scrambled away from another kick, protecting her ribs as best she could with her arm.

She needed to get on her feet. She needed to get Tilly off hers.

"For five years, I've looked after him." Tilly slammed in another strike, thrashing it about when Rowan wrapped her arm around her ankle until it was free again. "Doing what needed to be done." She punched her heel into Rowan's ribs. Rowan let out a strangled gasp, her grip on the woman's leg faltering.

Tilly broke free, a wild laugh tearing from her as she smashed her foot down onto Rowan's fingers and then slammed a kick into her side again.

"He only needed *me*," she snarled, her stare venomous. "And then *you* came and tried to mess with my plans!" Each word was punctuated by a savage kick to Rowan's ribs. Each kick detonated splintering white-hot pain in Rowan's side.

She curled in a ball, desperate to shield her injury. Desperate for a chance to strike back.

"But. Nothing. Fucks. With. My. Plans," she yelled with a savage kick to Rowan's ribs. "Ever."

She swung her foot back farther, her eyes wild, her stare locked on Rowan's face.

It was the split-second break Rowan needed.

She lashed out with her own leg in a low sweep, smashing her ankle into the side of Tilly's knee.

The young woman staggered sideways, hand going to her shattered knee, hateful glare fixed on Rowan. "*Cunt!*"

Rowan flipped herself to her feet. Agony ripped through her ribs, but she ignored it. She had to. Slamming out a side kick, she drove her heel into Tilly's chest, driving her backward. Followed it with another. And another. Each one harder than the first. Harder. Harder.

Tilly screeched, stumbling over her heels, her arms pinwheeling.

*"Rowan!"*

Aslin roared her name, his voice the thunder of an approaching storm.

Her heart leapt into furious flight. *He's here. Oh God, he's here.*

Tilly's stumbled, the Glock she'd pulled from her tote dropping from her grip. *"No!"*

Rowan didn't track its path. Nor look to Aslin. She kept her stare locked on Tilly.

"He's not yours," the young woman screeched, lurching sideways as her knee crumpled beneath her weight. "He's mine." She curled her fists and lunged at Rowan with murderous hate. "He's—"

Rowan threw herself into a jumping reverse spinning kick.

The world spun around her in a blur.

She saw Aslin run toward her. She saw Tilly try to duck her kick. The jolt of her heel slamming into Tilly's temple reverberated up her leg. She saw Tilly fly backward.

And then Rowan was standing again, staring down at the woman's motionless form on the ground.

*Thank fuck for that.*

The thought whispered through her mind on an exhausted gasp. She stumbled back a step, hissing as shards of searing pain sheared through her side.

Pressing her hands to her broken ribs, she raised her face to Aslin and watched him run toward her.

Closer.

Closer.

Closer.

"Chris is mine, cunt."

The whispered words lashed at Rowan, a second before the sound of hands and feet scraping on the ground.

She snapped back to Tilly in time to see her reach for the Glock.

Grab it.

Aim it at her head.

"*No!*" Aslin shouted. He burst into Rowan's line of sight, launching himself at Tilly. Slamming into her.

At the very moment the deafening crack of a gunshot shattered the air.

"*No!*" Rowan screamed. Her world went cold.

Ice.

She watched the man she loved crumple over the woman who'd tried to kill her, both falling to the ground. Her heart stopped.

*Oh God, no. No.*

She ran forward. To Aslin. It didn't matter her ribs were splintering with every move she made.

It didn't matter Tilly held a gun.

All that mattered was Aslin.

Aslin.

She ran, unable to breathe. To think.

To live.

She stumbled to a halt when Aslin slowly rose to his feet, the Glock in one hand, a writhing Tilly in the other.

"Lemme go!"

"You're one more word away from me ending your life, love." Aslin glared at Tilly, his British accent the most menacing Rowan had ever heard it.

A choked laugh burst from Rowan. Or maybe it was a sob. She ran to him, needing to be closer. To touch him. To prove to herself he was really alive.

Oh God, how could he be alive?

She quickened her limping gait, her stomach churning with sickening horror at the bright red stain beginning to bloom over his right side.

"You're—"

"Police! Don't move!"

Tilly began to thrash in Aslin's hold. Rowan flinched and stumbled to a halt. She turned, another warm wave of relief washing over her at the sight of two police officers running toward them, guns drawn.

"Drop the weapon," the closest officer yelled, leveling his gun on Aslin. "Now!"

Aslin slowly bent enough to drop the Glock to the ground, keeping his attention fixed on the approaching cops.

"*Rowie!*"

Rowan jerked around at the sound of Chris's shout, biting back a wince when pain shot through her ribs.

Her brother ran toward her, relief fighting with worry on his face. Nigel and more than a dozen cast and crew followed.

"*Chris!*" Tilly wailed, her feverish stare locking on Chris. "I just wanted what's best for you, that's all. She was stopping me. Please, Chris. Tell them I'm better for you. Tell them. Tell them you need..." The plaintive cries turned to wordless sobs, and as Rowan watched, Tilly slumped in Aslin's grip, her face wretched with grief.

"Are you okay, miss?" one of the cops asked Rowan, gun leveled at Tilly as his partner snared the sobbing young woman's wrists and cuffed them behind her back.

Rowan nodded.

The officer turned to Aslin, his stance making it very clear he was ready to shoot if needed. "You, sir?"

Aslin dropped a quick glance at the small, but slowly spreading bloodstain on his side. "I'll live."

"Paramedics are on the way."

Aslin chuckled, pressing his hand to his side and hissing in a breath. "Good."

Before Rowan could close the distance between them, her brother slammed into her. "Jesus, sis," he burst out, engulfing her in a hug. "I told you not to—"

"Chris," she laughed. Or at least tried to. It was hard when he was holding her so tight. "You're hurting me, squirt."

He let her go with his own laugh. "Sorry."

"Mr. Huntley?" Tilly's whine made Rowan stiffen. "Please, Mr. Huntley…"

"That's enough," the cop holding her cuffs snapped.

Chris pulled Rowan back into his arms. "I'm sorry, Rowie," he whispered into the top of her head, ignoring the whimpering woman he'd trusted for five years behind him. "I'm sorry."

With a wince and a snort, Rowan gave his chest a slight shove. "Shut up, you moron."

"I saw you in the newspaper," the officer not patting Tilly down said, his eyes narrowing on Aslin. "You're Nick Blackthorne's bodyguard, right?"

Aslin's gaze slid to Rowan. "Not anymore."

The cop raised an eyebrow at Aslin. "No?"

"About to embark on a career change." Aslin returned his gaze to the officer. "Thinking personal trainer for a world-champion martial artist."

Rowan's heart, already pounding far too fast, thumped faster. Her breath caught in her throat.

"She's clean," the other officer said, tugging on Tilly's now-cuffed wrists. "Time to go." He looked up at Aslin. "We'll be in touch, sir. Based on both your current states—" he gave Rowan a pointed glance "—there are quite a few questions to be answered."

"In other words—" Aslin's deep voice stroked over Rowan's fraying senses, "—don't leave town."

The cop chuckled. "Not for a while, at least."

"Are you sure you're okay?" his partner asked, frowning at the blood still seeping through Aslin's shirt. "You're a big bugger, but a bullet wound isn't something to brush off."

Aslin lowered his attention to his side, raising his stained shirt with steady hands. "I'll…" He stumbled back a step, his legs buckling beneath him.

Rowan was at his side before he could fall, sliding her arm around his waist. Supporting him. Holding him even as pain tore at her ribs. "I've got you."

He looked down at her, his lips curling into a slow smile. "Hope so."

She smiled back. "Know so."

Somewhere in the distance—or maybe it was right beside her, she'd lost track of anyone else—someone cleared their throat.

"Get a room you two," Chris said.

"You were right." Rowan gazed up at Aslin's face, unable to look away. "Someone *was* trying to hurt me."

He brushed his thumb over her split lip, a deep rage simmering in the back of his eyes. "She *did* hurt you. She's lucky I didn't kill her."

"*You* got shot," Rowan murmured, touching her fingers to the sticky red stain on Aslin's side. It was a ridiculous thing to say, but she couldn't think of anything else.

Aslin's answering grin was crooked. "I've had worse."

Rowan's eyebrows shot up. "Worse?"

He nodded. "This is just a flesh wound. A bloody stubborn American put me on my arse a week ago and I still haven't recovered."

Warm joy flooded through Rowan. "A bloody stubborn

American, eh?"

His dark eyes twinkled, his hands smoothing over her backside to hold her closer to his hips. "Thank God I love her, or I'd be forced to point out the fact she didn't listen to me when I was trying to—"

"Yeah, yeah, soldier boy," Rowan muttered, rising up onto tiptoe as she tangled one hand in his hair and tugged his head down to hers. "We've got a whole life ahead of us for you to tell me you were right and I was wrong. Now just shut up and kiss me, will ya."

"Yes, ma'am," he whispered with a smile.

And he did.

Carefully.

# Epilogue

"How many years were you Nick Blackthorne's bodyguard? I would have thought you'd be used to a red-carpet event by now."

Aslin shifted on his seat in the stretch limo, fighting the urge to pull at his black bowtie. "Sixteen years counting this one." He slid Rowan a sideward glance, unable to hide his wry grin. "But when I walked a red carpet as Nick's bodyguard, no one was remotely interested in looking at me."

Rowan leant across the seat a little and placed a soft kiss on his jaw. "I don't know how anyone could *not* be interested in looking at you. Especially when you're wearing a tux." She smoothed her palm up his thigh, the tips of her fingers brushing the bulge of his groin in a caress Aslin had no doubt was planned. When it came to turning him on, his wife knew *every* possible tactic, no matter how seemingly innocent. It was, he'd conceded, a gift. One she utilized often. Very often in the most inconvenient of places.

God, he loved her.

"But as sexy as you *do* look in it," she went on, her voice a husky whisper in his ear as she danced her fingers up the line of his rapidly responding dick through his trousers, "I can't wait to go home and strip it off—"

He turned and captured her lips with his in a ferocious kiss before she could finish the wholly arousing promise.

She burst out laughing against his kiss, the throaty sound almost undoing Aslin's control. The far-from-gentle scrape of her nails against his scalp as she tangled her fingers in his hair in response didn't help.

He had half a mind to tap on the screen dividing them from the driver and tell the lad to take them home. Pronto.

Any decision so self-serving was taken away from him however, when the limo came to a halt and the screen was lowered. "We're here, Mr. Rhodes."

Rowan groaned into Aslin's mouth. "Dammit."

Aslin chuckled, pulling away from her soft lips. "Thanks, Jeff," he said with a smile at Jeff Coulten.

"Your timing is impeccable as always, Jeff," Rowan grumbled, giving Jeff a disgruntled glare as she straightened the cherry-red slip she wore.

Jeff grinned at them both in the rearview mirror. "Of course it is. Now hurry up and get out. Chris is just about to arrive on his Ducati behind us, and I can see Nick Blackthorne waiting at the end of the carpet."

Rowan turned to Aslin. "Ready?"

He brushed a quick kiss on her lips before letting his fingers trail a tender path over the growing swell of her stomach. "Always. Haven't you figured that out yet?"

She snorted and gave him a shove. "Get out of the limo, soldier boy. The *Dead Even* premier is about to begin and your ex-boss is waiting for you."

He flipped her a salute. "Yes, ma'am."

Rowan's eyes narrowed. "Watch it. I may be six months pregnant, but I can still put you on your ass."

Aslin laughed and then turned to the door. With a deep breath, he counted to ten and stemmed the smile threatening to spread across his face. He had a reputation to uphold after all. Rowan Hemsworth-Rhodes' husband was—at all times—a menacing, serious man. It wouldn't do the world's press to know otherwise.

The door opened to reveal Jeff standing on the sidewalk, grinning at him as he stepped out of the limo's backseat. "Enjoy the movie, Aslin."

Camera flashes ignited in Aslin's face, but he ignored them.

Nick grinned at him. "Looking good, Uncle As," he called, sliding his arm around Lauren's waist.

Dropping them both a quick nod of greeting, Aslin turned back to the limo and held out his hand to help his wife alight from the transport. "In case I didn't mention it," he murmured in her ear, smoothing his hand over the lush curve of her hip before settling it on the small of her back, "you look stunning tonight."

She smiled up at him. "You did. But feel free to say it again many times tonight if you like."

Aslin couldn't help himself. He laughed. And the camera flashes fired around them.

# About the Author

Lexxie Couper started writing when she was six and hasn't stopped since. She's not a deviant, but she does have a deviant's imagination and a desire to entertain readers with her words. Add the two together and you get erotic romances that can make you laugh, cry, shake with fear, or tremble with desire. Sometimes all at once. When she's not submerged in the worlds she creates, Lexxie's life revolves around her family, a husband who thinks she's insane, a indoor cat who likes to stalk shadows, and her daughters, who both utterly captured her heart and changed her life forever. Having no idea how old she really is, Lexxie decided to go with 27 and has been that age for quite some time now. It's the best of both worlds – old enough to act mature, young enough to be silly. Lexxie lives by two simple rules – measure your success not by how much money you have, but by how often you laugh, and always try everything at least once. As a consequence, she's laughed her way through many an eyebrow raising adventure.

*Check out Select Contemporary's newest releases...*

## BOUND TO THE BOUNTY HUNTER
### a *Bound* novel by Hayson Manning

Harlan Franco lives by his own rules: be in control, be detached, and never mix business with pleasure. These rules are tested when he's being paid to secretly guard the sexy, unpredictable, pain in the butt, Sophie Callaghan–a woman determined to stay away from him. Sophie is on a mission. What she doesn't need is hot, broody, and controlling Harlan barging into her life. After a night where both live out their darkest desires, Sophie tries to fight the explosive chemistry between them. But the ties that bind her heart to this bounty hunter are tight and tangled.

## HARD PLAY
### a *Delta Force Brotherhood* novel by Sheryl Nantus

Ex-special forces ranger Dylan McCourt is a stone cold killer who cares only about his military brothers and doing what's right. He's used to giving orders and has zero patience for bullshit. Most people tremble when they look him in the eye, but not his infuriatingly sexy new rescue mission, Jessie Lyon. She just juts her chin and says she's not leaving without clearing her father's name, to hell with his rules. And was that a one finger salute he sees in her eyes or his imagination? Either way, he knows this is one job his training might not have prepared him for.

## RULES OF PROTECTION
### a *Tangled in Texas* novel by Alison Bliss

Rule breaker Emily Foster just wanted some action on her birthday. Instead she witnessed a mob hit and is whisked into witness protection, with by-the-book Special Agent Jake Ward as her chaperone. They end up deep in the Texas backwoods. The city-girl might be safe from the Mafia, but now she has to contend with a psychotic rooster, a narcoleptic dog, crazy cowboys, and the danger of losing her heart to the one man she can't have. But while Jake's determined to keep her out of the wrong hands, she's determined to get into the right ones—his.

## HER STAND IN BOYFRIEND
### by Kelly Jamieson

Event planner Lexi Mannis has a busy life in Chicago—too busy to have a boyfriend. For special occasions, she has her Stand-In Boyfriend, Mac Northrop. Mac offers (almost) all the perks of a real boyfriend—furniture assembly, a date to big events, and someone to cook for. But they've never been "with benefits"… until one wickedly hot night crosses the line.

Mac's been in love with Lexi for ages. He knows he should probably end it, but dammit, he just can't. When things get deliciously down and dirty, Mac is certain that he's made the leap out of the friend zone…until Lexi decides she wants to remain friends. With benefits.

What Lexi doesn't know is that she's running out of time. And if she won't promote Mac to Real Boyfriend, she might just lose her Stand-In Boyfriend to someone else…

CPSIA information can be obtained
at www.ICGtesting.com
Printed in the USA
LVOW12s1102311217
561408LV00001B/22/P